ABSOLUTE ZERO

WHEN A RECON BECOMES A RESCUE THERE IS NOTHING ABSOLUTE!

PHILLIP TOMASSO

SEVERED PRESS
HOBART TASMANIA

ABSOLUTE ZERO

Copyright © 2017 Phillip Tomasso

WWW.SEVEREDPRESS.COM

ISBN: 978-1-925711-33-2

PRAISE FOR ABSOLUTE ZERO

"Absolute Zero is classic sci-fi terror in space."—Simon Wood, USA Today bestselling author of *The One That Got Away*

"Absolute Zero is an outright sci-fi thrill ride that doesn't let up from the beginning. Tomasso has zeroed in on the perfect blend of supreme action with the foreboding helplessness of the darkest reaches of space. A non-stop page-turner that's sure to satisfy the need for epic sci-fi adventure." —Michelle Garza, Co-author of Bram Stoker nominated *Mayan Blue*

"Reminiscent of Alien, once Tomasso's Neptune gets up to speed, it's a head-down charge to a satisfying conclusion." —Shawn Chesser, author of the Zombie Apocalypse Series

"Great storytelling from the first paragraph. People say a book is hard to put down, but don't mean it. I mean it. This one was hard to put down!" —Jake Bible, Author of *Roak: Galactic Bounty Hunter* and *Z-Burbia*.

"A pulse-pounding sci-fi horror novel, Philip Tomasso's ABSOLUTE ZERO takes readers on a thrilling journey to the surface of the Solar System's outermost planet, where dark dangers lurk outside a mining colony. A corporate mission to salvage the operation soon turns lethal, leaving Captain Anara Meyers to wrestle with situations she never expected to find herself in. Meanwhile, a crew of space pirates, seeing an opportunity to loot the colony, lingers nearby. While the book has no shortage of horror thrills and action scenes, it also features some fantastic sci-fi world-building and poignant character moments... not to mention a refreshing number of well-drawn, prominent women characters in positions of leadership. If you like the darker side of sci-fi, I highly recommend you give this one a read." —Mary Fan, Critically Acclaimed sci-fi author of the Jane Colt series

"Aptly titled, *Absolute Zero*, will chill your spine. An amazing contribution to the military Science Fiction Genre! Action, running, gunning and plenty of alien monsters to keep readers at the edge of their seat. If you enjoy space marine adventures with all the blood and guts included, then buy this book." —WJ Lundy Author of *Donovan's War* and the Invasion Trilogy

"Phillip Tomasso pens a fast paced sci-fi novel, full of alien landscapes, and far off worlds. But it is so much more than that as he delves into the personalities that comprise the crews of the Eclipse and Cutlass as they do all in their power to save each other from the extreme weather and a hostile race that wants nothing more than their demise. If you're looking for action and a thought provoking, gripping read, you need not venture any farther!" —Mark Tufo, author of the award winning Zombie Fallout Series

This one is for my kids.

For all they do, and
all they have accomplished—
they inspire me!

PROLOGUE

Planet Neptune
Euphoric Enterprises Colony

The alarm sounded, a high-pitched wail combined with a deep honking horn. The warning blared throughout the facility. Gumball lights spun at hallway intersections and above doorways, casting everything, everywhere, in an amber hue.

Sandra Carter ran toward her work area. Her eyes darted this way and that, trying to make sense of the alarms. As the assigned astrophysicist, her fears naturally strayed toward some catastrophic climate issue.

Neptune's orbit brought the planet close to the sun once every one hundred and sixty-five years. The sun softened ice. Melted it. Although the colony was built on what had been surveyed as land, the temperature change affected everything on the planet.

Flooding?

The colony, built on ice at least three miles thick, should be stable. Had glaciers melted and ocean levels risen? Something like that could prove catastrophic. The colony would be forever buried. Lost.

As she reached her lab, through the glass walls, she saw her assistant. Calvin Friedrichs saw her. He moved for the door. He depressed a button on his side of the wall. The door between them swooshed open. "Sandra, what is going on?"

"I was hoping you could tell me." Carter stopped at her desk. She thumbed a toggle on the communicator. The screen came to life.

"Yeah?" It was far from a professional response. Ralph Johnson, the mining supervisor, was often anything but. After spending months together, she had grown used to it. He gave her a friendly, if not frantic wave.

"It's Doctor Carter. Talk to me, Ralph."

Johnson rolled his eyes. She knew why. She had identified herself, even though he could see her and she him. "Not sure yet," Johnson said. "Waiting on a body to return. Something happened out there. I'm headed to the storage area now. I got guys screaming bloody murder down there.

I can't make heads or tails of what's going on." The mining equipment was large. The machines vacuumed the planet surface. They called the machines The Bodies. The mouth siphoned up whatever was in front of it. The natural diamonds were sucked into the belly, while the snow, grit, and useless layers were discarded as waste out the back end.

"I'll meet you there," she said.

"Where are you, the lab? Why don't you stay there? Let me sort this out. I'm sure it's no cause for this much alarm. As soon as I find out, I'll let you know what's what."

Sandra Carter wasn't sure how to proceed. If it were some kind of mining accident, she couldn't offer much help anyway. Her medical training was limited to bandaging a wound, or splinting a broken bone. Shaking her head, she agreed. "Okay. I'll wait here. As soon as you figure out what's—"

"As soon as I figure it out. You have my word."

Learning early on, Carter was not impressed by taking the supervisor at his word. Oftentimes the smell of alcohol on his breath immediately negated any sincerity in what he said, and, like his speech, his actions were often slurred and stilted. "I'm not joking around, Ralph. The minute you figure out what's going on, we want to know."

"I just want to deactivate these alarms first. Have to do that from where they were activated. Should have had a way to silence them from here." He threw his hands up. "So, give me a few minutes. Okay? I'm going to silence the alarms, and then talk to my crews and see what's what."

"And then you call me."

"Got it. I got it, Doc. Then I call you." There was a soft beep. The screen went black. He'd ended the transmission from his end. It was his thing, always first to break the connection. That was the other thing. He was a last-word-kind-of-guy.

"What do you think is going on?"

Carter grew increasingly more concerned about Neptune's orbit around the sun. The closer the planet was to the sun, the more unstable the surface. The more unstable the surface, the more dangerous their mission became. "Could be any number of things. The geysers have been active. Volcanic eruption? Earthquake?"

Friedrichs grinned. "Would you call it that?"

"Call it what?"

"An earthquake. I mean, we're not on Earth."

Doctor Sandra Carter sighed, but smiled. "No. I guess you wouldn't call them earthquakes."

The sirens quit screaming.

The amber lights stopped spinning.

For a moment, there was silence, and darkness, and then the overhead lights came back on. The lab once again bathed in a soothing, normal, iridescent glow. "There," Carter said. "That's much better."

Maybe it was nothing, she thought. She hoped.

"And what should we do now?" Friedrichs asked, his weight on one leg and arms crossed.

"We get back to the sample testing. Ralph, if he doesn't have this thing sorted out, will figure out what's going on and get back to us. You heard him. There's no reason to let whatever's going on over there impede on our work over here. Agreed?" There were diamonds in need of grading and sorting; ocean and air samples, which required analyzation. At least a dozen other tests needed to be run on ground samples, as well as work with the medic on biometric scans of the colonists for health reasons. The dangerous and dense atmosphere would wreak havoc on a human body. Prolonged exposure guaranteed it.

"You got it, Doc." Friedrichs leaned forward, over the table. He pressed his eyes against the dual lens on the microscope, his hands spun the turret, and stopped on the objective lens before spinning the coarse and fine focus knobs until the specimen below came into crisp, sharp focus.

Then three things happened almost simultaneously. The main lights went out. The amber lights came back on, and began spinning. Wailing sirens screamed and honked. The alarms reactivated.

Doctor Sandra Carter held up a calming hand. "I'm sure it's a glitch with the system."

"What?" Friedrichs held a hand behind his ear.

"I'm sure it is just a problem with the system! It happens sometimes. My grandfather was a fireman, back on Earth. When someone tries resetting an alarm, it triggers. I'm sure that's all it is."

Carter was not sure she believed a word she had said. It was all for Calvin's benefit. Her mind raced. So many things could go wrong; could *be* wrong. Someone might have gotten seriously hurt. She imagined a suit tear. A miner with exposure. They would be dead almost instantaneously, worst case. Immediate frostbite best case. Damage from a nearby geyser may have burst through the hull of the colony. The geysers were unpredictable. The spray was poison ocean water, and jagged, sharp diamonds shrapnel.

A major air leak. They would all be dead before long if they did not isolate the source and seal off the area.

"Where are you going?" Friedrichs called out.

She could not remain in the lab with the activation of the alarms, a twisting knot in her gut made it near impossible. Carter needed to know what was happening, and if there was anything she could do to help. "Wait here. I'll be right back!"

———

Sandra Carter moved down the narrow hallways. The colony was a simple maze. The structures sat on, or were anchored into, what was best perceived as planet land mass and not just frozen ocean. Best recon calculations prior to building the colony also indicated their particular spot was the most stable. There were no reports of volcanic activity in the area, but unpredictable geysers did spot the land.

Before she realized what she was doing, Carter was jogging toward the storage area, maneuvering her way through the corridors. She was well aware of her increased heartbeat, and the sound of her breathing. The anxious knot in her gut now felt as if it had grown teeth and was gnawing at the inner lining of her stomach.

Back when she *Euphoric* approached her with the idea of trekking out to Neptune for this assignment, she had thought it was like a dream come true. Her lab on the Nebula Way Station was state of the art, and although she received samples for testing from across the galaxy, she jumped at the opportunity to gather the samples herself. Well, since arriving on the planet, she only ventured out with the miners once, but it had been exciting! The vacuuming operation was nothing shy of impressive. Regardless, she was here, on Neptune, working with harvested diamonds first-hand.

Only now, with the ambers flashing and the sirens screaming, did she realize the true level of danger inherently infused into the mission. They were millions of miles from home.

What if something did go wrong?

How would help ever reach them in time?

Okay. She was not naive. She knew a mission of this undertaking ran the risk of becoming potentially perilous. Like a teenager, she supposed, Carter felt invincible when she accepted the assignment.

Carter waved her I.D. in front of the door lock and punched in a four-digit code. The door *whooshed* open, and Carter charged into the storage area. The giant dome reminded her of ancient Earth films she had watched of sporting events held inside covered arenas. Football, soccer, and baseball. Eighty-thousand plus fans filled stadiums for three to four hours watching while others played a game. She did not get it at first. Streaming old footage, however, she found herself sucked into the excitement, respected the rivalries, and eventually appreciated the competitions.

The dome on Neptune was different, much, much different. There were no stadium bleachers, announcers, or athletes running amuck with a ball. Instead, piles of harvested diamonds filled the storage dome. There were randomly parked black bulldozers and dump trucks.

Then out of the corner of her eye, she saw something else.

Moving, it descended down from the top of a pile of diamonds on her right. Scaled, and slithering, it brought down along with it a rolling landslide of gems. Its footing slipped, and for a moment it rolled toward her, but then it regained balance, control. It continued down the side of the pile as if nothing had happened.

Carter wanted to jump back, get away, but she could not move. She knew she should turn and run and slam closed the storage door on her way out. Instead, she just stood there, her eyes not believing a thing they saw. She could not look away from the thing. Besides, her stiff legs could not feet that suddenly felt cemented in concrete. Her breath caught in her chest. Of all the scans performed there was no evidence suggesting any lifeforms lived on this planet.

When the second thing slalomed down the pile of diamonds on her left, coming at her fast, efficient her immobility spell shattered.

As she ran for the exit, her mind screamed over and over. *We're not alone on Neptune! My God, we're not safe inside the colony.*

PART I

THE DISTRESS SIGNAL

CHAPTER ONE

Aboard the Eclipse
Outside the Reach of Neptune's Gravitational Pull

Commander Anara Meyers stood with legs shoulder width apart, hands clasped together behind her back. Tall, thin, she kept her dark hair short in the back, long on top, but away from her face with gel. A small nose and high cheekbones accented overtly pale skin, but altogether brought striking contrast against emerald green eyes. Her uniform was crisp, pressed. Her white uniform shirt was tucked into tight, black pants. The royal blue collar indicated her rank.

The bridge, and the entire *Eclipse* vessel, was under her command. It was not her first flight in charge, however, it was the first with such a large crew, and the failure or success of the mission would greatly impact the future of her career with *Euphoric Enterprises,* or *E.E.* The bridge consisted of two tiers. The porthole was floor to ceiling.

The ship now hovered in open space just beyond Neptune's gravitational pull. With the sun at the ship's stern, the face of the planet was bright, brilliant blue, and well-lit. The planet, furthest from the sun, had seen some action. The surface had been battered and beaten at some point, surviving past a raining assault committed by a passing belt of asteroids. You wouldn't know it to look at the smooth, almost glassy surface of the planet from the space just beyond its moons. Neptune was, indeed, a remarkable sight.

Neptune's magnetic field is tipped on its side in relation to the axis the planet rotates around. At a forty-seven degree angle, the axis is not positioned at north and south, but east and west. The planet did not spin so much as roll. Additionally, the meteor-sized ice crystals which formed rows of thin rings, circled around the blue planet more from top to bottom instead of as if a belt racing around the center.

Although Neptune possessed fourteen moons, Commander Anara saw only two from where she stood on the bridge. Nearly seventeen times the mass of Earth, the planet's mammoth girth blocked from view the remaining moons on their orbits.

Commander Meyers had enlisted in the North American Alliance Armada (NAAA) immediately after school. After completing her fourth year, she had planned a life-long career with the military branch, just like her father and grandfather had done. However, *E.E.* came at her hard. On the table, the company offered a nearly quadrupled salary over what the NAAA paid her, an amazing pension plan, and profit sharing. Then there was the promise of immediate promotion from lieutenant to commander, and as an added benediction, they wooed her with the allure of a position that would place her in charge of the *Eclipse*, their newest, state-of-the-art, high-tech starship. Meyers did not know of a single commander, or lieutenant, or *any* officer for that matter, who did not dream of flying the *Eclipse*.

Her decision still had not been simple. *E.E.* gave her time to consider the options, which was thoughtful. She knew if she hesitated too long the opportunity would be snatched out from under. While making a call on the fly was a talent she possessed, leaving the NAAA for employment with *E.E.* required something more than a split decision. She was thankful they removed added pressure. In her heart, she knew she wanted the new position. Her mind was what kept her from immediately accepting. It made lists for her. Pros. Cons. These were things her heart failed at when contemplating decisions. The first person she called with the news about the job offer was the last person she wanted to discuss it with—her father, Retired Admiral Matthew Meyers.

Lt. Mark Windsor, her First Officer, sat beside the ship's Conn Officer, Robert Bachand. The two manipulated an array of touch-screen controls on a continuous, wide, flat, yet curved panel. The ship ran from the controls on the board, the throttle for engine speed and direction, ship and galactic communications, life support and weapons.

Neptune filled the view from the porthole high-temperature quartz glass. The rings were portside. Mass amounts of ice crystal debris, moving fast, orbited the planet. The passing shards seemed almost violent and treacherous passing beyond the glass of the bridge porthole, while the planet surface misleadingly resembled something more tranquil, and was blue with a sparse spattering of white clouds.

"How are we looking, Lieutenant?" Meyers asked.

The planet's dense atmosphere contained large levels of methane under layers of hydrogen and helium. With the high-temperatures and the amount of pressure, it oftentimes rained diamonds. *E.E.* built a colony on the planet's frozen surface. Mining for the precious stones had been going on for roughly the last four years.

Six months ago, a distress signal reached *Euphoric's* Nebula Way Station. There were two mega-constructed space stations beyond Earth.

A conglomerate of corporations raised funds and built together the Nova Way Station, which sat between Venus and Earth; the second, fully funded by *Euphoric* was the Nebula, situated between Mars and Jupiter. The mission, assigned to the *Eclipse*, which was docked at a Nebula bay, was dispatched as the first rescue response team.

Easily over six feet tall, Windsor's muscles filled out the *E.E.* gunmetal gray uniform nicely. His skin was coffee-bean brown, with even darker eyes. Meyers hand-picked Windsor for the crew, because he was the kind of lieutenant a commander wanted in their corner: competent, creative, and loyal.

"We're locked in on the distress beacon, Commander." Windsor touched a finger to his ear where a transmission bud fit just inside the canal. "It's a steady beep."

"Any luck reaching a contact, Officer Gaines?" she asked.

"Nay, Commander." Communications Specialist Nathaniel Gaines sat off to the right. His *E.E.* uniform was crisp, freshly pressed. The officer kept his blond hair short and spiked in a wave on top. His left eyebrow had a scar slashed through the center where no hair grew. His work area faced a series of monitors, high-definition receivers, and transmitters. "I've generated a loop. Our request for a response is always transmitting. If anyone hears the recorded loop, I should suspect they would be compelled to reply, Commander."

"Second you hear something, anything, let me know." The instruction was understood, and Meyers knew she had voiced the command needlessly. The way she saw things, it was better to state the obvious and avoid confusion, just in case.

"Aye, Commander." Gains took it in stride, his tone of voice calm, confident.

"Officer Bachand?"

"Commander?" Bachand kept his deer-skin brown hair shaved on the sides, long on top and combed back into a ponytail. Although a little extreme, it certainly would not be permitted within ranks of the NAAA. That was the beauty of it though, Meyers realized. This wasn't the NAAA, it was a private funded mission and although a dress code existed the limits were broad, accommodating, and better fit individual personalities. Growing up as a military brat, some things would definitely take getting used to. For the most part, though, Meyers appreciated the open diversity.

"Can we keep *Eclipse* a safe distance, outside the gravitational pull, and still launch our teams to the surface?" Meyers knew the flight from the Nebula bay to Neptune was the easier part of their journey.

Launching the first rescue response team through the volatile planet atmosphere was another matter altogether.

"Aye, Commander. The issue is maintaining a radar-visual with the colony once our squads land." Bachand pivoted around in his chair. "As you are well aware, Neptune completes a full rotation in just sixteen hours. She's turning fast on us."

"Can we match her speed?" the commander asked.

"Aye. Working on settings to do just that, Commander. Should be no issue with jockeying along beside her."

The one thing Meyers knew better than nearly anything else was formality. She was raised with it. Conversations with her father—when her father had been home to converse with—sounded exactly like sound bites from the bridge of a spacecraft. Always. Their talks came off almost like formal banter. There were times, perhaps too few to recall, when she longed for normal conversation with regular people. She knew how people perceived her. Rigid, stand-offish, and by-the-book. She intimidated people, peers, higher ranks, and subordinates alike. Having overheard others talking, whispering, and laughing together generally left her feeling ostracized and inadequate—a chink in her otherwise impenetrable armor.

"Even from here, Commander, I can tell the planet's surface is nothing short of one massive blizzard." Unflinching, Windsor's eyes locked on the porthole. "Look at those clouds. The swirl patterns. I can't imagine landing on that surface. The mining ships were enormous compared to the shuttles our pilots are flying. It isn't going to be easy at all. Doable, Commander, just not easy."

The colony was invisible from space. It was more than likely still invisible once the shuttle breached the atmosphere. The entire colony couldn't be more than a mere pinprick on the planet's massive surface. The storms on Neptune were expected. During the briefing before the launch of the mission, they learned about the near constant tempest-like conditions. Hearing about them and then witnessing the vehement condition first-hand were two entirely different things.

Meyers believed *E.E.* wanted a success guarantee. She knew the mined diamonds were the thrust of the colony program, but was certain the company she now worked for feared the impact of negative press should anything happen to those stationed on the planet's volatile surface.

A guarantee oftentimes proved anything but.

There were too many variables. Regardless, Meyers had faith in her pilots. Between starfighter patrols around Nebula, Earth, and countless hours spent in flight simulators, the *Eclipse* crew possessed some serious talent. "Your job will be keeping the *Eclipse* away from asteroids and moons, and all of that high velocity floating ice." She arched an eyebrow, her way of providing a visual exclamation point, and then tried a smile. "The squads are well trained."

Meyers did not think her smile worked, though. Bachand's simple: *Aye, Commander,* sounded more as if he was not sure whether he had just been chastised, or not.

Meyers leaned on the rail, standing behind Bachand, and relaxed her shoulders. "The opposite side of the planet is where the Great Dark Spot is, anyway. Did you know that storm system has been raging for hundreds of years? The storm was recorded about a hundred and thirty years after the planet was discovered in our solar system. Hasn't stopped yet. Or let up, for that matter. Winds were logged at thirteen hundred miles per hour. Sustained."

"Glad we're not landing anywhere near that storm front," Windsor added. He must have sensed his tone as too casual. He sat up straighter, and said, "Commander."

With lips pursed, Meyers unfolded her hands and left them at her side. Her subtle attempt at improving the crew's perspective of her did not seem to be working. "I agree with you, Lieutenant. Unstable ice and rock, and a sea of water and ammonia to contend with … it will prove trying enough, as you said, landing the two shuttles on this side of the planet."

Lt. Windsor nodded in non-verbal agreement.

The crew under her command needed time for adjusting. While loyalty was expected from day one, rapport and camaraderie took time. Missions could last years at a time, and even though respect was fine, she already longed for the kind of friendship she'd witnessed serving on other vessels. She knew, however, it couldn't be forced. The key was not to sacrifice respect for friendship. At least that was a lesson her father continually impressed on her when she was both in school, and enlisted.

When *E.E.* assigned her with this mission, she was given command over two squads. They, like her, were employed by *Euphoric*. Most of the detail had been recruited directly out of the North American Ground Defense (NAGD), just as she had been from the NAAA.

The armed para-military squads were essential on any vessel, but the commander was especially thankful having them on this particular mission. The likelihood of anyone attacking a vessel like the *Eclipse* was barely conceivable. Commander Meyers knew the former NAGD were well-trained pilots and soldiers, and that provided her with plenty of solace. One could never be too careful. Pirates existed—under the guise of Salvage, naturally, but attacks, hijackings, and murder *did* happen.

CHAPTER TWO

Commander Anara Meyers stood over the table display inside the War Room. A loose strand of hair kept dropping over her left eye, and with a finger, she kept swiping it over the back of her ear. "This is the last live satellite feed of the mining colony on the planet's surface," she said, though the crisp image was self-explanatory.

"There are seven structures." Lt. Windsor circled the encampment with a sweeping hand motion. Six structures, joined by enclosed walkways, encircled a large dome. "The smaller three over here are housing, mess hall, gym, that kind of thing. These three are for the mining equipment, a repair shop, and their shuttle. Right here, in the center, this large dome is where they store the mined diamonds."

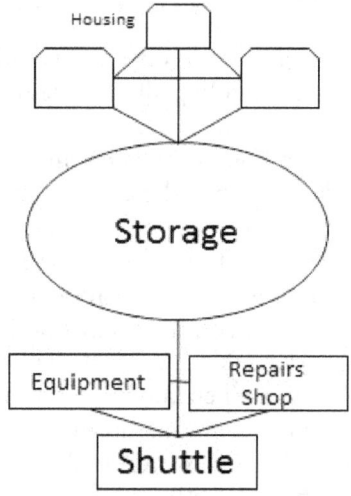

Frigid temperatures made extended outdoor exposure, despite perceived safety inside a spacesuit, dangerous, if not reckless.

"Where the shuttle is housed, there's a landing strip, here." Meyers pointed at the rectangular box on the image. "Captain Stanton. Rivers. We're launching one shuttle to the surface. Alpha Squad, where do we stand?"

"Aye, Commander." Danielle Rivers was in charge of Alpha Squad. Standing straight, hands clasped together in front of her, Rivers nodded with confidence. A stripe of white hair, *poliosis*, streaked from right temple to behind the ear, shocking otherwise raven-black hair. "Alpha team is prepped, and ready to deploy. I've debriefed them with blueprints and dossiers complete with images of each of the miners and specialists stationed inside the colony."

Commander Meyers appreciated the dedication Rivers and her team exhibited. "It's a total of thirty-five people on the planet. Miners and planetary experts. They, folks, are our mission. We are here because we have been unable to establish direct communication with anyone on the planet, within the colony. Obviously, what we are hoping for is a malfunction with the alarm system. A quick fix might be a simple reset, and we turn this ship around and head back home." That was the unpretentious hope, anyway. "And Captain Stanton?"

"Aye, Commander." Adam Stanton, dark hair, broad shoulders, and icy blue eyes, stepped up closer to the display table. He set fingertips onto the table edge. "Beta Squad has four starfighters prepped and armed ready to escort the Alpha Squad to the surface. We'll recon the immediate area, flying here and here, until the shuttle is safely on the surface and Alpha's crew is secure inside the colony."

The colony's distress beacon, activated and steadily signaling, started six months ago. The beacon was set up as the colony's last resort. Whoever initiated the beacon must have realized doing so was like ringing a dinner bell, calling out to pirates from around the Milky Way, and perhaps, beyond.

Blood in the water. Injured prey.

The universe, filled with countless predators that survived and thrived on the wounded, was not as safe a place as some might suspect. Priceless diamonds were being mined on Neptune, and there was not a soul in the galaxy that did not know as much.

The commander pressed the com-link on her wrist. "Officer Bachand?"

"Aye, Commander."

"Estimated time for shuttle launch?"

"We'll be in position by zero-one-thirty hours, Commander. This will give the shuttle and her escort the clearest passage from the *Eclipse* to Neptune's surface. The best window for launch will between forty-five and seventy-five minutes from now, Commander."

"Roger that." Meyers looked at the group gathered in the War Room. "Any questions?"

No one had any.

"Captain Rivers, I'll be riding down with you and Alpha Squad."

Lieutenant Windsor moved forward half a step, a clear objection to the announcement. "But, Commander—"

A wave of her hand silenced him. "You'll have control of *Eclipse*, Lieutenant. I don't expect we'll be on the surface long. Won't take longer than a few hours to assess the issue, search the colony, and return. By this time tomorrow, I'd like to be formulating our journey back home."

She left no room for arguments.

"Anything else? Anyone? Okay. Finish final preparations. We'll launch the shuttle and escort in sixty minutes. Thank you."

As the room cleared, Lieutenant Windsor said, "Commander, if I can have a moment?"

CHAPTER THREE

"Commander?" Lt. Windsor did not hide the apparent unease in his tone of voice, but at least waited until the others cleared out of the War Room before voicing his concern. "Permission to speak freely?"

Anara Meyers thought about stopping her first officer right then, right there, but ground her teeth, and kept her mouth shut. She knew without Windsor saying a word what the conversation would revolve around. He deserved the chance to speak his opinion. It would not change her mind, but allowing him a chance mattered. "Permission granted."

"I think you should let the Alpha and Beta Squads handle the initial recon. The distress signal has been active for months. We have no idea what's been going on down there. Reliable Neptune readings only go back three orbits around the sun. If the ice is melting due to the planet's tilt and direct location to the sun as it makes its way around, then everything on the surface could be unstable." Windsor had paid attention during the briefing prior to their dispatch. The risk was real, the undefined planet surface a potential issue.

Once a century Neptune's orbit brought the planet close to their sun. Actually, it was a one hundred and sixty-five-year orbit. This made planetary research difficult for climatologists and astrophysicists. The colony would change that, giving scientists first-hand exposure to the elements, and conditions on the planet. Either way, the science teams clearly had their work cut out.

"I understand the risks, Lieutenant." She wanted to speak frankly. "We're a new crew. This is our first major mission working together. I can't reasonably deploy my people into unknown circumstances and expect them to expose themselves to unknown hazards if I am not willing to subject myself to the same."

"But you can. It is your role as commander to make exactly those types of decisions, and your role as commander to keep yourself safe so that you can continue to lead the rest of us in the unlikely, or unexpected event of an emergency," he said. "I just think—"

"I appreciate your concern," she interjected, lips pursed, and she *did* appreciate his concern. However, her mind was already made up. "I will be joining Alpha Squad, riding in the shuttle. You will take control of the *Eclipse* until I return. Is there anything else, Lieutenant?"

He looked as if he might say more, but his jaw set, and he shook his head. "No, Commander."

She took a calculated chance and set a hand on his shoulder. "Thank you," she said, and then exited the War Room. She wanted a moment alone to mentally prepare for the deployment. She would be a fool if the idea of the mission did not frighten her. The way her belly flip-flopped and fluttered, though, led her to believe she was past fear and bordering on sheer panic.

———

Captain Danielle Rivers sat at the shuttle controls, and her First Lieutenant, Murray Bell strapped himself in beside her, while Commander Anara Meyers rode in the shuttle's jump seat. Secured in the back hull were the other two Alpha Squad crew members, Lt. Gordon O'Hearne, and the Field Medic, Lt. Marshall Weber.

Meyers would be lying if she didn't admit, at least to herself, she felt slightly out of place. The jump seat, positioned behind co-pilot Lt. Bell, faced the wall instead of the front windshield. She could not recall the last time she was not a lead pilot. It had to have been back when she first enlisted in the NAAA. Putting as positive a spin on the experience as possible, Meyers decided she would use the time and observe her crew operate.

The first time the commander had ever flown a ship, it had been a two-person fighter. Her father co-piloted in the seat beside her. She was less nervous about navigating the galaxy than she was about having him next to her, analyzing and commenting on her every move, decision, and indecision. The retired admiral had been gentler than expected, surprisingly. He remained silent and observed, adding little by way of vocal suggestions about the way she flew the fighter. It was only after they returned to Nova, and over hot drinks, when he finally provide her with usable and thoughtful feedback. It fit, though, because the admiral always found ways to surprise her. Good. Bad. Indifferent. The man had a way of always doing the unexpected.

"Officer Bachand, this is Alpha Squad." Rivers manually punched out commands on the panel in front of her. Bell mirrored his captain, relaying control readings while his fingers entered information to the navigation system.

"Alpha Squad, go ahead."

Rivers sucked in a deep breath, exhaled, and said, "Requesting clearance for takeoff."

The shuttle, made for transporting cargo, was an open-floor design. This left room for filling the vessel with equipment and, or personnel. Mounted seats with safety harnesses lined the starboard and port sides of the ship. The shuttle was nothing like the *Eclipse*. While the *Eclipse* was a long shaft with a non-rotating wheel and four engine turbines at the stern, the shuttle was boxy, almost rectangular; however, neither was made for extreme speed or fancy maneuvers. The *Eclipse* was made with unparalleled power and could hit hyper speed with ease; the shuttle seemed almost to float toward any targeted destination.

"Alpha Squad? This is *Eclipse* control. You are now clear for takeoff in five, four, three, two, and go."

"All systems a-go," Bell said.

"Roger that." Rivers pushed forward on the control wheel while her feet manipulated the rudder pedals. "And we are dropping from the belly of the *Eclipse* in three, two . . . Hang on, Commander."

Meyers re-checked the taut belt strapped across her shoulder and chest. Again came the unsettling flutter in her belly, and as casually as she could, she put her arm across her stomach. Meyers could not tell if the sensation came from the idea of landing on a mostly uncharted planet, or if it stemmed from the idea that an entire colony had not been heard from in half a year. Quite possibly, it was an off-balance combination of both. If she were honest, neither idea was very promising. Remaining optimistic seemed unlikely.

The stern ramp lowered from the *Eclipse*, and Rivers moved the boxy shuttle out of the bay and into open space before igniting ion thrusters, propelling the shuttle forward.

Ahead of them was nothing but blue. The enormous planet loomed in front of them with so much beautiful allure it was almost impossible to fathom the worse than Antarctic-*like* conditions below.

While ahead Neptune awaited them; surrounding them was nothing but cold, black space.

Meyers involuntarily shivered. A premonition passed through her mind. She closed her eyes against it, figuring if she did not acknowledge the foreboding feeling she felt, maybe she could wish it away instead.

CHAPTER FOUR

Aboard the Cutlass
On the moon Larissa / Neptune VII

Loud music piped through strategically placed speakers filled the *Cutlass*. Heavy rock with deep bass would rattle the walls if they weren't made of steel. The inside of the ship was dark except for the red glow from the auxiliary lights. All systems, except life support, were in standby. The idea was to go undetected while perched on the odd, oblong-shaped moon.

The *Cutlass*, built for speed and maneuverability, could turn on a dime, was equipped with a modified cloaking feature, and could hit hyper speed with a moment's notice—as long as a course had been charted out first. The last thing a pilot wanted was to pop out of hyper speed in the middle of an asteroid field, or worse, popping directly into where a planet already filled the said space. Simple physics told even nonscientific-minded people who would win in that kind of king-of-the-hill round.

Erinne Cohn enjoyed her position on the *Cutlass*. The hours were long, the work was dirty, and the rewards near non-existent. None of that mattered. She loved the small crew and the excitement that filled her as they embarked on dangerous mission after dangerous mission. She could not help but consider herself an explorer. Each day brought something new. She was not stuck on the sidelines working eight-hour shifts in some office, or in some manufacturing plant stuck on a mindless assembly line where robots were her peers.

Traversing the galaxy was where it was at, and nothing could be better. Nothing.

When her display detected motion from just beyond Neptune's thin rings, she spoke into the comlink on her wrist. "D'Rukker, we have movement from the *Eclipse*." She sat at the controls, leaned forward in her seat, and punched in the ship's startup sequence, readying her for launch. Her metallic left arm and robotic hand did not interfere with the smoothness of her performance. She took pride in that and knew the respect she received from the others on board was respect she had earned.

The cockpit door swooshed open.

A large, dark-skinned man ducked his head as he entered. Aroldis D'Rukker wore a faded olive-green tank top, showing off rounded shoulders and lined abs that revealed muscles Erinne did not even know existed over one's stomach. His skin was covered in pink scars. They were knife wounds from not that long ago. He'd been held prisoner on another salvage ship and was tortured for weeks before escaping. It was all Erinne knew, all he'd shared. She never pressed for more. When he was ready to talk about what happened, what led up to his getting captured, she'd listen. Until then, his past was just that. *His* past.

D'Rukker wiped sweat away from his brow with a swipe of a forearm as he set down a wrench on the floor near the co-pilot seat. D'Rukker belted himself in beside Erinne. "What do we have?"

"Looks like a standard shuttle. Just launched from the belly of the *Eclipse*," she said. "I've restarted systems. Cloaking shield up. Shouldn't be able to detect us while we are still perched on this moon."

"We've done nothing wrong, Erinne. Just, like them, we're merely responding to a distress call. Hardly a crime, good Samaritans that we are." His deep voice made everything he said come out with a ring of genuine conviction. The arched eyebrow was the only hint of sarcasm, that and the way he half-smiled at her.

"Wait. What's that?" Erinne pointed at the radar where blips appeared around the shuttle.

"Armed escort. Starfighters, more than likely. Standard procedure, I guess," D'Rukker said. "Tell you what. Why don't we hang on the moon for a little bit longer? Give them some time to see what's what before we move. There really isn't a rush. Not at this point."

She knew the starfighters gave D'Rukker pause. With good reason. She felt the same. Following a shuttle down to Neptune's surface was one thing if the shuttle was unprotected—not that they expected or planned on starting any kind of trouble, but going in when starfighters circled the shuttle probably wasn't the brightest idea. It didn't matter that there were only four starfighters. The *Cutlass* would have no trouble in a fight against them. Thing was, no one knew how many more starfighters sat inside the belly of the *Eclipse*. Hard to get into a fight when you didn't know exactly what kind of resources your enemy possessed. The *Eclipse* was a new ship, and therefore it was something of an unknown. Far safer to wait and see how things played out. "Last thing we need is one of them radioing back to one of the Way Stations a description of the

Cutlass. We're simple scavengers. We need to keep it that way. Makes our work easier staying under the radar, wouldn't you agree?"

"Agree completely." Erinne powered down the *Cutlass* once again. "Think they're going in to retrieve the people?"

"Can't say for sure. Haven't picked up any actual transmissions." D'Rukker sat back in the seat, arms up, hands clasped together behind his head. He looked tired. Dark bags cupped the bottoms of his eyes. "Keep hearing the *Eclipse* trying to make contact."

"Heard that. Nothing from the planet, though. No response." She wondered if there was anyone still alive on Neptune's surface. And if they were all dead she couldn't help but wonder what might have happened to them.

"Could be dead." He shrugged his shoulders, and his exposed biceps bulged with the motion. "Either way, right? Doesn't really change anything far as we're concerned."

He left the rest unspoken. It was common knowledge *Euphoric Enterprises* was mining Neptune for diamonds. The rare gems extracted from just below the surface were stronger than terra-extracted diamonds. Neptune's diamonds were not for rings and jewelry. *E.E.* used the precious gems for creating drill bits that could be used for other mining expeditions on other planets within their solar system. But that did not mean the stones weren't valuable. They were. Quite priceless, actually.

CHAPTER FIVE

Open Space
Between the Eclipse and Neptune Atmosphere

"Beta Leader to shuttle: Beta Squad falling into formation," Captain Stanton said as his team dropped out from the belly of *Eclipse*. The four starfighters flanked either side of the shuttle, two per side—two in front, two behind.

The starfighters adopted the sleek look of the ancient American Stealth Bomber design. Triangularly shaped and flat. The hard steel and titanium construction was coated in Kevlar, strengthening and protecting the ship, making it virtually puncture resistant. The outboard and inboard elevons and split rudders allowed the ship to roll, climb, and descend with sharp, agile turns. Stanton loved his fighter. It was by far his favorite ship to pilot. "Standby for roll call. Beta Leader to Red One?"

"Red One, over," Lieutenant Angela Ruiz said.

"Beta Leader to Red Two?"

"Red Two, over," Lieutenant Robert Reilly said.

"Beta Leader to Red Three?"

Lieutenant Jane Cornwell said, "Red Three, over."

"Beta Leader to shuttle?"

Captain Rivers answered. "Shuttle here, Beta Leader. Go ahead."

"Squad is in position. Ready to roll. Atmosphere breach dead ahead. Over."

"Roger that, Squad Leader."

Stanton always preferred the view of Earth from either Nebula or Nova. Didn't matter. Each of the Way Stations gave a unique perspective of the planet. There was no denying Earth looked beautiful from the stations, either. It had been over a decade since he'd been on the plane. *E.E.* required employees to live on Nebula, as Nova was something of a competitor. He was often dispatched on an assignment at a moment's notice, so spending time on Earth didn't make much sense. Time off was limited, but he considered maybe vacationing in New Zealand at some point.

Other than homesickness, there wasn't much need to return to Earth. There was no one there for him. His family was gone. The memories of Earth were far better than the realities. The wars had ruined most everything beautiful down there. The oceans beyond polluted, the death and decay rampant, contagious. If anything, he was thankful *E.E.* had hired him, that he'd escaped to space and that he had a life worth living. The road he'd been on when on-planet would have gotten him jailed, or worse, dead.

"Tight formation." Stanton eyed his control panel. Systems checked out. He didn't expect trouble. Didn't mean he wasn't ready for it. He was. His crew was top notch. Gentle reminders, a word to nudge here and there reminded them to remain on alert during an escort despite the unlikelihood of an ambush or attack was still essential. Lives depended on them always being on the ready. Those inside the shuttle were defenseless. There was a bow and stern gun, and Alpha Squad was more than capable of using the weapons; the problem was with the shuttle itself. It was slow, sluggish, and moved like a cardboard box.

"Red One to Beta Leader," Angela Ruiz called out.

"Go ahead, Red One."

Static. Hiss. Squawk. "Thought I caught a blip on radar, Captain."

Ruiz was an outstanding pilot. Confident. Although it was not official, she was more or less his right hand. Getting half of the things he got done could not have been accomplished without her help. She did not just understand the theory of flying, she knew nearly every nut and bolt within an array of starfighters. It would not surprise him if she could dismantle and put back together an entire ship blindfolded.

Stanton looked at the sweeping arm on his radar panel. He saw the *Eclipse*. Some moons. The shuttle. And their squad. "Not seeing anything, Red One."

"It was by the moon. Eight o'clock. It is gone now, Captain. Like I said, it was just a blip. There one sweep, gone the next."

Stanton re-checked the radar. There was no activity. Nothing. "Might have been an asteroid," he said, but thought more than likely it was a malfunction the *Eclipse* mechanic, Officer Mandy Kadera, would have to check on when they returned. He let his eyes roam across open space. Aside from the distant sun at their back, black darkness enveloped him, *them*. It oftentimes played tricks on the mind. While he actually saw only infinity before him, it felt more like the space was closing in on his ship. Crushing it.

Within moments the lights inside the small fighter cockpit seemed dim when compared with the bright blueness of the planet in front of them. Stanton's warning lights flashed. "Beta Squad," he called over the air. "Planet's atmosphere ahead. Reset warnings. Ignite heat shields for entry on my count. Four. Three. Two. And heat shields on." Switches flipped. Buttons pushed. "Shuttle, copy?"

Captain Rivers said, "Shuttle copies. Heat shields ignited for atmospheric entry. We are a-go. Over."

High heat caused what was known as a bow wave. It resembled the shield a gladiator or Viking warrior carried into a fight. Only, the bow wave arced across the nose of a craft. Stanton loved the shake and heat and excitement of racing through a planet's atmosphere. Hypersonic speeds caused the strong shock wave. Traveling only at Mach 5— because they wanted the shuttle keeping up—the atmosphere rapidly compressed; the 6000 k gas impinged on the front of the starfighter, transferring heat to the surface. The result was a hypnotic fiery red and orange curling across and below and around the bow, as if threatening to disintegrate the entire ship, him included, in the blink of an eye.

The force made his cheeks flap and eyelids flutter. He ground his teeth and tightened his grip on the yoke. People lost consciousness at speeds like this, in ships like his starfighter, or on something like the shuttle. Even in training, Stanton had never blacked out. The pressure built inside his skull, and he knew he came close but he held on, kept awake, and exhaled once safely through.

———

First Officer Mark Windsor remained on the bridge of the *Eclipse*. From the front porthole, he watched the starfighters and shuttle breach the atmosphere. With all coms monitored, the crew on the bridge listened to the conversation between ships, followed by an uneasy silence when they awaited the announcement of a successful landing.

Communications Specialist, Officer Nathaniel Gaines, turned away from his workstation. "Sir, we're receiving a call from *Euphoric's* home base on Nebula. Shall I connect?"

"Transfer the call to the porthole." Windsor walked across the bridge, closer to the tempered and forged glass before it crystallized, and then became defined. The video conference call revealed a man in an expensive suit. Tie. Gold-rimmed glasses. Windsor did not recognize the person. Not uncommon, since *E.E.* employed nearly one hundred thousand people. Standing rigid, hands clasped together behind his back, Windsor introduced himself. "This is First Officer Mark Windsor of the *Eclipse*."

"Officer Windsor, I am Crispin Gunther, the Neptune Mission liaison. I'd like to speak with Commander Meyers, please."

Windsor wondered if Gunther was the liaison for the mining mission on Neptune or just their recon mission. He supposed it didn't really matter right then. "Mr. Gunther, the commander is escorting the shuttle onto the planet surface. They just passed the atmosphere. Should be landing by the colony shortly, sir."

Crispin Gunther gave a slight nod. "And you're in control, Officer Windsor?"

"I have command of the *Eclipse*. Yes, sir."

"Has there been any communication between the colony and *Eclipse*?"

"Not yet, sir. We are continually reaching out to them, hoping someone will answer." It didn't seem likely, though. After all of this time, no one had heard from the colony. There was only the constant of the activated distress beacon. It didn't look promising for the colonists. That, however, was the point of the mission. Investigate the alarm and ensure the colonists were okay. Everyone hoped it was a mere malfunction. Computer error. Maybe those inside the colony weren't even aware a distress signal was strobing.

Again, not promising, but possible. Remaining optimistic was key, Commander Anara Meyers continually stressed.

"We have put together an addendum to your mission. Information has been sent to the system. Please ensure your commander receives the delivered instructions. Because she is occupied on the planet, we will go ahead and assume everything's a-go, unless we hear differently." His eye twitched, as if he was not pleased learning the commander had tagged along on the surface portion of the mission. Windsor couldn't argue the point. "Is that understood, First Officer?"

"An addendum?"

"Altered the primary. Understood?"

"Clear," Windsor said, his curiosity piqued. He fidgeted, anxious about reading the revisions. "I will get the data to the commander as soon as the shuttle lands."

"I won't expect to hear back from you unless there is some unforeseeable issue, understood, First Officer?"

Windsor did not like this guy. He could not help wondering if Crispin had spoken to his commander the same way. Would Meyers put up with someone like this suit? Windsor could not imagine Meyers taking attitude from anyone. Ever. "Understood, sir."

The screen went white. Black. The crystallized screen vanished, and once again Neptune came into view, and became clear, and focused.

Windsor could not see the shuttle, or the starfighter escort.

Wouldn't be long before the ships landed.

"Officer Gaines?"

"Aye."

"Have we received documentation from *Euphoric*?"

"Aye, we have, sir." Gains tapped the screen in front of him. "Sealed. Confidential, sir."

Windsor went to the commander's chair behind Conn Officer Bachand who manned the flight control panels responsible for flying their vessel. "Send it to my screen, please."

Swiveling the monitor arm around, Windsor leaned forward and touched buttons on the screen, opening the message from *Euphoric*. It was addressed to Commander Anara Meyers. By rights, he should forward the revision directly to the commander. He was in charge of the *Eclipse*; however, and as the acting-commander, he needed to know what was contained in the memo. The information might have been meant for her eyes only, but in the current situation he knew he had a legal right reading the revised documentation.

Rationalization complete, Windsor tapped the screen. The electronic document opened. He scanned the document first, and then read through it more thoroughly a second time. His breath caught in his chest.

It couldn't be right.

Euphoric couldn't be asking them to do this.

Commander Meyers would never agree to this!

"Sir?" Officer Gaines stood at his position.

Windsor looked up, distracted. "Yes?"

"The shuttle, Squad Beta—they're headed into a storm." Gaines kept a hand on the face of his controls. His eyes darted back to the monitor. "It is a blizzard with terrible force. Winds on the planet shifted. Storm wasn't anywhere near the colony when the ships launched. We couldn't have known ahead of time when making the calculations, sir."

"How soon until they land? How close are they to the colony docking area?"

"The captain is most certainly relying on her global positions system. She's most likely snow-blind. She's drifting off course. Not much. But if she lands, they'll never be able to walk even one hundred yards in the declining temperatures. The winds appear relentless. I'm afraid even in their suits they'd freeze to death before ever reaching the colony."

Windsor tried ignoring his rapid heartbeat. He stood up, and leaned on the rail between the tiers of the bridge. His white-knuckle grip did not go unnoticed by the crew. "Establish a link with the shuttle. I need to get a hold of the commander. I want to know what's going on."

"Aye. Will do, sir."

CHAPTER SIX

Space Station Nebula
Between Mars and Jupiter

Crispin Gunther sat behind his desk. His office was sandwiched between floors of the *Euphoric Enterprises* corporate building. His position did not even allow him a window. Or a sofa. He had a desk, three chairs, which included his own, and the computer. Not much larger than a prison cell, Gunther did his best to make the office homey. Spending ten to twelve hours a day here, adding small comforts felt essential. Not least of which was his personal coffee pot. He drank coffee like water. For years, he took it with heavy cream, mounds of sugar. Once when out, and with no opportunity to immediately replenish supplies, he forced down cup after cup black. The acquired taste was developed, enhanced, and now he could not imagine drinking it any other way. Unless adding a shot or two of whiskey was an option. He could most certainly imagine drinking it that way. Whiskey clearly … enhanced the natural bean flavor. Everyone knew that.

Employed with *Euphoric* most of his adult life, Gunther rose through the ranks. His initial position as an administrative assistant in Human Resources came at a perfect time. Fresh out of university, he dedicated himself to the job, menial as it proved to be. Showed up early, stayed late. He made coffee and copies. He coordinated travel plans, booking rooms and flights, and was eventually relocated from Earth to Nebula where his hard work paid off. At the time he was promoted to a Human Resources Representative, *Euphoric Enterprises* had begun phasing out the admin roles. The positions were filled by robots. Clanky, loud, and unreliable robots.

Euphoric was determined to make the project work. Everyone knew they'd never admit failure, and eventually, as was mostly suspected, newer generations of the robots were released, improved, and made more dependable.

Now, as a liaison manager, Gunther's right-hand man was a robot, and he couldn't imagine getting done the things that needed doing without him. "Egor?"

Egor, a *Euphoric* Generation-12 Operations Robot, walked into the room. He was dressed in a solid blue suit. White shirt. Thin blue tie. There was a constant whirring sound—the fans keeping his computer systems cool were on the sides of his neck. "You called, Mr. Gunther?"

"I want you to monitor any communications between the *Eclipse* and their shuttle." He absently tapped a finger on his desk, knowing he'd need ducks in a row on this one. Getting the work done wouldn't be the issue. It was the undesired media coverage he loathed. "All communications are then to be scrambled and password protected. For my ears only. Are we clear?"

"Crystal."

"Can you monitor all mike-to-mike conversations. Start a log. Again, confidential. No one has access other than myself. Are we clear?"

"Crystal." Egor tilted his head to one side. "What is it we're looking for, or hoping to hear?"

Gunther pulled his chair away from the desk and sat down. "Key words will be anything that mentions or has to do with diamonds. But I don't want it limited to that. Just highlight those portions of conversations. I want everything, every word spoken.

"Won't every transmission be automatically recorded by the ships themselves?"

"I do not wish to wait until the Eclipse returns for the data, Egor. I want you recording a live feed, giving me, let's say, hourly updates." Gunther wasn't at all comfortable with the new directive. It was far too easy working in an office, sitting behind a desk, to remove oneself from a situation. Thing was, he had a good job, worked hard to get where he was. If he didn't do as directed, management could bump him down a peg or two. They could label him as insubordinate and fire him, even. He most certainly didn't want that. What would he do then? Where would he go, back to Earth?

The thought made him shudder. Earth was so desolate, so dirty.

Gunther processed it all in his mind. He tried seeing both sides of the coin. *Euphoric* had a vested interest and wanted said investment protected. He understood that, and couldn't fault the company there. It made sense. What they failed to grasp was the simple fact their change in priority affected lives and, in all likelihood, posed a direct threat to those the *Eclipse* was being sent to check on.

No one knew for sure the status of the colonists. Those living on the planet the last several years might very well be alive and okay. That was what Gunther hoped, what he imagined everyone was hoping for. Or, perhaps, there *was* some kind of an emergency which could be easily rectified thanks to the resourcefulness of *Eclipse's* crew. The problem became apparent when *Euphoric* didn't plan on waiting for an assessment or report from *Eclipse* on how the colony was fairing, but instead went all greedy.

Recover the diamonds.

Return with the diamonds.

Nothing in the new primary addendum mentioned the people of the colony; there was nothing about making contact or rescuing or retrieving the people. This made Gunther uneasy and led him to speculate.

Did *Euphoric* know more than they were sharing?

Did management know what had taken place on Neptune six months ago? Had they reassembled a transmission learning more about the situation? Were those living in the colony dead? Had something gone terribly wrong?

Gunther could only surmise something had gone terribly wrong.

Why else would they adjust the primary mission to focusing just on the retrieval of diamonds without any mention of saving lives?

"Egor? I would love some coffee, please. I have a feeling we're not going home tonight," he said, taking a seat behind his desk. Resting his elbows on the desktop, he closed his eyes and let his thumbs massage his temples.

Egor tipped his head slightly to the left. "I stay here twenty-four-seven. It is always a long night for me, sir."

CHAPTER SEVEN

Eclipse Shuttle
Neptune Atmosphere

As the shuttle breached the planet's atmosphere, Commander Anara Meyers lurched forward. Restrained, the belt across her shoulders cut into her neck and across her gut. When her head snapped forward, her chin slammed into her chest. The commander bit down hard on nothing but teeth, quite thankful her tongue was not caught in between the mashing collision. The muscles in her neck went taut, and as the shuttle stuttered, she banged the back of her head on the rest behind her. With a white-knuckle grip on the jump seat arms, and said, "Captain?"

"We've dropped ourselves into a storm." Captain Danielle Rivers held the control wheel in both hands. The yoke shook and rattled. Meyers watched the captain fight for control.

"I can see that." Meyers' eyes were opened wide. Zero visibility confronted the tiny shuttle. The wind whipped. What looked like snow swirled all around them. The ship was tossed, turned, teetered, and tottered. Meyers couldn't tell if they were right side up or upside down.

"Losing altitude fast. We're caught in a down shaft. Wind shear is near impossible to navigate." Lt. Bell's fingers tapped the control displays in front of where he sat beside the captain.

Outside, it was whiteout conditions. They were in clouds. Something like hail pelted the shuttle. It reminded Meyers of an Earth-storm in early spring when cold and warm fronts crashed together. First thought coming to mind was of twisters in the mid-west of the old Americas. She cringed, realizing there probably weren't many warm fronts passing along Neptune. They were inside a beast of a blizzard.

The shuttle dropped.

The commander's stomach dropped with it. She worried about their escort. The smaller starfighters would fair far worse in these conditions. "Was this storm on radar?"

Lt. Bell shook his head. "No, Commander. It caught came out of nowhere."

That wasn't good enough. Success depended on preparedness. A mission onto another planet's surface would always present unexpected dangers. Weather should have been the one constant they could at least predict. And now they didn't even have that.

"Thrusters are jamming," the captain claimed. She worked the throttle left and right. Her feet stepped on the rudder controls, to no avail. The shuttle barely responded. Instead, it tipped. With the nose up, wings listed to the left, and then overcorrected and tilted right. "We are going into a freefall."

Meyers felt helpless. She wished she were seated at the controls. Her faith was in her team, but she trusted herself more than anyone else. She trusted her training and reaction more than anyone else's ability to respond equally. And yet, there was little she could do strapped into the jump seat behind the captain and co-pilot except trust.

"Commander to the *Eclipse*," Meyers spoke into the comlink on her wrist.

The shuttle vibrated, and shuddered. She knew her voice was contorted with quakes and quivers. She only hoped the sound of fear wasn't as apparent in her tone of voice as it was inside her chest. Her heart pounded. It was never becoming for a commander to display fear. The great leaders, although she knew they felt afraid more often than admitted, knew how to keep the reactions hidden from their crew. Reigning in her emotions, she tried contacting the ship mustering up a sense of counterfeit courage and authority. "This is Commander Meyers. *Eclipse*, come in. Over."

It was an order. She demanded Officer Windsor answer her.

Only he didn't.

"The storm is blocking the signal. Any attempt at communicating with the *Eclipse* is jammed at the moment, Commander," Lt. Bell said.

The shuttle tipped forward.

They went into the promised freefall, and spun out of control. Meyers yelled, "Captain Rivers!"

"We're in complete failure. Every system is offline. I have no way to steer or control the ship, Commander. Brace yourself. We're going to crash."

Captain Rivers spoke in a matter-of-fact way that Meyers found unnerving. A chill raced along her spine. There was more to worry about than just the three of them packed into the shuttle cockpit. "Lieutenant Bell, hail the Beta Squad Leader."

Bell turned toward her, hands off the control panels, as if there were no longer a need for him to perform his job. "I don't think you understand, Commander. We have no power at all. Must be a magnetic storm. It's as if every system is as good as fried."

Just then, Captain Rivers pointed toward the front shield. "We're out of the clouds!"

They still fell fast.

It was not necessarily good news. From clouds to the surface, cracks of brilliant white lightning shot forward. The sky split in all directions as bolts of lightning connected with the ice below.

"We may have been hit by a bolt or two while inside the clouds," Bell said, as way of an explanation on why the systems may have failed. "At this point, I really can't be certain."

At this point, Meyers thought, the matter was moot. Knowing why everything was broken was not going to help them when it came to making a safe landing.

"Captain Rivers," Meyers said. "Will you be able to set down the shuttle?"

It was the only thing that mattered at the moment. Landing. Crashing was not an option. The commander did not even want to think about what would come next, or after that, or how they would find their way to the colony—surely they were miles off course. Right now she needed to focus on one issue at a time. All that mattered was landing, and safely if at all possible.

"The rudder and flaps are manual," Rivers said. "Now that I can at least see where we are, maybe I can steer the shuttle somewhat. This is not going to be easy. It's going to be a hard landing, at the very best, Commander."

The planet surface rushed toward them.

Meyers could barely distinguish the sky from the ground.

Most everything was blue, white, and blinding.

The raindrops, or hail, were fist size. The sound of them smashing into the shuttle left no doubt the hull was, at the very least, getting dented from impact. "Those are diamonds falling, aren't they?" Meyers said, talking to herself. The commander realized she had asked the question out loud. No one answered, though. It had not really been a question. It was not rain or hail. *Diamonds.*

She had, overall, been skeptical of the claim. It did not matter a colony had been out on the planet for years mining for the precious gems. With minimal time on Earth over the last two decades, she just was not used to weather in general. Not with climate control on the Nebula Way Station. So the idea of ...

Diamonds *did* rain from the clouds on Neptune.

Just below them a geyser gushed. The unknown blue spray rocketed toward them. With only limited navigation abilities, the most the commander could hope for was that they would miss contact. The captain threw her weight to the right, taking the yoke with her, sidestepping past the gushing geyser. The motion made Meyers' breath catch in her lungs as her stomach lurched with the change of force and then a sudden sense of weightlessness ensued during the tail end of their fall.

"I can't see *one* fighter," Lt. Bell said. "I can't see a single one of them!"

CHAPTER EIGHT

Eclipse Bridge

First Officer Mark Windsor, acting commander while Meyers was on board the shuttle, sat in the commander's chair in the center of the bridge and watched the *Eclipse* crew profusely work at re-establishing communications with the shuttle and the starfighter escort. He leaned forward in the seat, an elbow on the arm of the chair while he talked with Officer Nathaniel Gaines. "Keep attempting to contact the shuttle," he said, needlessly, "and Captain Rivers."

They had lost all digital and visual contact with the shuttle and starfighters, as well. Last images they saw on the porthole display depicted an out-of-the-blue storm. There were lightning flashes and then static before the connections were completely severed.

"Aye," Gaines said. "Continued attempts are proving futile at the moment, sir."

"Don't stop trying." Windsor felt panicked. The mission involved investigating the safety of the colonists. Initially, anyway. If the shuttle crashed, everything changed. No longer would they focus all they had on investigating the colony's distress call. Instead, it would become a full-blown rescue mission. Trouble was, Beta Squad was unreachable, as well. Nearly half the crew would be in trouble. With limited resources, he would have to find a way to get everyone back on board the *Eclipse*. If the shuttle and Beta Squad starfighters were destroyed, then he was not sure how he would be able to save any of them.

From where they were, the porthole revealed what resembled nothing more than a serene blue planet. The view was misleading, at best, and downright deceiving, otherwise.

The bridge buzzed with activity.

Aside from Gaines and himself, Conn Officer Robert Bachand was up and about, checking terminals at different positions on the bridge. "Commander," he said, addressing Windsor. "Best I can tell from my readings, the shuttle is either without power, or the storm is blocking us from obtaining any kind of readings."

The shuttle was in trouble. That much they all knew. Windsor didn't fault Bachand for the report. The officer was merely confirming what they all had suspected.

"And the starfighters? Captain Stanton?"

"Our radar is not showing any activity. It's almost as if the five ships have vanished, the shuttle and all four starfighters."

They could have crashed. That was the reality of it all. The skeleton crew left on board the *Eclipse* may have to send a pilot on the remaining shuttle after the others. "I need better updates on the weather conditions."

"Aye," Bachand said.

"Gaines, call down to the bay. Have them ready the second shuttle."

"Commander?"

Windsor thought about the message he had received from corporate. Crispin Gunther. Their liaison. With the mission primary altered, the new instructions did not allow for this particular scenario. He considered that fact the perfect loophole. Orders might be orders, but saving his commander took precedent over not just the diamonds, but also the colonists.

There was a chance his use of a loophole would be considered disobeying orders, insubordination, but working for *Euphoric* was not the same as serving in the North American Alliance Armada. Disobeying orders as an enlisted person carried a stiff prison term. Once sentenced to Mars, one might as well consider themselves forgotten. The barren wasteland of a planet was more of a drop-and-run, as opposed to a penal institution meant for the rehabilitation of the criminally convicted. Worse *Euphoric* could do was fire him, which was bad, but far better than serving a life term on Mars.

Windsor said, "If they've crashed, they are going to need our help. We will have to go down there and rescue the crew."

If any of them survived.

Windsor closed his eyes and mentally pushed the grim thought out of his mind. He had enough to worry about without letting negative thoughts impede his position, and his decision making.

Someway, somehow, remaining optimistic was essential.

CHAPTER NINE

Cutlass Bridge

"They're in trouble. All of them." Erinne Cohn shook her head. She watched the radar. Where there had at one moment been five blips on the screen, there were now none. She tapped the screen, wondering if it was a malfunction. Nothing changed. "Yeah, they're gone. Just gone."

Aroldis D'Rukker said, "Got a blizzard taking place down there. Been raging on for a while."

"I didn't notice any kind of storm."

"Look here. See this solid mass? That's the storm." He pointed at the center of the radar and swept his finger around a circular image. "It's encompassing. Sustaining. See how it doesn't move, but just hovers in the one area? Makes it seem like standard weather. When in fact, that is what blizzards on Neptune look like. Nothing. Normal. Would fool most, even the best meteorologists, unless they knew what to look for. Not to mention, in the last hour or so, the winds had shifted. Moved right over where that Nebula colony is stationed. I've been keeping an eye on it. Kind of surprised the Eclipse crew missed it."

"You just said even then best meteorologists could have missed it, but you know what to look for?"

He shrugged, smiled. "I do."

"And where'd you get your meteorology degree?"

"School of hard knocks, sister. School of hard knocks." He ran fingertips over the center console keyboard. Reaching above his head, he flicked toggles from front to back and back to front. "Can't pilot a ship if you don't know how to monitor the weather. There was a time, on Earth, when I navigated the oceans with nothing but the stars to guide me."

He rarely talked about his past. The fact he had been the captain of a ship, one that floated on water, did not surprise her. She did not know the background, the details, but she was not at all shocked. She did, however, wonder if he had been a pirate then, too, but did not ask. "Okay. So, what's the plan?"

"Same as it was when we lifted off the moon. We're going in."

Erinne's eyes drifted back to the radar, studying the circular mass. "We're going to help them?"

D'Rukker laughed. "Are you trying to be funny?"

"They could be in trouble, I mean serious trouble." Erinne knew her argument would be lost on D'Rukker. He practically owned the rights to tunnel vision. Once on target, getting him to see anything peripherally was a battle in and of itself.

Unless it came to safety. D'Rukker could, and would, protect his ship and crew even if sound asleep. However, when she thought about, security was also a form of his tunnel vision. So, actually, that only solidified her opinion.

"The Corporations hired us to do a job. Saving those people was not part of it. Nova is not a customer we want to let down, either. They have deep pockets. We stay in their good graces and we get steady paychecks. It's not like we have to follow a bunch of rules. They know who we are. They know what we do, and how we do it."

And there she had it. As expected. "I'm just saying. We can siphon all the diamonds we want and still save the lives of that crew. If we do nothing, any survivors will freeze to death."

"What did we count? The life force scan showed what, like nine, ten people? Know how much space they take up? We're going to fill the hull with diamonds and high-tail it back to the Nova Way Station. Payments for the job aren't deposited into our accounts until delivery is made. You know this, Erinne."

"I know it, but even ten people won't—"

"We're going in fast, grabbing up diamonds, and getting out." D'Rukker made a face Erinne knew too well. It was his *that's final* face. Jaw set, brow furrowed. "The storm is something of a blessing. Caught them off guard. Unlucky for them. Lucky for us. They're going to be preoccupied a-plenty with repairs to their shuttle, and make heads or tails out of directions, I imagine. Won't even see us coming, *or* going. It kind of makes up for the difference in our arrival times. For a while there, I was thinking we were far too late to collect. Now, it's as if time is on our side ... for once."

CHAPTER TEN

Eclipse Shuttle

Commander Anara Meyers knew, by all rights, the shuttle alarms should be sounding. Red lights flashing. The situation had escalated. They were in dire straits. The shuttle had cruised through Neptune's atmosphere and into the heart of a storm. The severe weather damaged the shuttle's computers. Systems shut down. Nothing worked. They were a free fall and were heartbeats away from crashing into the planet's unstable surface.

Captain Danielle Rivers refused giving up. With both hands, she fought for manual control of the shuttle's rudder, and wing flaps. "I may not be able to stop the fall, but if we can catch the right wind, I might just be able to glide us in for a landing."

Lt. Bell said, "I'm attempting a complete system reboot. It could take several minutes. If I can get us back online, that should help."

The commander knew several minutes was not something they had. The reboot might work, but it would never work in time.

The ground rushed up at them.

All the commander saw was blue. Snow. Ice. And opaque blue liquid. The rolling waves of the water-ammonia ocean pushed jigsaw piece icebergs around. The storm raged blowing in from all directions. The edges of icebergs smashed into one another, ends crumbled.

The ocean would swallow the shuttle completely if the captain could not set them down somewhere on frozen ground. Being jolted about inside the cockpit, Commander Meyers couldn't see clearly enough to locate any stationary piece of land. Everything looked as if it were moving about beneath them.

Lt. Bell's jaw dropped open. His eyes went wide as he pointed. "Geyser!"

They headed directly toward a sudden gushing spray of ammonia water. It erupted from out of a crater and shot straight into the sky.

Captain Rivers yanked back hard on the yoke. Her head lifted up and tipped back as muscles in her neck went taut through to her shoulders. Thick, they protruded and pulsed. She strained, gasping and groaning, as she fought for control of the shuttle. Hopefully, the flaps on the wings responded, but the commander couldn't differentiate River's manipulation from the gale force winds tossing them about.

Rivers gave a yell as she leaned all of her weight into the turn. The shuttle tipped, and nearly skirted past the expanse of the geyser. Before anyone could exhale in relief, spray clipped the end of the left wing and the solid impact sent the shuttle into a roll.

The commander reached out with both arms; right palm flattened against a wall. Her left hand latched onto the back of the jump seat headrest. The shuttle shuttered, metal moaned. It sounded as if the vessel might crumble—the extreme cold, the ice, the wind—might be more than the design specs allowed.

Rivers, despite the roll, never let go of the yoke, never stopped her fight for control; Bell's hands flew across the dark panel, toggled switches, and pressed buttons.

"Captain?" Anara Meyers wanted an update.

Lights inside the cabin flickered on, some of the ship's power restored.

"We're going down, Commander. Fast," Rivers said. "Lieutenant, transfer ninety-percent of whatever life support energy we have to the thrusters."

"Captain?" The commander heard the clear warning in Lt. Bell's voice, apparently not thrilled with River's plan. Leaving only ten percent of life support in place sounded risky. If they could not stop the ship from crashing, all the life support in the world wouldn't make a difference. The commander agreed with the captain's call, and believed she would have made the same decision if she sat in the captain's chair.

"Do it!" Rivers barked.

"Aye, Captain."

The shuttle whined as wind rushed wild against the hull. It sounded as if the shuttle were screaming aware of its inevitable demise.

They plummeted toward the planet's surface.

Bell said, "Eighty-percent. Eighty-five…"

They were not going to have time. They would crash before life support was fully converted.

"Punch it now," Rivers ordered. "Now, Bell!"

The commander watched Lt. Bell depress buttons and toggle switches. She heard the fire ignite and the thrusters engage in a whoosh.

"We have power, Captain."

Rivers slammed feet on foot pedals, twisted the yoke left and right, and then eased it between her thighs as she regained control of her ship.

They would run out of oxygen soon, true enough, but they needn't worry about suffocation. If they did not find somewhere safe to land, they would freeze to death long before the breathable air depleted.

CHAPTER ELEVEN

Beta Squad

Captain Adam Stanton opened his eyes. His vision was blurred, and so he blinked a few times hoping it would clear, that things might come into focus. He ran an arm across his forehead. He suspected beads of sweat mopped away, but it turned out to be streaks of blood on his sleeve. His hands touched his face. There was a gash above his right eye. The blood dripped into his eyes, hence the blurred vision. He blinked several times in an attempt to rid his eyeballs of the blood.

He smelled smoke. He knew he had crashed the starfighter. There was no telling where on the planet he had ended up. He thought about unfastening his seatbelt and getting out of the fighter, but gave pause.

There seemed little point.

He would die if exposed for too long outside in the elements. The sub-zero temperatures and heavy winds would kill him in minutes.

If the starfighter caught fire, he would die inside the cockpit.

Stanton's eyes roamed over the control displays. Lights were on. Flickering, but on. Systems were up. Running. He did not think the ship would fly again. It looked as if he had buried the craft in a snowbank. Without a tow, he could not figure out how he would free a two-ton ship. At least there was life support. Air.

He depressed his comlink. "Captain Stanton. Beta Squad Leader. *Eclipse*, come in. *Eclipse*?"

Static. Then nothing.

He tried again. "This is Captain Stanton to the *Eclipse*. *Eclipse*, come in?"

"Beta Leader to Red One. Red One?"

Nothing.

"Beta Leader to Red Two. Red Two?"

Static.

"Beta Leader to Red Three? Red Four? Beta Leader to the *Eclipse* Shuttle? Someone? Is anyone there? Anyone?"

Nothing, and then static, and then nothing again.

The wind howled outside. The hail pelleted his ship. He no longer smelled smoke. Maybe the starfighter wouldn't go up in flames. That might not be a good thing. Although the thought of burning alive sounded beyond horrible, suffocating inside the ship would take longer. It would be a slower death.

He thumbed the distress beacon.

A light just outside the cockpit came on. Red and flashing.

The signal would travel hundreds of miles. If anyone else was out there, they'd have the ability to lock onto it. The call was transmitted on any and all open frequencies. Worse case, the colonists might be in a position to pinpoint his location if, in fact, there was anyone still alive inside the colony.

"Beta Leader to Red Two. Red Two?"

There was no reply. No static.

Just nothing.

———

Eclipse Shuttle

Commander Anara Meyers knew she was screaming. The ship dropped fast, and it felt as if her stomach launched up into her throat.

They all screamed. The shuttle toppled end over end now. Restraints bit into the commander's shoulders and her chest ached. She wanted to press her hands to the sides of her head. It felt like her brain had jarred loose and slammed around inside her skull.

"Brace yourselves!" Captain Danielle Rivers shouted over the terrified cries.

Meyers could not see clearly. She did her best to look out the front window porthole. There was blue and white. And it spun beyond the thick glass. Everything appeared to spin out of control. There was no differentiating up from down, down from up.

Her stomach rolled.

Rivers let out a cry, defiant, and brave, determined even, but a cry nonetheless.

Meyers saw her father.

The admiral.

He was in the path of her mind's eye. He stood in front of her. Dressed in his military uniform, he wore a scowl and shook his head. The disappointment in his expression was clear. He never wanted her working for the private sector. This accident was a direct result of her leaving the NAAA. That was what his expression said. She left the NAAA, so she had this coming.

The shuttle slammed into something.

Meyers' head snapped back. It felt as if her loose brain crashed against the front of her skull, where shots of sharp pain raced for her temples.

When everything went black, when all of the whining engines and signaling alarms were silenced, Meyers felt no shame in quietly welcoming death.

CHAPTER TWELVE

Eclipse Shuttle

Commander Anara Meyers opened her eyes. She expected white lights. Harp playing angels. Trumpets. A stairway into the heavens.

Instead, red lights flashed. A siren squawked. Her ears throbbed in beat with the wail.

"Commander. Commander?"

Captain Rivers stood over her. She had a gash on the bridge of her nose. Blood dripped off her chin. "Are you okay?"

Meyers let her hands roam over her chest. It felt as if every rib were broken. When she coughed, she winced. "I'll be fine."

Rivers helped her with the safety restraints. "Take a minute before getting up. Okay? Let your body get a hold of the situation. It needs time to adjust, just like your mind." Rivers looked around. "Bell, how are we doing?"

"Switching what I can back to life support," he said, but did not sound at all hopeful.

Meyers moved, shifted her weight and rose out of the jump seat.

Rivers had her by the arms. Steadied her. Meyers was thankful for the support, and tried smiling in a way that expressed her gratitude. "Nice and easy, Commander."

Her legs worked. Her arms moved. Meyers' internal assessment revealed little more than a sore chest. She might bruise some, but would otherwise survive. Realizing the people in the shuttle cockpit were okay, she asked, "The others? The crew?"

"Haven't gone back there yet." Rivers kept a hand under the commander's arm.

Meyers mentally braced for the worst. The fact the three of them were alive, and for what seemed like the most part, unbroken, was a miracle. Rivers' piloting had saved their lives. No doubt about that. The woman was highly skilled at the controls. "I'm fine. We should check on them."

"Aye, Commander."

Captain Rivers tried the door separating the flight deck from the rear of the shuttle. It would not budge.

"Captain?" Meyers said.

"It's stuck."

Bell, draped over the instrument panel, sat up straight. "It's done. Wasn't easy. I managed to convert every last bit of energy I could, and re-routed it all to life support."

Rivers nodded. "How long do we have?"

"Twelve, fifteen hours tops."

Commander Meyers knew even twenty-hours of air would not be enough. They were stranded on an alien planet. God only knew how far away they were from the colony. They would use up fifteen hours of air just brainstorming an escape plan. First things first. "Let's get this door open, and check on the rest of the crew."

Lieutenant Bell fidgeted with the door's control panel. He opened the cover, disconnected wires, rubbed bare ends together trying to spark life into the ends. With the power re-routed, it took several attempts. "This might not work."

The door swished open.

Bell stepped back, eyes wide. "Well, what do you know?"

Amber lights lit the short passageway. There were sparks in the left corner. Live, exposed wires. Captain Rivers pushed forward, and retrieved the extinguisher from where it hung mounted on the wall. She pulled the pin, aimed the nozzle, and squeezed the handle. CO_2 doused the area in a plume. The immediate threat diffused. Danielle tossed the spent canister aside. With a wave of her hand, she stepped past the cloud and into the back half of the shuttle. "O'Hearn? Weber?"

"Captain?" It was Lt. Marshall Weber. The field medic. "We're good. O'Hearn broke his nose."

O'Hearn sat restrained in a seat. He wore a goofy grin. Pressing a blood-soaked cloth over his face, he said, "I'm all good, Captain. Not as pretty as I was an hour ago, but all good."

Commander Meyers let relief wash over her. Her crew was what was most important. Above all else, she was in charge of their safety. "Glad you guys are okay."

Weber asked, "What happened up there?"

"A storm came up out of nowhere. Knocked out our systems," Bell said. "We were snow-blind. Did all we could to steer the ship. The captain landed us best she could."

"Crashed us," Rivers said.

"Hardly," Meyers said. "Could have been a lot worse. By all rights, we should be dead. You piloted this box of a ship with amazing skill. Design engineers could never have fitted the shuttle with the ability to move the way you handled her. Well done."

"Thank you, Commander."

A short silence cascaded over the group before Anara Meyers cleared her throat. "We're in a bad situation. I think that much is obvious." Her first officer was on the *Eclipse* with a basic skeleton crew. They could not hold their breath and expect a miracle rescue from space. Survival came down to how they handled the situation. Their chances were slim. Anorexic. If they did not device a plan soon, then they were as good as dead. "We have to figure out where on the planet we've landed, and how far off course we are from the colony. Getting from the shuttle to their commune is not just our best chance at getting through this. It is our only chance."

"Before transferring complete power to life support," Bell said, "I was able to lock in on the colony. We most certainly overshot the compound. I was able to pin down our crash site, excuse me, Commander, our landing, and quickly map a course back toward the colony. I downloaded the coordinates onto my pad."

"Wonderful. How far away are we?" Commander Meyers remained as hopefully optimistic as possible. There was little left for them to hold onto. Bell's bit of good news was a spark she did not want diminished. The distance between the shuttle and the colony, however, would determine how optimistic things looked overall.

Murray Bell pursed his lips. He let his head nod left and right, as if gauging his answer carefully. "We've got ah, well—"

Meyers insisted, "Lieutenant Bell?"

"About ten clicks south of us," he answered.

Ten clicks. Just over six miles. It was whiteout conditions. The temperature was far below zero. There was no telling what kind of consistency surface of the planet was in. In fact, the shuttle could be on the verge of sinking into the toxic ocean. The planet was the closest it has been to the sun in a century and a half, and frozen areas were melting, exposing more and more of the oceans that normally remained below the ice.

She needed the idea of six miles to be a good thing, a positive. Was there a way to put that kind of spin on the trek ahead of them? Grin and bear it? That would not be enough. She had to sell it. The commander needed the crew to buy it.

"Outstanding work, Lieutenant Bell. Outstanding." Commander Meyers took solace in the ability of her team. She did not hide the swell of pride she felt about each of them. *Euphoric* did not skimp when recruiting talent and the company did its best ensuring the success of her crew when assigning members to the *Eclipse*. "We've got limited air on the shuttle, but plenty to do what needs getting done."

"We taking the rover?" Bell asked.

"We're not. Be a tight fit for all of us. We were sold on a luxury model that seats four comfortably. Have you sat in that thing? *Salesmen*." She smiled, shook her head, pleased for the opportunity, brief as it may have been, to lighten the mood some. "The combined weight of passengers and machine. No. No, I don't like it. Think we have a better chance on foot. Sounds drastic. If the rover falls through thin ice, we're dead. It's just not a risk I'm willing to take with my crew."

"So what is it? What are you saying? Are we going out onto the surface?" O'Hearn asked. His words came out muffled from behind the cloth he held over his nose. It did not help that he talked while keeping his head tipped back in an attempt at controlling the bleeding. "On foot?"

"We are. With the exception of Lieutenant Bell," she affirmed and turned her attention. "Bell, I want you to turn all of your efforts on finding a way to make contact with the *Eclipse*. We've got to find a way to let them know that we're okay, but also inform them about the dire straits of our circumstances. You have extra air in the tanks. Should it get to that point, where we haven't returned with help, put on one of the suits. Use the air from there, as well. Understood?"

"Aye, Commander," Bell said and gave a nod. "I'll find a way to get communications up and running. You can count on it."

"Good. Because I will be," she said. "And Lieutenant, I will return for you. One way or another. As soon as we reach the colony we will be back for you."

"Aye." The acknowledgment was there, but the sincerity attenuated.

Weber, still squatting beside the lieutenant, dug around inside his medical bag. "With permission, Commander, let me get his bleeding under control and set the bone. Then we'll both be in a better position pull our weight."

"Of course." Meyers nodded. "By all means tend to his wounds. And take a look at the captain's nose as well."

Rivers said, "I don't think it's broken."

"Let Lieutenant Weber have a look, regardless. I have no idea what kind of a journey we're getting ourselves into. It can only go better if we are as healthy as possible. The conditions are certain to be treacherous. If our medic here can clean us up before we head out, it might make his job that much easier once we're underway. Agreed, Lieutenant?"

"Commander." Weber nodded, and stood up. "I also noticed you holding your sides. May I?"

Anara Meyers would have deflected the attention, but after her little speech, she reluctantly raised her arms. Weber touched around her stomach, and then along her ribcage. Unexpectedly, she winced, and then cringed at allowing him to expose a weakness.

"That hurt?"

"A little tender," she was forced to admit.

Weber applied pressure here and there. "I don't think anything is broken. Thing about ribs, even if one *were* there isn't much we could do about it. But like I said, I don't think you broke anything. If they took a knocking, they are bruised. Might hurt like hell now, but by tomorrow," he looked up, and grinned, "they are going to feel a million times worse."

O'Hearn raised a hand. "Commander," he said.

"What is it?"

"How'd Beta Squad fair in the storm?"

CHAPTER THIRTEEN

Starfighter, Beta Squad

Captain Adam Stanton remembered back to a time when he was new in the cadet academy. Flying fighters was always his dream. As soon as he'd finished high school, he'd enlisted with the NAAA. A year of intense training did more than prepare him for flying fighters, it turned him from a boy into a man.

One day, the sergeant called him down to his office. When Stanton arrived, he knew immediately something was off. The sergeant had a strict open door policy. In fact, even when giving a cadet a dressing down, the office door remained open.

Hesitant, Stanton knocked on the door.

It opened immediately, and the sergeant stepped aside. Seated in front of the sergeant's desk was the colonel.

Stanton's mouth went immediately dry. His tongue felt swollen and thick inside his mouth. Swallowing became a chore. He stood at attention and saluted.

"At ease, cadet," the colonel said as he rose from the chair.

"Cadet Stanton," the sergeant said, once again closing the office door. "We just have a few questions for you."

"Of course, Sergeant. Colonel. How can I help?" At ease in the presence of a colonel was anything but relaxing. Feet shoulder-width apart, hands clasped together behind his back, Stanton worried his muscles might cramp up from tension alone.

"We know that you have been seeing a lot of fellow student, Irina Vasiliev," the colonel said.

They were not asking. They were telling. They knew. For some reason, his activity on campus had been closely monitored.

He had met the Russian woman at the beginning of the semester. Stunning. Long, silky blonde hair. Big, dark eyes. Soft, milky skin. And flexible beyond just being limber…

"I have been. Yes, sir."

"Are you aware she can speak many different languages?"

"Eighteen fluently," I said. "Twenty-three conversationally."

"For reasons of Armada security, we'd like you to call it off, or you can pack your things and leave the academy."

It was then he noticed a thick manila folder on the sergeant's desk. The truth was he planned on calling it off with Irina, regardless. Despite amazing looks and astounding brains, she lacked an imagination, or motivation, or vigor in bed. "Consider it done, sir."

"No questions asked?"

"None needed." The implication Irina was a spy, or under suspicion of *something* big enough to attract the colonel's attention, was more than enough by way of explanation for him. "Are we all set here, then?"

The colonel saluted. "Carry on, cadet."

It was a few years later when he saw Irina's face on the news. She was a wanted fugitive, potentially responsible for a café bombing over in France. Far as Stanton knew, his old flame was still on the lamb. In a way, he thought, good for her.

A radio crackled. The static-hiss pulled him away from his thoughts. Had he fallen asleep? The sound filled the cramped cockpit. In the mix, faintly, just barely audible, Stanton thought he heard a familiar voice.

Someone was on the portable, a short-distance frequency.

He should have thought to use the hand-held. He increased the volume, held the communicator close to his face. "Red One? Ruiz? Is that you?"

Stanton could not recall a time when he had ever been as excited to hear the sound of anyone's voice. "Ruiz?"

Again, faint. He heard her voice, and she had heard his. She sounded as elated as he felt. "Captain? Stanton? I can see your starfighter."

The fighters were easily identified, and differentiated from one another, because of the markings. His bore one thick red pinstripe. The other ships had thinner stripes. Ruiz's ship had one. Reilly two. Cornwell three.

"Any sign of the shuttle, Red One?"

"No, sir. No sign of them."

She was close. He could not see a thing from where he sat. Best he could tell his ship had frosted over, at least his windows were for sure, and quite possibly the entire starfighter was encased in ice by now.

"I'm in trouble, though, Captain. Front glass on my fighter is cracked. Cold's getting in."

Stanton heard the fear in her tone of voice. It sent a chill through his body. He closed his eyes, needing a minute. She could see his ship, so they couldn't be too far away from each other. If she stayed inside her fighter, she would die. There was no way they could both fit inside of his. The cockpits in the ships were small, tight, and meant for a single person. He was wedged in place as it was. He needed a plan, a way he could save her life. "You have your suit on?"

"I do, Captain. All snuggled in."

"Helmet? Faceshield?"

"Helmet's on. Faceshield is up while we talk." She laughed. "I can feel the tiny hairs in my nose icing over. Feels a bit like glass shards inside my nostrils."

There was nothing funny about it. "Ruiz, stand by." Talking into the portable, Stanton said, "Beta Leader to Red Two. Reilly, come in. Red Two?"

He waited, hopeful. "Red Two?"

Nothing.

"Beta Leader to Red Three. Cornwell, you there? Jane, can you hear me?"

He waited. "This is Beta Leader, Red Three. Answer me. Damnit, answer me, Jane!"

Silence was the only reply.

"Captain?" It was Ruiz, timid. It was as if she did not want to disturb the moment, or risk talking over Red Two or Red Three if they were attempting to respond.

A good amount of time had passed, however. And neither Reilly nor Cornwell had chimed in.

"Go ahead, Ruiz."

"I ... I think I can see the colony," she said. "It's just beyond your ship. Yes. That must be what it is, what I'm seeing. Sir, it's got to be the colony."

She had a visual? That was a good thing. Promising. It meant a chance existed. They might get out of this. "Are you sure, Red One?"

"Unless there are natives on the planet we didn't know about, I'd say I'm fairly positive what I see beyond your fighter is *Euphoric's* colony."

Beyond was vague. He would have loved a more precise position. She could see the colony, though. He knew how bad the storm was, and the fact visibility was extremely limited. Beyond would have to be good enough. There was hope in the statement. Right now, a glimmer like that, of hope, he would latch onto it. Tight. Both hands. "Here's what we're going to do, Ruiz ..."

CHAPTER FOURTEEN

Cutlass

Erinne Cohn hated her metallic arm. It was fully functional. The fingers responded, the arm bent. She could grasp and grip, scratch and dig, poke and point. Doctors assured her in time she would forget it was prosthetic. That was more than five years ago. She could not recall a single day she was not reminded about what she had lost.

Being with Aroldis D'Rukker might be why she could not forget.

She lost the arm in Tennessee. Although originally from New York, Tennessee was where she had wandered off to after her father passed away.

There was a time when those on the planet feared something known as global warming. Scientists assured people the icecaps were melting. The fear of major cities getting swallowed up by a swelling ocean moved nations into action. Money and resources were dedicated to research. Countries scrambled toward finding a solution. Instead of ocean levels rising, they declined. The limited bodies of fresh water all but vanished. Planet Earth became something of a wasteland. Globally.

They called it an apocalypse. Plagues, violence, famine, and war wreaked havoc across continents. All that remained when everything was said and done were small pockets of survivors. Scavengers. Gangs. Inbred societies. And people like her. Wanderers.

Each vied for a piece of pie that was not worth cutting, and certainly not worth eating.

It did not matter that in the heavens two massive Way Stations existed, where hundreds of thousands of people lived more normal lives … Earth continued on, quality dwindled down to savage bare bones, but continued on as best it could.

Earth was where she was born and raised. Her father was the only parent in her life. When she was three, her mother was raped and murdered on the way home from a corner store. Erinne was far too young to understand the loss, and far too young to retain any worthwhile memories of her mother. Like what she looked like. Like what she sounded like. When she thought of her mother, her mind conjured up a blurred image that could more easily be confused with a blob than with a person.

Some niche communities did their best at restoring some semblance of normalcy. Where she was raised there was something of a local government and a police force. They were allowed authority, but it was limited. And, eventually, corrupted. When it came to her mother, no killer had ever found if one had ever been looked for in the first place.

Geno's was a pizza place in Gatlinburg. Hungry, but with limited money, Erinne entered the small shop. The person behind the counter asked her what she wanted. He spoke in some foreign accent so thick she almost could not understand a word he had said.

"Do you sell pizza by the slice?" Erinne asked. She couldn't recall the last time she'd had pizza. Or real food. She wasn't delusional. The ingredients in any prepared food were questionable. As long as it tasted better than mere roadkill scraped off the road, and if she was lucky, roasted over a makeshift open flame, she was game. The thought of real pizza made her stomach growl and the aromas inside *Geno's* made her mouth salivate.

"I make whole pizza for you."

"But I don't want a whole pizza. Just two slices."

"You want I should cut two slices out of the pizza for you? But then what do I do with the rest of the pizza?" He held back a laugh, barely. "I cannot make just two slices of pizza for you. How would I shape the dough that small? Two slices. You joke with me."

Erinne had a hand in her pocket. Her jeans were torn. Tattered. Her fingers pushed around the few coins inside the pocket lining. She could not afford an entire pizza. She could certainly eat one, but she could not afford one. "Thank you, anyway."

Walking toward the exit, she could still hear the man behind the counter. "How can I cut two pieces out of a pizza and just sell them? I'd never make money ruining an entire pizza that way!"

Pissed, she snatched a loaf of bread off the rack and sprinted for the door.

Somehow, the man behind the counter moved with unsuspecting stealth and speed. He leapt over the counter, a machete in his hand. He chased her out of *Geno's*. Erinne made a dash down the street, and though she thought if she dropped the loaf, and the guy might let her go, her stomach growled with encouraging protest, as if insisting she could make it.

The mistake came when she chanced a look back. He was not that close, but clearly gaining on her.

And then she tripped.

She had not been looking where she was going and she went down. Hard.

The man was on her in a flash. He seethed as he straddled her hips. Saliva oozed in strands from the corners of his mouth and leaked from behind rogue teeth that barely gripped diseased gums.

Without warning, without even a scolding, the man from *Geno's* raised his arm in the air, the machete over his head, the blade reflected sunlight like a white laser into her eyes, and then he swung. It happened fast, although it felt as if time moved in slow motion.

She could not remember the pain.

What she recalled was the spray of blood as it coated over the man's face and spattered already pizza sauce-stained clothing.

Making heads or tails of what had just happened was nearly impossible. She knew the man had just cut her. What she did not immediately realize was that her arm had been severed off from the rest of her body, just above the elbow, and then she slipped into shock.

Two things happened before she blacked out.

She saw her wrist in the mouth of a large Shepherd. She recognized her mother's wedding ring on her own finger. What she could not understand was how the dog, backing away, was now running from her with her arm clenched between its teeth. This was when she caught on. The guy cut off her arm, and a starving dog just swiped it.

When she woke up, several days later, Aroldis sat in a chair beside the bed she found herself in.

He had saved her, scooped her up from the street gutter, and run with her in his arms to the nearest medical facility. In time, he even footed the bill for surgery. She had him to thank for the metal that was now a permanent limb.

Erinne never let him know how much she hated the prosthetic; because she was certain living without one would have made life even worse.

Monitoring the *Cutlass* control panels, Erinne depressed the intercom switch. "D'Rukker?"

After a moment, the intercom light came on. "Yeah, Erinne. Go ahead?"

"Picking up two new distress beacons. Also coming from the planet's surface. All within close proximity of the colony. Far enough away, though, that it more than likely isn't coming from within the compound."

"The fighters, or the shuttle?"

Erinne nodded even though D'Rukker was elsewhere on the *Cutlass* and could not see her doing so. "Either. Both. That's what I'm thinking.

Add to that the colony distress signal, and I don't know about you but—"

"Not having second thoughts, are you?"

Erinne imagined her boss grinning. What she was thinking was that maybe they should consider seeing if anyone needed help. She'd never say as much. D'Rukker may have saved her life, took her under his wing, but that was as far as she had ever seen his charity extend. Not to mention he had already made it clear any available space on the *Cutlass* was for diamonds, and not passengers. "Not at all. I was thinking maybe we should hang back and wait for the storm to pass. No reason to penetrate the atmosphere right now. We stand a better chance of detection by the starfighters, and it really won't make much of a difference if we swoop in tomorrow, or even the next day and take the diamonds. Way I see it, we wait a day or two, the people from the *Eclipse* will have their hands full. Guards will be down. They won't be expecting an attack. We go in now, with distress signals activated everywhere … every single one of them on the rescue is on high alert, wound tight."

D'Rukker said, "That's an excellent point. Set us down somewhere. Keep us out of *Eclipse* radar range if you can. I want you to continue monitoring frequencies. Has there been any verbal transmissions?"

"None I've been able to detect," she said, eyes looking for a large asteroid or another of Neptune's moons. They had been safely hidden on Thalassa. "D'Rukker, Naiad is just ahead. I can give the thrusters a final push, land us on her with minimal effort. Gets us closer to Neptune to boot."

"Naiad. Sounds like a plan. Get her done, Erinne."

Get her done, she thought. Her arm squeaked when she reached for the control panel. She ground her teeth. Joints needed regular oiling. Her other elbow never needed oil. Okay. A little lotion now and then, but when she did not use any lotion the damned thing did not squeak.

Erinne pushed thoughts of her mechanical arm out of her mind, or tried anyway. She placed one hand on the control wheel, the other on the thrusters. Her feet sat on the rests, beside the rudder and brake pedals. The moon, identified by her system information display, was named Naiad. Not quite round, it was fifty-nine by thirty-seven by thirty-two miles around. Nothing huge, plenty of room for landing and staying well hidden.

The *Cutlass* pushed forward, and when Erinne disengaged the thrusters, she allowed for inertia to take over. Limiting system electronic activity, with the exception of life support, Erinne knew detection was not probable. Possible, but not probable. With the number of distress signals bouncing about the crew on the *Eclipse* would be plenty busy. The number of asteroids and the rings spinning around the planet set off the *Cutlass* sensors countless times. Same false-positive readings had to be occurring on the *Eclipse*.

At least, that was what she was banking on.

Sooner or later, the crew of the *Eclipse* would know they were there. Close by. In striking distance. The element of surprise remained key.

The *Cutlass* coasted toward the moon surface. With some throttle and rudder manipulation, Erinne expertly set the ship down.

"Smooth." She powered down the ship. *Got her done.*

CHAPTER FIFTEEN

Eclipse Shuttle

Commander Anara Meyers remembered when she was a girl. Her father, the admiral, was stationed on Earth. The military compound was a training facility for special forces. The elite. Platoons spent weeks in the elements with minimal gear. Survival the objective. Even the highest skilled and best qualified oftentimes failed. Initially, Anara remembered feeling devastated about the deployment. The Way Station was and always had been home. How could her father expect her to up and leave friends?

She'd always viewed Earth from Nebula portholes with little more than a passing glance. The planet was an orb in the galaxy. She felt no allure, no kindred connection to ancient ancestors. Nothing. Its oceans, landmasses, and patterned white clouds were as inanimate as a flat painting, something frame*able* and hung on a wall.

Everything changed once their ship launched from Nebula and they were en-route to Earth. In awe, strapped in her seat beside a porthole, she saw Earth in a new light. Sunlight lit half of the planet and left the back half in darkness. Anara noticed, for the first time, the swirling movement of the clouds, and as their ship flew closer and passed around the planet's moon, she noticed vibrant greens and deep jagged browns. Plains, mountains, white—that the admiral explained was snow, whatever that was—and giant moving bodies of water.

Their ship landed along the coastline of Anchorage, Alaska, by the Cook Inlet. It was snowing. Hard. Getting off the ship, she was almost fearful. The large flakes rained down from the sky. When the ship's doors opened and she descended the staircase, the sound of howling wind amazed her. There was a sting from the cold on any part of exposed skin, but she didn't mind. The snowflakes melted on her wrists and the end of her nose. One flake lodged on her eyelashes and she laughed.

"Try this," her father said. They were on the plowed tarmac, making their way toward the main facility. The admiral tilted his head back, opened his mouth, and stuck out his tongue. A snowflake fell into his mouth. He looked at her, grinning.

She gave it a try, and spun around, moving her head back and forth.

"Just stand still," he instructed.

Standing still, mouth open and tongue out, a snowflake landed on the tip of her tongue, and she ate it up as if a gourmet meal.

Way Station Nebula had always been home.

The climate was controlled. It didn't rain or snow.

"The air tastes funny," she said, breathing in deep through her nostrils.

"That's because it doesn't come out of a can. It isn't fresh down here. Toxins everywhere, but it isn't recycled like back home, either," the admiral said, sucking in a deep breath himself. Anara knew the expression he wore then. It was similar to the one when he took a bite of some new amazing entree. The admiral was savoring a breath of fresh air.

She remembered thinking, *I love it here!*

"Commander?" Captain Danielle Rivers tucked her hair into her helmet and adjusted the mounted side LED lights. The black nylon tricot, spandex material of her suit form-fit her body perfectly. The sub-freezing temperatures would eventually penetrate the layers. If outside too long, they'd die. The boots worn were special. They'd keep them grounded. The wind should never be able to lift them off the ground. *Euphoric* knew how to design wonderful equipment. However, Neptune was doing its best to prove the corporation's efforts ineffective.

Meyers secured the end of the gloves over the forearms of her suit. "Captain?"

"I was asking if we should use a static rope, securing each of us to the other?"

"That's exactly what we'll do. The terrain will be unforgiving. But if the storm keeps up, visibility will be non-existent. It will be easy to get separated, lost." If the whiteout condition wasn't bad enough, the commander was also worried about footing. The ice was melting. A wrong step could let one or all of them plunge into the poisonous ocean. The ammonia-base would kill them. Even with a static rope, a rescue might not be possible. The rope would come into play simply as a means of keeping them tethered, preventing any one of them from wandering away from the small herd.

Trying not to sigh, or let show her own personal doubt, the commander realized death seemed almost certain. "Make sure your side-arm is secured. Lock the holsters. We don't want unknown elements interfering with firing ability."

"Aye," they said.

If—when—they reached the colony, God only knew what they would be walking into. Going unarmed was not an option. Meyers has been firing a weapon since she was old enough to grip to trade a rattle for a blaster. Anara Meyers knew her blaster was loaded and safe on her right hip, and her Ka-Bar combat knife sat inside a sheath belted around her left thigh. Also safe and accessible.

Regardless—that was the key!—Regardless, they needed to keep moving, to keep trying. Although she never went through the training on Anchorage, she did learn from the examples and tests set forth. They could not succeed, could not survive if they stayed stationary. Knowing this tidbit, the only obvious option was making a break for it. The danger of losing their way, of freezing to death, was real. Even if Lieutenant Bell reestablished contact with the *Eclipse*, she was not sure there was anything they could do to help from space. At least not until the storm passed. *If* the storm passed.

"How's the nose, O'Hearn?" Rivers asked, punching him in the shoulder.

Gordon O'Hearn removed a wad of rolled tissue paper from each nostril. "Good as new," he said. He sounded as if he had a cold. The "d" in good and the "w" in new became silent letters in O'Hearn's pained pronunciation. He smiled as if he knew he sounded funny. "Doc fixed me up good."

"Radio check," the commander said and placed the black helmet over her head and closed the UV protective face shield. The others followed suit. "Commander, check one, check two."

In less than a minute, they confirmed by way of checks that the short-range communicators worked perfectly. They could hear one another clearly inside the security of the helmets.

They put on backpacks filled with supplies, and double-checked the air supply levels for each other.

The time arrived.

Commander Meyers did not like the idea of leaving Bell alone with the shuttle. Someone needed to stay behind, and he was the best candidate. His skillset trained him for scenarios like this. She had complete faith he would find a way to fidget rerouting power from something to something else and make contact with the *Eclipse*. As the only person on board the shuttle, there would be more air. Hopefully, he'd have longer than the initial twelve hours once they were out of the shuttle and on their way. Well, twelve, and he could also don a spacesuit and have additional air from the tanks. Even with twenty-four hours of air available, without a means for rescue, it did not really affect the undesirable outcome.

They affixed the static rope through carabineers on the belts around each suit. Commander Meyers on point. O'Hearn stood next. Then Rivers. Medic Weber completed the small train.

"You understand it is going to be zero visibility out there." The commander stood by the hatch. Bell, safe inside the cockpit, would re-stabilize cabin pressure after they had exited the shuttle. "You heard the sound of rain, we'll call it rain, hitting the hull? The helmets are going to protect us not just from the cold, but also from having our skulls bashed open, okay? We keep in a nice line. Any issues give the rope a tug. We've got coordinates to the colony. The maps should be displayed on your UV shields?"

"Aye," they said in unison.

"The shortest distance between two points is a straight line. Unfortunately, I have a sneaking suspicion we aren't going to be that fortunate." The commander held up a six-foot pole. "The trek is going to prove slow and tedious. I'll be checking the solidity of the ground before each and every step. It will be vital no one step to the left or the right. I am only testing the steps directly in front of me. Are we clear?"

Again, they responded, "Aye."

Meyers gave them what she hoped resembled a reassuring smile. "Okay. Then let's do this."

Turning around, taking a deep breath, Commander Anara Meyers opened the hatch door.

CHAPTER SIXTEEN

The commander stepped out of the *Eclipse* shuttle and into a raging storm. She switched on the helmet's side LEDs. The bright light barely cut through the snowsquall conditions. The wind roared, fierce and constant. Visibility was worse than expected. Had it been a clear day, she had no doubt the landscape would look spectacular. She could not help wonder how many moons would have been visible in the sky, otherwise. Instead, something like snow and hail rained on her.

Inside her helmet, Anara Meyers was conscientious of three things: her breathing, the beat of her heart in her ears, and the GPS map displayed in the right corner of her locked faceshield.

The breaths came fast, shallow. If she could not regain control, she'd use up her air. Who knew how long the trek from shuttle to colony would take? She did not want to deplete her oxygen if she could help. As she concentrated on calming her nerves, the sound of her heart beating slowed and her breathing regulated.

Digitally projected onto the glass in the right corner of her faceshield was a three-dimensional survey of the land in front of them, as well as the best route for them to take from the shuttle to the colony.

There were variously sized peaks. Shallow valleys. Might only be, roughly, six miles, but nearly all of it was uneven. Uneven and with no direct path. The visible terrain was not the issue. Whether they walked across solid ground or on thin ice over a poisonous ocean was what most troubled Meyers.

Poking the ground in front of her, Commander Meyers conducted a quick par with her crew. All accounted for, she pressed on.

Six miles. Snail's pace. Spending over six hours in the inclement weather would not bode well. They had air enough for twice the time, but Meyers considered twelve hours of air still cutting it close. So far, the suit did its job blocking the cold. If anything, if nothing at all, Meyers was working up a sweat. The beads of perspiration came from stress, fear, and desperation.

And yet, she felt exhilarated. The NAAA boasted promises of adventure, danger, and rewards. Her time spent in the branch of the military validated, at times, the claims. However, *Euphoric* guaranteed action. As the exploration of space became more routine, talks of traveling beyond the galaxy into other galaxies was even more attractive a sell.

Having spent most of her life on a Way Station and on the NAAA base, Anara Meyers didn't just long for the threat of peril, risk, and taking a gamble with her own mortality; she banked on it. Only this was different. As a commander, as *the* commander of the *Eclipse*, it wasn't just her own life in jeopardy. It wasn't just her life she gambled with.

There was the game changer; that small fact made the difference. This was also where the fear she felt originated. She was not afraid of dying. It came with the job. Failing was what bothered her most.

The crew depended on their commander. It reminded her of an old book she once read. *A Brave New World*, written by Aldous Huxley. The basic dystopian premise focused on a scientifically bread race of people. They infants were sorted. Alphas grew up to be doctors, and lawyers. Betas were assigned positions as managers and bosses. Gamma's worked mid-management. Deltas filled the blue-collar jobs. Epsilons emptied trash, and scrubbed toilets. The unique thing about the story is that each class of people were engineered to believe their role was essential, and they never longed to do anything else. The Epsilons were happy being Epsilons because they knew (were programmed to know) Deltas and Gammas had far more stress, and too much responsibility. The Gammas were happy as Gammas knowing that Betas and Alphas had far more stress, and too much responsibility.

Meyers felt like an Alpha now. It was not a great feeling. Part of her longed to be a Beta, or a Gamma. Part of her wished someone else were in charge. Rather than chew on that during the walk, she folded the thought up, tucked it away, and hoped she could pretend it had never entered her mind in the first place.

The people on *Eclipse* depended on her.

A small part of her has always worried about disappointing her father, the admiral. A larger part could not help but focus on ever having to hear him say *I told you so*. Hearing those four words went beyond disappointment. They signaled complete failure. In death, she'd be spared the sound of his voice saying, the look in his eyes, and the crushing sensation inside her chest, but she suspected even once in the *beyond* the realization would haunt her long into the afterlife.

They moved steadily. Slow, but steady. Thankfully, the iced over ground was solid. Footing sound.

Meyers did not let her attention wander. She poked and prodded ahead of each step. Carelessness could cost one of them their life. The tediousness of the task did grow daunting, however. Meyers switched the pole from hand to hand, providing what little variety she could.

The wind picked up. It surged down and raced toward them from several directions. An icy hail came with the wind, raining at them sideways. The foreboding sky was grey and white. There was a brilliance to it all. A blinding brilliance. Even with the UV faceshields in place, Meyers squinted against the brightness.

Collectively, they stopped walking. Meyers lifted her shoulders and tucked her chin to her chest.

Someone screamed behind her.

When she spun around, she caught Gordon O'Hearn flailing. The wind had knocked him off balance.

Captain Danielle Rivers reached for O'Hearn's arm.

The lieutenant's foot slid on ice. His arms pinwheeled.

He fell backwards.

When his back slammed onto the ground, the ground gave.

The ice shattered. Jagged pieces rose into the air. O'Hearn plunged through and splashed into the ocean underneath.

"Gordon!" Danielle lunged forward.

Weber positioned his feet and wrapped gloved hands around the rope tethering them all to each other. "Danielle, stop!"

Weber yanked on the rope, halting Danielle's momentum and jerking her to an arm-winding stop.

"Back up! Everyone, back away from the hole!" Commander Meyers grabbed onto Danielle's arm and pulled her further away from where Gordon fell through. "The rope. We've got to pull together. Danielle! Pull together!"

They stood in a line. Meyers last, Danielle, and then Weber.

The wind fought against them, rushing in at their backs, trying either desperately to push them forward toward the hole in the ice, or to knock them off balance.

Weber grunted and used all of his strength holding on to his length of rope.

The sides of Danielle's shoes bit into the ice. She stood at an angle, and put all of her weight into the work.

Meyers secured the rope around her waist, tied a knot in front, and then used her legs to pull. She battled the wind and won some ground. She took small steps backward, step after step.

O'Hearn had been under for some time.

The cracked ice around the hole moaned, cracking more, spider webbing toward the others.

They were putting too much stress on the surface.

It wouldn't hold much longer. If they didn't pull O'Hearn out fast, they all risked crashing into the ocean.

Too much time had passed. Meyers didn't want to give up.

She refused to surrender. "Pull!"

There was a small splash near the edge of the hole. A hand rose out of the water. The palm slapped down onto the ice. There was no handhold of any sort.

"Keep the line taut!" Weber's order boomed inside Meyers' helmet. She didn't ask questions, but quickly reset her footing and double-wrapped the rope around her wrist, bracing for whatever Weber had in mind. "Don't let go of the rope."

It was a plea.

Meyers had no intention of letting go.

On his belly, Weber slid forward on the ice until he was inches from the hole, inches away from O'Hearn's hand. In one motion, Weber reached for O'Hearn. He locked his hand over O'Hearn's wrist.

Weber moved closer, still. The ice groaned in protest. Meyers saw the ice underfoot web in cracks. They were all going to plummet into the ocean. Meyers didn't see a way around it. The ammonia would fill their lungs, the poison would kill them. It would burn; a painful death.

O'Hearn was under for far too long, but then Weber, his hands on O'Hearn's forearm, pulled O'Hearn up from beneath the water. He shot forward and clapped his hands onto O'Hearn's back, gloved fingers scratching around for a handhold.

Danielle crawled forward. She reached for O'Hearn's arms.

"No," Weber shouted. "Don't touch him! Help the commander. Use the rope. With both of you pulling, we can fish him out!"

Meyers held her ground, the rope in her hands. Feet set. Rivers joined her.

The three of them worked together, and at last, yanked O'Hearn out of the ocean.

CHAPTER SEVENTEEN

"I was born and raised on Earth." Adam Stanton set a steady pace. He kept one arm up, as if it worked better as a shield against the weather than his faceshield. He and Angela Ruiz walked side-by-side, their starfighters left abandoned behind them. "Most of my time I spent in New York. Place always had something of a bad rap. Even going back centuries, you know?"

"I've heard. Seen movies. Documentaries." Ruiz matched his stride. "Doesn't seem at all like a safe place to grow up. Were you scared?"

Stanton worked at keeping his breathing even. They used air talking. The silence, otherwise, was maddening. He considered it a fair trade-off, as long as he kept his breathing even. "Scared? Me? Nah. We lived in a one-bedroom apartment on the sixth floor of Bedford Park in the Bronx. Manhattan was just south of where we lived. Heard of it?"

"The Bronx or Manhattan?"

"Either."

He heard her laugh. "Both," she said. "There are files on record of New Year's Eve parties in Manhattan."

"That's the place. See, I took care of my dad. He was disabled. My mother left us when things got tough. At the time, I hated her for leaving. Oftentimes, I wondered how a mother could leave her son; a wife her husband, just because things got tough. Thing is, after a year without her, it only got worse. When I was like fifteen, I was responsible for everything. My dad, the bills, finding food. Everything. And I found that my hate toward my mother had evolved into something more, something worse. I resented her. I knew if I saw her again, I might not be able to refrain from socking her in the jaw."

"I'm very sorry," Ruiz said. "That must have been extremely hard for you at that age. You were just a boy."

He wasn't looking for pity. It wasn't the point of talking. Stanton was not sure why he had started the story. He knew he needed to talk, that it would help both of them pass the time while walking, without focusing on the likelihood they would never survive the short trek. "See, my dad suffered a stroke. The doctors explained what happened. The blood flow to an area of my father's brain was suddenly cut off. The cells, deprived of oxygen, died. His brain became under attack. The stroke left the left side of my father's body paralyzed. His speech was slurred and his left eye drooped. He was unable to walk, and, I guess, all of that real life stuff was just too much for my mother to handle. Granted, it was a lot. My dad needed constant attention. I even found him a wheelchair, well, found is kind of a loose word, you know? Point is, it helped me get my father around, but didn't provide him with any independence. With no mobility or fine motor skills in his left arm and hand, I was forced to push him around everywhere we went."

They didn't go out much. "My dad preferred staying home. In public, people stared. He always ran into someone he knew. My father would smile and retell what happened—because everyone always wanted to know what had happened. The medical talk had people speechless, intently listening, you know? But shaking their head, like, how sad for you. Then they'd talk for a bit, catch up on old times, but as soon as the conversation ended and they continued on, my father, he'd brood. I mean he would fold his arms, lower his head, and demand to be taken home. Right then."

Ruiz was quiet. Stanton wondered if he'd gone too far, opened up too much. He regretted getting into this topic. It was more than most needed to know. He was committed now. There was more. Stopping before reaching the end wouldn't do. "On one particular humid June night, I found myself free.

"We had this rusty fire escape I used as a balcony. It was off the bedroom window. Even though I slept on a sofa in the family room, I'd often wait for my father to fall asleep before sneaking through his room and out onto the fire escape. I'd spend the night listening to the sounds of the city, watch the people pass under the window. In New York, no one had much of anything. There wasn't much point in robbing each other. I think most of us, most people, longed to have things the way they once were. Back, you know, before the planet went to hell. You said you thought New York was a tough town, yeah. It was, but I felt safe. It was the only New York I knew, I didn't know much different. And where I was, that was home.

"My father, he passed quietly. It was more than I could have hoped. My father had suffered for a long time, you know? First the stroke, then my mother leaving him, and then the humiliation of having his son caring for him. I had to bathe him, and sometimes, wipe his ass.

"An easy death was the least life owed him, the very least. And you know what? Do you know how many times I wished I could trade places with him? I would have, you know. I would have traded places with my father in a heartbeat. I would rather have been the one stuck in bed, an invalid. It just wasn't something I could do. As much as I wanted to sacrifice myself for him, there was nothing I could do." Stanton knew crying would use up his air faster. The tears rolled down his cheeks. There was no way to brush them away.

"Captain, you okay?" Ruiz asked.

"There's a point to this." Stanton chuckled, regaining control. "See, that night, with my father in the room, his body on the bed, I sat out on that fire escape with my knees up, my head back against the rail, and just stared up at the heavens, at the stars. I knew that above me were man-made worlds. Starships. And I saw it, Ruiz. I saw a chance for a new life, new beginnings. So, after burying my father, I set into play my plan for getting off Earth, away from having nothing." Stanton stopped walking. Ruiz stopped beside him. "I decided I'd get a job, any job, and leave for the stars as soon as they would have me. The idea served two purposes. One, I'd be off the planet, away from the famine and hunger and crime. And, two? I eliminated the random chance of ever having to see my mother face-to-face ever again." Captain Adam Stanton did not want to die on Neptune, but if he did, he had no regrets. Not a-one. He'd had a dream and accomplished his goals.

"Adam?" Ruiz backhanded his arm before she snatched the sidearm from the holster. The blaster held steady in an outstretched arm. "Over there. Did you see that?"

Adam looked around toward where she pointed. The ocean moved between two banks. Free. Flowing fast. Reminded Stanton more of a river. Same difference, he supposed. More of the acrid body of water was below where they stood as well. Thankfully, the ice was thicker. He hoped. Either way, he didn't see anything. "What was it?"

"Something. I don't know what, but I saw something, and it moved. It jumped out of the ocean."

"A moving chunk of ice. Probably looked like it was something alive, you know? But it was more than likely a mini-iceberg, dipping and rising in the current." Although Stanton had his hand on the butt of his blaster, he kept it holstered. His breathing was faster. Shallower. In all of the briefings he could recall, he knew the planet to be lifeless. Nothing they knew of could survive in this constant cold, with ammonia-saturated oceans. Nothing *they* knew of. "I'm not seeing anything. What did you see?"

"It was no iceberg, Adam." Ruiz shook her head, as if maybe she wasn't sure even she believed her own eyes. "It was in the water. And then it jumped out of the water, I think."

"You think?"

"Or it was already on the bank. But I know for certain it—whatever it was—was on this side of the water." She pointed at her own feet.

It was not uncommon for people to come unglued under high-stress situations. They were in a calamitous situation. That was after prolonged exposure in an extreme circumstance. Had enough time passed to qualify Ruiz's seeing things? He was no doctor, and did not know if there were rules or timelines for an acceptable timeframe when a person could come unglued. He figured it just happened when it happened. If breakdowns were more predictable, they could be stopped. Breakdowns happened all the time. This led Stanton to believe there was no predictability at all.

"How's your air?" Stanton said. If her trimix, nitrox, and oxygen levels were off, an unbalanced combination could cause hallucinations, or be flat-out lethal.

"It's fine. Readings are normal," she said, without hiding obvious frustration. Her response might have answered his question, but Stanton read between the lines. What she really was saying was, *I'm not crazy, Captain. I'm not seeing things that aren't there!* "I'd have an alarm on the faceshield display if something were off kilter."

"That's true, but you never know. After the crash, any number of things can be wrong with the systems. Here, turn around. Let me check your gauges." He put hands on her shoulders as she turned. They were wasting time, and, as it so happened, air. He eyed the digital displays.

Ruiz's arm shot up, blaster aimed at the vastness of white and blue. "There!"

Adam Stanton stood up straight.

Something slithered on the ground, skirted around a blue, icy boulder. "What was that?"

"You saw it?"

As improbable as it seemed, Stanton admitted: "I saw something."

CHAPTER EIGHTEEN

"Is he breathing?" Danielle Rivers knelt beside Gordon O'Hearn's body. The spacesuit was drenched.

"I can't tell. Ammonia and water are one of the worst possible mixes." The medic, Marshall Weber, knelt across from Rivers. Without touching O'Hearn, his hand passed over the body from head to toe. "The two produce what is known as ammonium hydroxide. The chemical is corrosive and damaging on contact. The integrity of his suit . . . it's been badly compromised."

Had Commander Meyers noticed the deterioration of O'Hearn's spacesuit? Weber wondered. Smoke rose from the fabric, from shoulders to ankles. The ammonium hydroxide ate away at the suit. It reminded him of one of his first rides on a rescue as a newly licensed paramedic. There had been a fire in the engine compartment of a starfighter. The ship was still inside the bay. Unfortunately, the pilot was still inside the cockpit. The fire fried the ship's operation systems. The hatch not only would not open, but by the time help arrived, the hot metal had welded the hatch shut.

When they finally extricated the pilot, they had laid him on the floor. Before the suit was cut away from the body, Weber had in awe watched the smoke rise from the material. The pilot was dead, blackened and crisp beneath the layers of the suit.

It was not unlike the situation in front of them. Except, even if O'Hearn was still alive, they could not remove his suit—getting O'Hearn out of the suit would be the only way of protecting the lieutenant from the poisonous gas seeping inside. However, removing O'Hearn from the suit and exposing him to Neptune's elements would kill him instantly. It was a lose-lose predicament.

Weber scooped the snow and slush and began burying O'Hearn. "Don't touch him! The chemical is strong. Dangerous. We're not talking bathroom cleaning supplies here. The concentration is beyond anything you can pick up at a grocery store. Trust me, you don't want to get any on your gloves or your suit."

Meyers asked, "What are you doing, Weber?"

"I'm trying to counter the negative reaction, hoping I can rub off or wash away the ocean water. We need to get as much off of O'Hearn's suit as possible." Weber worked while he talked, moving the clumps of snow and slush over O'Hearn's suit as if giving him a sponge bath with ice.

Then it dawned on him. The frozen snow and slush was the same as the ocean but in solid form. He only hoped it made a difference since it was gritty and textured enough to use like a brush. So far walking in the snow, handling the snow, had not deteriorate his suit. Maybe the snow was less toxic in solid form. He could only hope.

Meyers had not seen O'Hearn move since being fished out of the ocean. Not a limb. "Weber, what can we do for him?"

"We're doing it, Commander."

"Is he breathing?" she asked.

Weber leaned in. He passed his gloved hand over the faceshield. "Hard to tell. Difficult seeing into the mask. All I can really see is my own reflection. Won't matter if he is or isn't if we can't somehow stabilize the ammonia effect. Once a hole's eaten all the way through his suit, he'll be dead. This is like acid burning through the materials. Won't stop when it reaches skin or bone."

Commander Meyers could have done without the details. She understood the potential for catastrophic results. She also knew Weber was exposed. He had put his own safety at risk pulling O'Hearn out of the ocean. The same ammonium hydroxide eating away at O'Hearn's spacesuit was also burning a hole through Weber's.

Lights on O'Hearn's suit flickered. Pulsed. Went out.

"Weber," Rivers said, pointing.

"I see it." The submerged suit was short-circuiting, or had short-circuited. Chemicals or not, the suit was not made to be submerged. The quick corrosion from the ammonia allowed tainted water into the computers. The areas impacted most by the ammonium hydroxide were thinning, vulnerable. The damage was as good as irreversible. They were far from the shuttle. Equally as far from the colony. Time was a moving factor against them.

"Do something." Rivers looked over at the commander. "Do anything."

Weber made fists. Smoke rose off his own gloves by the wrists and along the fingers. He punched his hands into the closest snowbank and twisted his hands around. He was not sure what else he could do. Were there any other options available?

"I don't think he's breathing," Rivers said.

Weber bent forward. If O'Hearn *was* breathing, he was inhaling toxic fumes. Looking around, he saw everyone staring at him expectantly. "Throw snow onto his chest," Weber commanded, keeping his own hands buried in the bank for as long as possible.

Rivers clawed with her hands and shoveled loose snow over O'Hearn's chest.

"What are you going to do?" Commander Meyers asked.

Weber pulled his hands from the bank. He slid over, closer to O'Hearn, and while on his knees, rose above O'Hearn's chest. "Compressions," he replied.

On the mound of snow covering most of O'Hearn, Weber set the heel of his right hand on the center of O'Hearn's chest between where the two nipples would be. He set his left hand over the right. Elbows locked.

"That's not a good idea, Weber," Meyers said. "The ice below us is thin already. If you start doing compressions, you could compromise the integrity. We could all fall into the ocean."

"Then all of you step back. Get back now! What else am I supposed to do?" Weber voice cracked. It sounded like he had just entered puberty. The hopelessness surrounded him. Nervousness almost made him laugh. "Commander, what am I supposed to do?"

Mere seconds passed, and Weber got as close to O'Hearn as he could. He looked up at the Commander.

Meyers saw her own figure reflected in the glass of Weber's faceshield, a distant sun, and blue sky behind her.

"He's gone."

"We have to leave him for now." Meyers knew it was an unpopular answer. She saw no other way. They could not drag O'Hearn the rest of the way. She saw nothing they could use for making a sled. Air was limited. Time worked against them. "We will come back for him."

CHAPTER NINETEEN

Captain Adam Stanton fired his blaster. A sixteen-inch red laser bolt exploded from the end of the blaster's barrel. The bolt slammed into a towering snow bank. Ice crystals sprayed from the impact. It reminded Stanton of something like a rock thrown through a storefront window. He had seen that type of vandalism day-in and day-out when in New York.

"You hit it?" Ruiz stood with feet shoulder-length apart, knees bent. She had both hands on her blaster. She swiveled left, right, and checked behind them.

He worried his eyes played tricks on him. The thing he shot at moved fast, low to the ground. It reminded him of a serpent, an anaconda, but with the head of a crocodile. Black, glistening, scales rippled through its body as it slithered. Or had he seen front and rear legs? Had it slithered for cover, or did it run? "I don't think so."

"But you saw it? You saw that thing?"

Did she think I fired my weapon for fun? "Yeah. Yes, I saw something."

Stanton still was not exactly sure *what* he had seen. He knew that didn't really matter though, because he had seen something. He was sure of it. His mind was not playing tricks on his eyes. That much he knew.

Ruiz had been correct. Whatever it was, it had moved to just beyond the banks of the ocean. For all intents and purposes, it moved toward them. Not straight on, but it took cover here and there. If it was actually taking cover, did that suggest intelligence, or simply natural born instinct? Was it in survival mode? Since he took a shot at it, did the thing now consider them the enemy? Would it have left them alone if they hadn't fired on it? Would it now feel compelled to attack them?

Whatever it was did it now considered them prey?

Stanton stepped forward.

"What are you doing?" Ruiz asked.

"It went that way," he said, and pointed with the barrel of his blaster.

"So we should be going that way." Ruiz indicated a direction away from the fast-flowing ocean, the small waves moving between wide ice banks. Her entire body language motioned toward where the colony should be located. "We have two things that are more important. We are here to check on the people stationed at this facility. That used to be number one. The other thing we have to do is get out of this weather, this cold, or we're going to die out here, Captain. With all due respect, that is now my number one mission. Reaching the colony. Getting inside out of the cold and staying alive. We can't complete any objective if we're out here wasting time hunting Neptunites."

"*Neptunites*?"

"What else would you call it?"

"I don't know. Extraterrestrial?" Stanton shook his head, his eyes still on the area where the thing slipped away. Best guess the creature was fifteen, twenty feet long. A head-to-head encounter might not go their way. Blasters or not. "Neptunites works."

"Adam, we're not going that way. I'm not going that way. I'm sorry, Captain. I know you're not asking me for my opinion, but I say let's get away from here. Let's just walk away from that thing. When we reach the colony, we'll report our findings to the commander. Let her figure out what she wants to do about it. She's rank. It's her mission. Her pay grade, Adam. We're pilots. We fly fighters. It can't just be me, but don't you feel like a fish out of water?"

Angela Ruiz was correct. It made no sense going after something when they had no idea what it was or what it was capable of. Advancing was nothing shy of idiotic at this point. For all they knew, the creature was harmless. Friendly. He had no business even firing at the thing. It was unprovoked hostility on his part, an uncalled for response to an unknown situation. Training taught him better than that. His knee-jerk reaction had been the wrong decision no matter what way someone looked at it. "Okay, Ruiz. You're right."

They took steps backward. Slow. Steady. They put some distance between them and the ocean; between them and the creature. (And yet, Adam still almost labeled the bizarre specimen *Monster* in his mind).

Stanton and Ruiz never lowered their blasters. They kept them trained on the general area. Sweeping arcs left to right and back.

Stanton kept blinking. He monitored the map displayed in the upper corner of his faceshield. He saw a red blip for himself and one right next to his for Ruiz. No other blips present on the map. As far as their technology could muster, for miles around the two of them were alone on the planet surface.

Had the creature dived back into the ocean? Was that why it wasn't visible on their indicators? Or did the alien just not register on the device because the thing was comprised of meat, flesh, and bone so different from humans the device scanning the immediate circumference had no idea what to look for?

His eyes played tricks. It seemed as if everything was moving, as if the entire planet surface might be alive. Crawling, closing in on them.

It reminded him of a road mirage. On hot, humid days in New York when he looked down a block, the street toward the horizon appeared wet and wavy, as if the pavement were moving. It was a refraction of light, he knew. It did not make the illusion any less … authentic. That was what he saw now, he hoped. A mirage. "Keep going, don't stop."

Ruiz said, "Don't worry about me. I'm not stopping."

"You are right. We'll get to the colony and fill in the commander on what we've found," Stanton said.

"We've already established that, Captain." Ruiz moved with caution, but speed. Her taut, lithe body pivoted this way and that. The weapon swiveled with her, ready to blast if a fight found them. "I didn't think anything lived on this planet."

"Nothing was ever detected," Stanton said and realized it reaffirmed his thought. The creatures did not show on the map. And apparently went undetected from earlier space probe missions. Amphibians suddenly came to mind. A thing that could survive both on land and in water. Even if the water was irrefutably toxic to humans, it apparently did not negatively affect the *Neptunites*. "Wasn't supposed to be anything alive here. The air, the atmosphere, none of it is conducive to life."

"None of it is conducive for human life. Seems like aliens might have different basic needs than oxygen and H2O. This toxic planet might be like the Florida Keys for them."

"Them?" Stanton said. "I saw one. How many did you see?"

Ruiz stopped walking. "You saw only one? I saw two, maybe three."

CHAPTER TWENTY

Lieutenant Murray Bell sat in the pilot seat of the downed *Eclipse* shuttle. He left as much re-routed power as possible for life-support, while transferring the rest for operations. The temperature inside was a blistering forty-nine degrees Fahrenheit. He could manage fine in the cold. He was a big guy and prone to sweating whenever it was over sixty. Keeping the thermostat at forty-nine conserved energy.

He changed out several circuit breakers. Installed new wires where older ones looked fried, and with a multimeter verified voltage and current levels were where they should be. It was the moment of truth, he supposed, as he used the ship's communicator.

"*Eclipse* Shuttle to *Eclipse*: come in. *Eclipse* Shuttle to the *Eclipse*: can you read me?"

He sat motionless, waiting. Anticipating.

Was he holding his breath? Breathing would not change the response. Either the *Eclipse* picked up the low-frequency transmission or they didn't. And so he sighed, and then breathed as regularly as possible. In. Out. "*Eclipse* Shuttle to the *Eclipse*: Do you copy?"

Nothing. He eyed the control board in front of him. Everything indicated a signal was available, he was transmitting.

Bell shivered. Shrugged his shoulders. Maybe it was a tad colder than he would have liked. It was when his lips quivered and teeth chattered together he realized forty-nine pushed it. He would not adjust the temperature, though. Heating the ship, even just the cockpit, drained power. Rationing as much as possible bought precious little time, but time it did buy.

He knew he had survived worse, gotten out of hairier situations than this in the past. Stranded on a remote planet, separated from his team and the commander, might seem daunting to most, okay it was a bit daunting, but Bell was confident he would get past this. He would establish contact with *Eclipse*, and then don a spacesuit and catch up with the others.

Bell stopped and looked up and out the front portal.

Something moved outside. His breath caught. And once again, he held it.

He let his eyes scan across the expanse of blue and white snow. The diamond crust shined. Light radiated in rainbows. The storm was ending. He could see beyond a few feet through the plated glass.

He could see, but saw nothing out of the … what would he call it? The ordinary? … He depressed the communicator on his arm. "This is Lieutenant Bell. Commander, is that you outside the shuttle?"

They should be long gone by now. Halfway to the colony, if not there already.

Unless something went wrong and they doubled back.

He took another moment, rising out of the pilot's seat and with his hands on the panel in front of him, leaned closer to the portal for a clearer view.

Nothing.

Freaky snow. Some wind.

Nothing was out there. No one was out there. His mind. His imagination. Now was not the time to come off the rails.

"I'm getting cabin fever," he said aloud, and then laughed. "And I'm talking to myself."

He turned his attention back to the work at hand. The leads from the multimeter touching wires he tugged free under the panel. Readings were spot on. He could not figure out why he was unable to contact the *Eclipse*. Could they be that far out of range? The storm above must be blocking the signal. That was the best explanation he could come up with, and it made the most sense.

There it was again.

Peripherally, he saw it. Something. Damned movement.

He looked up, but his view hadn't changed at all. Snow. Wind. Nothing else.

Shaking his head, Bell stood up, wiped his hands down the thighs of his pants. "This is nuts."

The hairs on his arm stood on end. It was a sensation he had not felt in some time. *Panic.* It was the only word he could relate the odd feeling with. Panic.

He could not shake the reaction. Breathing again, his breaths were quick and shallow. Something *was* out there, something *was* watching him. He did not know what it was, but he knew it was something, or someone.

"Commander Meyer?" He tried again.

Bell hated the sound of fear he heard in his own tone of voice. It reeked of cowardice. It was the being alone that bothered him. This was quickly turning into the worst situation he had ever found himself in, and thought scared him.

When he was a boy living on Earth, the plague spread fast. He lived in Alberta. Calgary, to be more specific. The Canadian government at the time put into place quarantine areas. The sick were rounded up and dropped off, kept behind barbed wire fencing.

When the soldiers came, conducting door-to-door, Bell remembered the terrified look in his father's expression. The knock thundered against the solid wood door. Bell's father's eyes darted around the small ranch house. There weren't many places for hiding.

Bell's mother was in bed, too sick to move. His sister sat on the sofa, coughing.

Bell's father placed a finger against his own lips as he shushed his daughter. "Please, angel. Please, don't make a sound."

Another knock.

The soldiers must have known someone was home, or they didn't care. Perhaps they had orders to search every house whether occupied or vacant.

When the door smashed open, wood splintered and the door casing came free from the drywall. Bell's father put his back to his children, protective, but ineffective.

Without wasting time, the soldiers ransacked the house. They collected the sick and left, ignoring his crying and pleading to leave his family alone. With shoves, kicks, and harsh words, the armed men knocked him out of their way.

Sitting by the window, back to the wall, Bell pulled his knees close to his chest and hugged them tightly. He had not moved the entire night. He had been terrified at the idea of moving. Instead, still and quiet, he sat listening. Every sound made him tremble. He worried the soldiers were coming back.

Part of him wanted them back. Let them take him. Then he could be with his family.

The other part of him was terrified at the idea of them returning.

He stayed inside his house for weeks. Alone. He ate the little bit of food left in the cupboards. He moved from room to room on all fours, afraid someone from outside would see him pass in front of a window and realize he was by himself.

His father had always warned him about the people outside. "The sick deserve our sympathy," he had said, "but the healthy get are dangerous. They will come and take for themselves what little we've saved."

The last thing he wanted to do was go outside.

When the food was gone, and there was absolutely nothing left to eat, he knew he faced a quandary. If he stayed inside the house, he would starve and die. If he ventured outside the house, he still could starve and might still end up dead. The thing was, leaving at least offered up some semblance of hope.

Some.

Shaking the memories out of his head, Bell yanked his sidearm from the holster. Someone or something was outside the shuttle. If it was the commander or someone from the crew, they might be in danger, or in need of help. They could be freezing outside. If it wasn't the commander, if it wasn't someone from the crew, then who in the hell was it?

Either way, he could not knowingly just sit idle.

He had to do something.

Bell knew he needed to check. "This is crazy. Absolutely nuts."

CHAPTER TWENTY-ONE

The only thing now on their side was the weather. The storm had passed. The wind still whipped, but not with the same ferocity as before. Thankfully, the insulated suits worked well.

Visibility had cleared and Commander Meyers saw the outline of the colony ahead. Despite the tragedy they had faced, they were now closer to sanctuary; they were a click or so away from the colony. For the first time since leaving the shuttle, Meyers actually believed they stood a chance.

Her heart was heavy, though. Meyers was not thrilled about having left Bell back with the shuttle, or O'Hearn's body lying on the unstable ground behind them. Those decisions troubled her. She kept second-guessing her call. Maybe they should have attempted dragging the corpse. They covered a lot of ground since leaving him, though, moving forward at a determined pace.

Meyers knew, once they reached the colony, the colonists would have a better, lighter rover. Dispatching the rover a retrieval of both Bell and O'Hearn would be underway. The miners must know the terrain better, where it was safer to drive across and what soft ice spots to avoid.

She hoped. Today was proving to be a day centered around hope.

Commander Meyers knew the Neptune mission would not be simple. Galactic travel always posed dangers, threats. There were far too many variables involved. Planet exploration was an entirely different layer of problems or of potential problems.

Euphoric recruited some of the best minds. Engineers mapped out the trips and held roundtables discussing scenarios. The bright people, the Alphas, worked long hours, ensuring superiors that every possible issue, hiccup, predicament, and outcome was thoroughly accounted for, with multiple resolution options available. They were good at what they did. Theoretically speaking, of course.

Commander Meyers' issue stemmed from one setback. They had lost all radio contact.

At least with radio contact, they could transmit the details of the crisis, let their powerful minds work on the problems, and await their solution.

They, instead, were stranded and left to their own devices.

Meyers was resourceful. Intelligent. You wouldn't have become the commander of a ship like the Eclipse, otherwise, she told herself.

Poking the ground ahead of each step, Meyers did not let her thoughts slow their progress. Her eyes monitored the air supply gage inside the faceshield. There was just over a quarter left. Should be plenty.

Once they reached the colony, the first thing she would do is dispatch someone to pick up Bell and retrieve O'Hearn.

That kept her going.

One step at a time. She didn't look back. They would be following her. She felt the weight on the rope around her waist. "I can see the colony," she said, hoping her words encouraged.

It was slow. Tedious. Steady.

They made easy progress. Without knowing for certain, Meyers suspected they were no longer just walking on an iced-over ocean but were now trekking on solid ground. Still frozen, but it was more like ground underneath. Why else would they have built the colony compound in this area?

The urge to pick up the pace was strong and she had to fight it. Salvation was so close.

The colony loomed just ahead.

She wanted to ditch the stick she probed with and make a break for it. Everything inside of her screamed, *"Run!"*

Safety was the detailed features of the colony as it became clearer with each step taken. The structure became one of the greatest sanctuaries she had seen in a long time.

————

First Officer Mark Windsor, now acting commander of the *Eclipse*, hovered just beyond Officer Nathaniel Gaines' workstation, with his arms folded. "That was them? That was Lieutenant Bell? Are you certain?"

"Aye. It was him." Gaines punched keys, and toggled switches. "Signal was faint, but he was calling from the shuttle."

"Can you get him back?" Windsor hated the way he felt. He had no control over anything. They had all been working at establishing contact with the shuttle, with the fighter escort, and all to no avail, until now.

It was a glimmer of hope.

"I continue hailing them," Gaines said. "It does seem as if there is a connection now. Signal seems strong. When the shuttle passed through the storm, something must have gotten scrambled. Think Lieutenant Bell must have repaired whatever was wrong on his end. But he is not hearing us responding."

"What about the starfighters? Captain Stanton?"

"I have not been able to reach his ship. Or any of the others in his squad," Gaines said.

"Keep trying. They could be trying to reach us as well. It's quite possible the storm merely blocked signals, and now that it is passing everything will go back to normal," Windsor said. His mind was in hyperdrive. There were limited options available. They did not have the resources, or the staff, for a second rescue mission. That wasn't exactly true. He could fly the second shuttle. Pile everyone in and get the hell off the planet. Shuttle was big enough. That wasn't the problem. The danger was if anything went wrong, he'd be leaving the *Eclipse* with a worse than bare-bones staff, just barely enough members to man the vessel for a return trip home. So instead, he clung onto the idea that communications would soon be back online. "We've got to reach them. We need to know what's going on down there."

Gaines swiveled around in his chair. "If they're no longer with the shuttle, they may not hear our calling them. The comlinks may, or may not have the signal strength for us to communicate together."

"Why wouldn't they be in the shuttle? How far from the colony did they land?"

Land was a relative word Windsor demanded using. He refused to accept that Commander Meyers and her crew had crashed on Neptune.

"Before we lost the signal, I showed them about six, maybe seven clicks out."

A *forever* distance away, Windsor thought. Venturing out of the shuttle was suicidal. With limited air and freezing temperatures, even in their suits they would be exposed, risk hypothermia, frostbite, or death.

Gaines had explained how they could not center on any readings for any of the starfighters. The fighters were small and more susceptible to bow to the sudden onset of a raging storm.

How could the radar not have picked up the weather front? They should have had some advance warning prior to launching the shuttle, or even minutes before the wind struck. Minutes would have given them time to abort or redirect. Windsor knew he would forever blame himself for the oversight.

Right now, there was no point worrying about the whys. Doing so changed nothing, but feed his personal anxiety.

"Sir, there is one other way of looking at this," Gaines said. "There might not be anything wrong with the communicators at all. The storm clouds may just be thick enough that all communication attempts are bouncing back."

"Is that possible?"

"Aye. Possible, and likely, sir."

"So, perhaps when the storm passes, we'll be able to talk to the commander, whether she is inside the shuttle, or in her space suit, or inside the colony?" Windsor hated getting his hopes up, but when he considered his second option … Radioing back to *Euphoric* was the last thing he wanted to do. It was more than admitting defeat or failure. His reluctance stemmed from the last transmission he had had with corporate. They were not interested in saving lives. All *Euphoric* was interested in was the recovery of the diamonds.

Not the people.

Windsor put a hand over his stomach.

"Are you alright, sir?" Gaines asked.

"Aye." Windsor removed his hand, looked at his own palm like as if an alien limb, and then quickly placed his arm behind his back. He returned to the commander's chair, and sat down. Although Gaines made progress, and Lieutenant Bell was indeed trying to reach them, the unanswered questions were what caused his stomach to flip and flop. He knew he was going to have to get a hold of *Euphoric* and inform them of their current situation.

Euphoric was the only one with the authority for the launch of their second shuttle.

The question was if they would authorize such a rescue mission?

CHAPTER TWENTY-TWO

Captain Adam Stanton and Lieutenant Angela Ruiz ran.

They pushed forward, the colony in their sights, but each kept looking back over a shoulder. The creatures that possibly had emerged from the ocean depths were nowhere to be seen, but that did not mean they were gone. It did not mean nothing followed, or stalked them.

"I feel like prey." Ruiz spoke between haggard breaths. Running was not simple. The loose gems crunched underfoot. Her next footfall crashed through, and her leg sank almost knee deep into a snow-like substance. She tumbled forward, grunting. "Adam!"

Stanton stopped, turned around. "Are you okay?"

He struggled, catching his breath as he walked back toward her, and extended an arm.

Ruiz clapped her hand onto his forearm. He wrapped his fingers around hers. As he helped her out of the hole and back onto her feet, his eyes caught sight of something slithering behind them.

It wasn't close, not too terribly close. The thing slid behind a dune of diamonds and snow.

"What?" Ruiz asked, and spun around.

Stanton slowed his breathing. He did not want to frighten Ruiz, not any more than she already was. "It's nothing. Sun must have hit a stone just right. Really, It was nothing."

Ruiz brushed snow off her lower legs and padded her hands against her thighs. "You know what? You're an awful liar."

Captain Stanton did not even attempt denying it. Instead, he turned Ruiz around. "Colony's dead ahead. Let's just keep moving. We're going to be there in no time. I don't know about you, but I am looking forward to getting out of this suit, and having a hot meal. All right?"

"Dead ahead, really? Did you just say *dead ahead?*"

He saw only his own reflection in her helmet's glass, and even that reflection was obscured by the planet brightness surrounding them. "Poor word choice. My apologies."

"Apology not accepted," she said. He wondered if she smiled. "Let's go."

Just then, from the mound on their right, a geyser erupted. The sound, like a starfighter engine roaring when it turbo-launched into space, startled them both. They fell over one another. Ruiz landed on top of Stanton.

Jagged, sharp diamonds sprayed into the sky.

Stanton and Ruiz struggled back onto their feet. Stanton took Ruiz by the hand. They ran, as best they could, away from the downpour. The diamonds could easily cut through their spacesuits. The shower of gems and poisonous ocean water presented a host of dangers.

The mist from the geyser rained on their faceshields.

Ruiz raised a hand in an attempt at wiping the spray away.

Stanton yelled. "Don't touch it! You don't want that concentrated onto your gloves. The ammonia might damage the integrity of the suit's material."

The geyser continued spitting contents skyward. The sound became nearly deafening. "Can it?"

"What? Don't slow down! Keep running!" A large diamond thudded against Stanton's shoulder. He winced. His hand touched the area, checking for a tear in the suit. It was difficult determining if one existed while wearing gloves. With his helmet on, he could not crane his head around for a closer look.

"I said, *can it?*"

Can it what? Then Stanton remembered. The integrity of the suit. "It could. We don't want to risk it."

"But it's raining down on us right now! You're covered."

"How's my suit?"

"What?"

They stopped running. They were just past the reach of the raining down gush from the geyser. Maybe they should have kept running. He was worried about his suit. Even if the material *was* compromised, there was nothing he could do about it. "Here." He pointed at his shoulder. "Is it ripped."

"I don't see anything." She ran a finger over the area. "No. Nothing. It looks fine."

Stanton sighed. His quick breaths fogged the inside of his faceshield and then cleared, and then fogged again. For whatever reason, all he could think about was drawing a smiley face in the collected moisture. "Come on. We have to keep moving!"

For the moment, just a moment, Stanton had forgotten all about the creatures still closing in on them.

CHAPTER TWENTY-THREE

Lieutenant Murray Bell, not thrilled about wasting air in one of the suits—the supply indeed limited—knew, beyond a doubt, something outside had passed in front of the shuttle porthole. If someone needed his help, he would be negligent not to at the very least to go out and give the ship a complete once-around.

Checking the perimeter did not mean he did not have to play it safe. He made sure the blaster was loaded and held the weapon with a finger over the trigger. Part of him suspected it had not been the commander or anyone else from the crew outside the shuttle. He tried not allowing his imagination get the better of him.

Colonists? Aliens?

He shook his head and concentrated on his breathing, keeping it to slow but shallow breaths.

The sound of his breathing, however, was loud inside the secured helmet.

The digital display showed his pulse and heartbeat in the upper right-hand corner. A map of the area in the left. The radar wasn't picking up any other signs of life. That alone made him feel somewhat relieved. It also made him think he might be crazy. He *had* seen something. If anything was out here, why hadn't his radar locked on.

He would rather find his mind was messing with him, as opposed to learning some creepy extraterrestrial lifeform was slinking about Neptune's surface, that some unknown *thing* might be circling the shuttle.

Standing by the hatch, about to exit the safety of the shuttle and step out into the icy cold, an involuntary shiver raced down his spine. He shook, freeing himself of the sensation, and blinked away a bead of sweat from the corner of his eye. It rolled down the side of his face. The damned helmet kept him from wiping it away. "Yeah. This is nuts. Absolutely nuts."

Hesitantly, Bell reached out and depressed the door lock. The door hissed, hydraulics engaged, locks disengaged, and then almost soundlessly, but smoothly, the hatch swooshed open.

The planet was bright. The crusted blue snow best resembled a thick dusting of crushed diamonds over layers of larger, fuller diamonds. The surface glittered and glowed. When Bell stepped out of the shuttle, his boots crunched on the ground. Only after looking left, and right, and then left again, did Bell venture out a few feet beyond the supposed safety of the shuttle, and then after a few heartbeats, he took a few more.

Bell's Basic Combat Training (BCT) took place on Earth, in Florida. Once Bell got off Earth joining with *Euphoric*, Earth became the last place he ever wanted to visit again. There was more than just memories of his family being taken by soldiers to the quarantined areas and him being left alone. Once abandoned, he received what he referred to as Basic Life Training, and it made *Euphoric's* program seem, and feel, almost trivial, if not academic.

There was downtime, sure. A long period where he let himself feel bad for himself. Leaving the house he'd grown up in (once all of the food was gone, and the area in general no longer felt safe), Bell went to the second place that felt most like home. Bow River.

Staying close to the river, a place his father had regularly taken him fishing, Bell accepted he'd now be forced to survive alone. With a backpack of essential belongings, his fishing pole, and some tools, Bell set to work.

First, he made a lean-to from leafy tree branches, garbage bags, and someone's discarded clothing. He kept it as close to the brush as possible, keeping the shelter naturally camouflaged. He set up a box trap near his lean-to, using scraps of fish as bait, and tied off the stick holding the box up, or open, with some twine.

He started fires at night, kept them small enough not to attract unwanted attention, but large enough to give off some heat.

On more than one occasion, Bell found himself on hands and knees snaring bugs between cupped hands and devouring them live, as if dining at a luxurious restaurant and the insect part of a delectable meal.

In BCT, they did not teach him how to survive as much as how to kill, and not get killed.

Bell supposed he was thankful for both training opportunities. Each served a different purpose, both contributed in making him into the man he was today.

Except, right here, right now, he didn't have the confidence he should have had. The mission seemed cursed from the get-go. He supposed all he wanted now was …

Something moved. No. That wasn't right. Whatever it was he saw slithered. *Moved* sounded too jerky and mechanical. That was not at all what he'd just witnessed. The thing he saw slipped, slinked … *slithered*.

While all of this ran through his mind, Bell spun around.

Again, there was nothing. It was somewhere. There had been something. Had it rounded a corner of the shuttle?

The lieutenant, hesitant about straying too far from the shuttle hatch, knew if he were going to do a walk-around, he would have to do it now. An entire pass could not take more than six, seven minutes.

Everything inside of him knotted, knowing that if he continued and walked all the way around the shuttle it could prove detrimental. He was confident it was not someone from the crew out there. It could only be one of the colonists, or an alien.

All of their gathered intelligence suggested nothing lived on Neptune.

Suggested. He supposed that was the key word.

He did not want to die. Not while on a mission in space, and not on some godforsaken planet at the edge of the galaxy.

Yet, none of it mattered. There was a job to do, and he was the only one here to do it. Maybe he should not waste time policing the area. Inside the shuttle was clearly safer than outside of it.

With his arm extended, blaster in front of his body, he turned over his arm and double-checked the bolts, ensuring the safety was off. If he ran into a hostile, he would tear it apart and ask questions later.

Bell pressed his back against the shuttle. He cautiously moved toward the corner of the shuttle where he had seen the thing, something. His eyes continually reverted to the map in the corner. He clearly saw the boxy layout of the shuttle. More importantly, he noted the lone red dot. He was that dot.

There were no other life forms present; none his equipment could detect, anyway.

That should have been some consolation. In a way, maybe it was. He would laugh aloud if it turned out he were just losing his mind, literally. Could going crazy be better than a lurking E.T.?

Yes. Why, yes, it could, he thought.

At the corner, Lieutenant Murray Bell peaked around the edge and screamed!

He had not properly prepared for what faced him. There had been no way to get ready for something as unexpected.

Black scales reflected light from the sun, from the diamonds, from the blue snow. The long snake-like creature was semi-coiled, ready to strike. The body was meaty and wide. The crocodile-like head looked as if it floated above the tail, supported by a thick, strong neck.

The thing had arms, or were they legs. There were more than four, regardless. Bell wasn't sure. All he knew for certain was in one bite this thing could easily swallow him whole.

Once the thought registered, Bell's training kicked in. His survival mode activated. His finger pulled the trigger. Bolts shot from his blaster. Red lasers *soared* past the thing.

One bolt struck it below the head.

The thing reared up, reached a towering fifteen feet high, and still more of its body slithered around on the icy ground.

Bell never moved his finger away from the trigger.

It seemed as if the bolts had little to no effect penetrating the black scales. It did not hinder Bell's response. He yelled, and screamed as his blaster kicked from the recoil in his arms. He felt the kick reverberate from his wrists, up his biceps, and into his shoulders.

There was no other choice but to keep firing. He had no other weapon to combat the creature.

And then the thing surged forward. It moved fast. Jaws opened wide. Bell saw every detail. Rows of large, sharp teeth. Saliva dropped from the ends of bowed fangs. A fat, thick tongue shivered inside its mouth as it roared.

Bell thought to take a shot into its throat.

Before he could find the mark, it was on him.

A shadow of darkness fell over him, and he turned to flee. Jaws snapped shut. The teeth punctured through his suit, and sank into flesh.

His hand released his blaster and Bell screamed!

CHAPTER TWENTY-FOUR

Seven hours had passed. Felt more like days. Commander Anara Meyers hated the time visible on her faceshield. The display had been a constant reminder time was running out. The indicator to the right of the time was a gauge. Air supply was dangerously low. The level was just above the red. Still in the green, but barely.

Thankfully, they had reached the colony.

The structure stood like a white, barren, but safe haven. It reminded Meyers of an abandoned ghost town. The walls were iced over and snow-spotted. They sparkled and shined. The jewels reflected every fraction of light touching the buildings. It was almost as if the colony *Euphoric* built was an ancient castle in some fantasy movie. If a unicorn galloped by, she wouldn't be surprised.

"We're there," she said. "We've made it."

As if to punctuate her proclamation, her air gauge fell into the red. She felt a slight stutter inside her helmet. It was part of the alarm system, and the gauge itself lit brighter on the faceshield; safety efforts made to ensure an astronaut knew the air was nearly depleted.

There was, maybe, an hour's supply remaining. Maybe.

Seemed like plenty of time; however, they were not inside the colony just yet. They were far from safe. There were limited entry hatches available. Where they now stood, looking at the facility, there were no doorways.

They would need to continue the trek around the buildings until they found an accessible entrance. Additionally, it would be easiest if they reached someone on the inside to let them in.

"Check out the sky." Lieutenant Marshall Weber pointed. "It's going to be dark soon. Very soon. As good as these suits are, we've got to assume temperatures are going to plummet even more when nightfall hits. I'm sure I speak for all of us when I say I'd like to be inside the colony before then."

A day on Neptune lasted sixteen hours. The night the same. Weber was right. The temperatures would drop drastically. Meyers knew they needed to get inside the colony and out of the cold sooner, rather than later.

"This is probably one creepy place in the dark," Captain Danielle Rivers added.

"There's no life forms on the planet," Weber said. "Nothing at all I can detect. No one. Not out here with us, and not inside those walls."

Danielle said, "Doesn't matter. There's just something not right here. I mean, don't you all feel it?"

Meyers would not admit anything, but she did feel it. There was something off. An odd sensation tickled her senses. It was almost as if someone were watching them or following them. Except that just did not make sense. Who would be following them?

Unless it was her escort, the starfighter pilots?

Sensors would have picked them up.

No. There were no signs of life anywhere in the immediate vicinity.

Commander Meyers spoke, asking the computer for a layout of the colony. In three dimensions, the blueprints of the colony displayed inside her faceshield. The three-dimensional image dominated the entire shield. "Show me the closest entrance?"

The blueprints became an aerial overview. A flashing X marked where they stood. The image shifted and spun. A dotted line gave the commander the quickest route from point A to point B.

The good thing, if bright sides existed, was that she no longer needed to prod the surface. The colony had been constructed on what was best defined as one of the limited Neptune landmasses. The poisonous ocean still surrounded them, and it did not mean they were any safer from falling into a crevice, or stream, but for the most part, the rest of the journey should be straightforward.

Meyers said, "Stay close. We'll be there before you know it."

"I'm low on air," Weber said.

"Same," Danielle added.

"We should all have about an hour left," Meyers said. "We're going to be just fine. All we have to do is keep moving. All right? Okay, then. Let's go."

———

Captain Stanton and Lieutenant Ruiz hooked arm in arm. They supported one another. Each step they took was tougher than the last. Once the sun set, the temperatures dropped and the wind kicked up again. Loose gems from the ground and on the snowdrifts whipped through the air in a frenzy.

"I'm running low on air, Adam."

He did not want her panicking. His insides felt twisted enough for the both of them. Visibility was once again down to nil. Except for digital data displayed inside his helmet, he could not see more than a few feet in front of them.

It would not be so bad if those ... *things* ... were not out there, and were not following them.

Worse, his air was equally low.

"We've got more than enough to get where we're going." He decided even he could detect the tremble in his tone of voice. If he heard it, Ruiz would have noticed it, as well. "Plenty," he added. Yes. That sounded far more authoritative and convincing, he convinced himself.

"There," she said, suddenly.

Stanton saw it. Upper right of the faceshield.

The colony. They were back on course. "What's that? Those blips on the side east side of the building?"

Stanton said, "Enhance."

A three-dimensional blueprint of the colony filled the glass of his faceshield, which was fine since he could not see where he was going, anyway. "Detect," he said.

The blips showed up on the left side of his faceshield. Three thumbnail-size photos. Rank and names under them.

"It's the commander," Ruiz shouted.

"And Weber and Rivers!" Adam could not contain his excitement any better than his lieutenant could. A wave of emotions ran through him. The captain had been reluctant to admit— *to even think*—the two of them had been the only ones to survive. But he'd thought it. He didn't want to tell Ruiz he believed the two of them were stranded. Alone. Or that he never believed they'd reach the colony in time.

The tables turned.

Optimism filled him.

"They made it!" Ruiz said. The similar revelation apparent in her own tone of voice. Stanton knew they each had the same thoughts, but decided to keep dismal opinions locked away from the other. Relief flooded from Ruiz's sigh: "They made it."

"But why are they outside?" Stanton said, immediately regretting he had spoken the question aloud.

"What? What was that?" Ruiz asked.

There was no taking back his words and maybe Ruiz didn't need or didn't deserve the unsolicited overprotection he provided. "The blips. Still see them? They are on the outside of the structure."

It didn't take Ruiz long to see the issue. "Can't they get inside?"

The question posed a plethora of concerns. He fought those dark thoughts back, back, out of the forefront. "The colonists will let them in."

"They're the reason we're here. It was their distress signal that called us in the first place. What if they can't get to a hatch? What if they're unable to let the commander in?" Ruiz stopped walking, clearly contemplating the situation.

Stanton tugged on her arm. "The commander will have a way in. A hatch code."

"Do you think?"

"Think? No. I know," he said. He lied. "But that's why we've got to hurry."

"Why?"

"Because I don't have a code." Stanton gave her the truth. "Communicators long distance aren't working. They don't know how close we are. When they get inside the colony, we want to be right there. Walking in with them." Instead of locked on the outside, beating on doors no one on the inside would ever hear.

Angela Ruiz began walking with vigor. Stanton worked at catching up. Purpose restored. Drive and determination inspired.

"Adam," she said, "Adam—if we can see them on display, doesn't that mean the commander can see us, too?"

CHAPTER TWENTY-FIVE

Captain Rivers shouted, "Commander!"

They had finally reached the colony. The trek had been long, dangerous, and deadly. The hours spent outside had taken a toll on them. The structure in front of them was a haven, truly a sanctuary.

They stood huddled around the hatch on the east side of the buildings. Commander Meyers faced the locked doorway, with Lieutenant Weber on her left, and Rivers on her right.

Meyers nodded toward Rivers. "I see them, Captain."

The commander turned around, facing the blue vastness beyond the colony.

Two dots blinked. They were located on the south-west portion of the map. Commander Meyers didn't want to get too excited. Not until she had some confirmation. In desperate times, it was sometimes too easy to grasp onto hope. While there was nothing wrong with reaching, the commander just wanted to be sure there was a handhold waiting. It wasn't so much for her own sanity, as much as for Rivers' and Weber's.

They deserved hope with a concrete foundation, or as firm as can be expected.

"Detect," Commander Meyers said.

The computer system responded. The images, ranks, and names appeared on the left of the faceshield.

"Captain Stanton. This is Commander Meyers. Do you copy, over?"

Silence answered.

Meyers wanted to make contact before going inside. She worried the short-range radios might not transmit through the walls of the colony.

Facing the lockbox and with a gloved hand, the commander lifted the lid protecting the keys and punched in the unlock sequence. The hatch rose.

"You guys, inside. I'll wait for the others." Meyers ushered them in. "When this door closes, you will be inside a recompression chamber. Strip out of the space suit. Activate the detox. You'll get sprayed down. Remove any foreign elements. After a final scan, if all is well, you'll be able to enter the colony. Thing is, we won't be able to enter the chamber—come in from out here—until the two of you pass through. So don't dawdle. Understood?"

"Aye, Commander," they said in unison.

"Once inside the colony, you stay put. Wait for us. No exploring on your own. Understood?"

"Aye."

"Get inside," Meyers said. She could not take her eyes off her own air gauge. Her helmet vibrated more frequently, letting her know she was dangerously close to suffocating.

Rivers and Weber did not wait. As soon as they passed under the hatch and into the recompression chamber, the door swooshed closed.

Meyers put her back to the door. The lights on her helmet barely penetrated five feet in front of her; the darkness and the storm were beyond crippling. She concentrated on the blips representing the others from her team.

They would be with her shortly.

"Captain Stanton. This is Commander Meyers. Do you copy, over?"

Silence. It was disheartening. They were alive, however. Alive and making their way closer and closer every second. She wondered if they were aware of her?

"Commander? Commander? This is Captain Stanton. I copy. How do you read my communicator?"

"Loud and clear, Captain! Loud and clear!" The two were in close enough range the communicators worked. While not thrilled about the limited ability of their technology on this planet, she was relieved and thankful just the same.

"Commander? Lieutenant Ruiz and I are nearly to the hatch. We are running very low on air. It's going to be close."

"Captain, I'm waiting right here. Right by the hatch. I'm not going anywhere without either of you." The commander was no longer as concerned with her own air. She was, for most intents and purposes, safe. The hatch was inches from her. She could hold her breath if the supply ran out, enter the sequence code on the lockbox, and be inside the chamber in seconds.

No. Now she let her attention center around Captain Stanton and Lieutenant Ruiz. They had to make it.

Her helmet vibrated. The gauge flashed with a red light inside her faceshield. She would hold her breath until they made it to the hatch. It was decided.

She was not going through the hatch until the others joined her.

They would enter together.

"Commander," Stanton said, "we're very low on air."

"Don't stop. Don't slow down. Don't talk. Conserve oxygen. I'm coming your way." Meyers started toward them. With her arms out in front, waving blindly, the commander picked up the pace.

The computer set a direct route for her. She followed it and hoped the captain was using the same program, and headed directly for her. The challenge was the distance between them. Time minus air equaled jeopardy.

She kept her breathing even, despite moving as fast as her weighted boots allowed.

The blips grew closer.

Progress on both ends made.

Meyers pushed forward, with a screaming wind at her back. The force continually threatened knocking her face first into the blue snow. Every bone in her body burned. Her legs ached. Time in space damaged muscles. Use of treadmills and stationary bikes maintained strength and bone mass. Exercise was not suggested; it was required for in-space living.

Perhaps she had taken shortcuts. For that, the commander knew she was paying the price. Never again. From this day forward, she would complete every second of the required cardiovascular workouts.

The two blips were so close. The commander looked past the map and out into the storm.

Wind sent snow and gems in a whirl pattern. It appeared as if she were walking directly toward a Black Hole, a vortex. She did not let the fear of the unknown stop her. Apprehension and fear never controlled her actions. She was prone to do the opposite of what others did when faced with uncertainty. Her training, her personality, told her to walk toward danger when natural instinct would be to turn and run.

And then she saw it. Four LED lights. They were in a line. She recognized the formation immediately. Two belonged to Stanton and two to Ruiz. They were the lights perched on the sides of their helmets.

The lights bounced with the steps her people took.

She quickened her pace. Any faster and she would be running. The excitement inside her convinced her she could indeed run if need be.

Then two of the lights dropped, vanished.

She ran.

"Commander," Lieutenant Ruiz yelled. "The captain's out of air!"

Meyers reached them. Her captain was face down in the snow. She knelt next to him, and with Ruiz's help, rolled him onto his back.

Thankfully, the dark sky eliminated a lot of the brilliant reflection in the faceshields, and Meyers was able to see that Stanton was awake.

Eyes and mouth open. "We've got to get him to the hatch. Now! I'll take his arms. Ruiz, grab his legs."

Meyers and Ruiz lifted Stanton. The man was dead weight. Ruiz led them. She faced away from Stanton, one of his feet at each of her hips. She walked forward, while the commander carried the brunt of the load. She cradled Stanton under the arms but kept in time with Ruiz's pace.

At one point, when the hatch was just ahead, visible in the soft glow of the security light over the doorway, Meyers stumbled.

Stanton went down. Thankfully, she had dropped the captain snow, and not rocks, or something less … fluffy.

Ruiz halted, turned her head, and seeing what had happened set down Stanton's legs. "Commander—"

"I've got this. We pick him up on three."

They counted. Lifted.

Hurrying toward the hatch, the commander's helmet alarmed.

There was no more air.

Meyers sucked at nothing. There had been plenty of warnings all along, but now there was not even time to take in a final breath.

Her lungs immediately began burning.

They reached the hatch. She hurried, dropping Stanton a second time as she lumbered past him, past Ruiz.

She struggled lifting the lid on the lockbox. Her fingers, clumsily, entered the sequence code, only nothing happened. Meyers tried a second time.

When the door did not open, she pounded a fist against the hatch. Her mind raced. She hoped Rivers or Weber saw them on a security camera, and that they would find some way to open the hatch for them.

There was no time for hoping. If the three of them were going to survive, it was up to her. She glanced behind her. Ruiz stood statue-still, holding her captain by the ankles.

Meyers closed her eyes taking a moment she didn't have, and couldn't afford to take, and calmed her thoughts, her nerves, herself, and then, when she opened her eyes again, she tried the sequence a third time.

There was a second of doubt, of dread and desperation, before the hatch finally opened, and stepping into the chamber, the commander collapsed.

PART II

THE SEARCH

CHAPTER TWENTY-SIX

Aboard the Eclipse

Chief Engineer Officer Mandy Kadera radioed the bridge.

"Bridge on," Acting Commander Mark Windsor replied.

Kadera, draped over her pad, pushed the image displayed with fingertips this way and that. "Commander," she said, addressing the First Officer as such out of respect and admiration. "Thanks to Officer Gaines, I've been able to re-establish a link with the shuttle."

"You've reached them? Are they okay?" Windsor kept an even tone. His words came out smooth and calm sounding. Kadera knew there was hidden concern, perhaps panic in them. It might not get picked up by the average ear, or maybe it was just because she knew Windsor better than most.

"No, sir. I have not been able to reach any of the crew. However, with the link re-established—"

"I believe that is because the storm has passed. The clouds are no longer blocking the frequencies. Not sure how long the lull will last. It's nighttime. Have to assume more storms could pop up at any time."

"I understand, sir."

"I didn't mean to interrupt you, Chief. Please, continue."

Chief. She loved her work. Good grades never came easy. She spent long hours and sleepless weekends studying. It paid off. Graduated top of her class. Proudest moment in her parents' lives, they had told her. Countless times. Maybe a little pride caused the puff in her own chest, as well. It did not matter. She didn't care. It was well deserved, she always thought. A bit of arrogance was really just a display of confidence, the way she saw it. Anyway, the point being, when Mark called her chief, he made the title feel sexy. She thought he did it on purpose. It was her title. And he was addressing her properly. It was just the way he said. There was a certain pronunciation when he called her chief that made her blush. She was blushing now. The heat in her face had her thankful the two were communicating over the radio and not via monitors.

"Chief Kadera?"

Except then. The blush vanished. She let her thoughts get away from her, got the better of her, and now she was embarrassed. She might not be blushing any longer, but she was most certainly flushed. "Ah, yes, Commander," she said. "I've been able to zero in on the shuttle. It still has systems online. I've run a remote diagnostics on the transporter, sir."

"And what did you find?"

"The ship went down due to engine failure."

"But, then why—"

"Remember when, on Earth, they used to travel by airplanes?"

"Of course. The Wright Brothers. History one-oh-one."

"Exactly. Well. There is file footage of a most famous crash. It was back in two-thousand-nine. A pilot landed his jet in the Hudson River. Apparently, a flock of geese was sucked into the engine. His amazing piloting skills saved the souls of the passengers on board. Killed a hell of a lot of geese, but I guess that's not what's important here," Kadera said.

"Are you saying that there are geese on Neptune ... that geese brought our shuttle down?"

"No. Not at all, Commander." Now he just sounded idiotic. How could he suggest that that was what she was suggesting? She was just getting geared up to explain the situation. All the work she had done analyzing data, what point was there to just getting to the point without some explanation, without some background? It took the fun out of everything, diminished the importance of the investigative work conducted.

"Chief Kadera, the point. Please."

Did he sound impatient? She felt like maybe he did. She heard the slight change in his tone of voice. She was definitely detecting some irritation. "There are no geese on Neptune, Commander. Not as far as I know. I'm pretty sure the planet is lifeless—"

"Kadera!"

Yes. Definite irritation. She actually took a step back from her worktable, from her pad. It was almost as if Windsor were in front of her, face-to-face, for the scolding. "Diamonds," she said, as if that were that, and she had given the acting commander what he wanted. A direct answer.

"Diamonds, Chief? What about them?"

Oh, *now* he wanted a more detailed prognosis? At least he sounded less hostile. That was much, much better. She exhaled a quick sigh, and answered, "You see the clouds on Neptune, everything inside the heart of that storm was crystallized or full-blown diamonds. As you know, the Neptune diamonds are the strongest known gem in the worlds. Considered absolutely unbreakable. Once sucked into the shuttle's engines, the gems did immediate, *and more than likely*, irreparable damage to the thrusters."

"And it is safe to assume the same thing happened to the four starfighters?"

"Quite safe, although even with restored networks, I cannot zero in on a single one of the four." She knew what that could mean, and was sure Windsor did as well. Some things were better left unsaid.

"The starfighters must have crashed and are beyond help."

Or said. Whichever. He was the acting commander. It was his prerogative to speak the unspeakable, she supposed. "Well. I am not sure I would jump to grim that fast, Commander. But I haven't had any success on my end," she said, and then added, "How about Gaines? Has he had any luck?"

"Thank you for the report, Chief."

There was a soft double beep. The connection terminated. Mandy Kadera pursed her lips and furrowed her brow. "Now, that was rude."

CHAPTER TWENTY-SEVEN

"Commander?"

Anara Meyers heard the voice. Soft. Caring. Male. "Dad?"

It couldn't be her father. He loved her. She had no doubt. He just never sounded soft or caring. It wasn't his way. Military pumped through his veins. Nowhere in any of his training, field experience, or background as a grunt, a lieutenant, a captain, or as an admiral was there ever room for soft. It didn't exist in the admiral's world.

It wasn't to say there weren't tender moments or tender memories. There were.

There had to be.

It was just, at the moment, Anara Meyers couldn't recall a single one.

She also knew her eyes were closed and realized she must be sleeping, dreaming. Her father was always more kind, concerned, and loving in her dreams when she was asleep. Dreaming or awake, it didn't really matter. Her father was there. And right now, with the way everything was going, the way life was going, having him close was good enough to offset her constant, uneasy feelings.

The best part was he stood over her, wearing his admiral's uniform. He loved the uniform and always looked handsome in it. Even at his age, he never let his mid-section soften, or flab over. Staying in shape and healthy was as important to him as discipline, determination, and dedication. His well-deserved medals pinned to the left breast dangled from short ribbons, making Anara smile.

"She's smiling," he said. "How are you feeling, Commander?"

"I'm tired, Dad. I feel so tired," she answered. And she was thirsty. She smacked her lips and let her tongue pass over them. "Wha—what are you doing here?"

"She'll be alright. Dehydrated. Exhausted. I don't think it's anything more than that."

Her brow creased. "Who are you talking to?"

"Commander, this is Weber. Your medic. Can you hear me alright?"

Meyers puckered her mouth. She nodded. "I can hear you. I hear you."

It came back to her. A rush of memories. It was all there. All of it. The shuttle crash. Their trek across Neptune. Reaching the colony. Running out of air. "Did I faint?"

Weber smiled. "You did. You ran out of air. It's to be expected. Thankfully, we made it. We're here. Inside the colony."

Thankfully. Yes. "Captain Stanton?"

She had helped Ruiz carry him to the hatch. The man had collapsed, as well.

"He and Ruiz are fine. They're right here."

"Hey, Commander." Stanton leaned over her. He smiled.

She tried sitting up. The inside of her head shifted. It felt as if her eyes flipped around inside their sockets before rolling toward the back of her head.

Weber placed a hand on her chest, another on her back. "Not too fast, Commander."

She sat still for a moment, and let her world come back into balance. When everything leveled off, took shape, she nodded. "I'm okay. I'm alright."

The medic took a hesitant step back. "Just sit tight for a few more minutes. Give your body a chance to recoup some."

It was solid advice, and she was not in a rush to neglect a doctor's orders. "How long was I out?"

"Minutes," Weber said.

"Where are we?" For the first time, the commander looked around. She was on the floor. They were in a grey metal hall. Floor lights and evenly spaced ceiling lights illuminated the hall in a soft, white glow. The recompression chamber stood across from them. "Everyone okay?" Four faces stared back at her. Flat expressions. Hard not to feel self-conscious. "Am I missing something?"

Captain Adam Stanton stepped forward and took a knee in front of the commander.

He wore a solemn expression, mouth frowning.

"What is it, Captain?"

"We're not alone on the planet, Commander." Stanton maintained eye contact, but his weight shifted from one leg to the other.

"The colonists? You've made contact?" she asked.

Stanton shook his head and looked over at Lieutenant Ruiz. "No, ma'am. We haven't. That's not what I mean."

Meyers didn't want this to resemble pulling teeth. For some reason, her captain was not explaining himself clearly.

"I'm not sure I follow," she said, but maybe she did follow. She remembered the odd sensation she felt while they had journeyed across the frozen tundra-like terrain. Although she could not put a finger on the feeling, it had existed just the same. A tingle on the back of her neck, a shiver up and down her spine. The suspicion they were not alone, that someone, or something, had been watching them. "What are you saying?"

Ruiz knelt beside the Captain. "We saw these ... monsters. I call them Neptunites."

Commander Meyers bit down on her lip. Her jaw set. She directed her attention back to the captain.

Stanton nodded. "It's true, Commander. Not just one. We saw a handful," he said, and then described the snake-like creatures, the black scales, and the crocodile-like heads. "But they have legs. Not a lot. Not like a centipede, but two, three, maybe four sets."

Meyers saw Stanton shiver. "Did the creatures appear aggressive?"

Ruiz said, "Curious, I'd say."

Stanton shook his head. "I'm not sure I agree with that assessment."

"You thought, what, Captain? That the creatures were more than curious?" Meyers tried filtering the information. A moment ago, she had been unconscious. Now, awake, she was hearing about beings on a what-was-supposed-to-be an otherwise barren planet. "Did they seem hostile?"

"Hostile? No," Stanton said.

Meyers asked, "Aggressive?"

"Well. Not really," he answered. "Thing is, they skirted around the area, always just out of sight. Hiding behind snow, but watching us."

"So, they didn't attack?" Meyers said.

"No, Commander."

Meyers pursed her lips. "Sounds like they were curious. Wouldn't you agree, Captain?"

"Aye, Commander," he said.

"This doesn't mean we let our guard down. We don't know anything about ... whatever it was the two of you saw. I'd rather err on the side of caution. The safety of my people is my first priority. But, I want you to understand this one thing: we're not here to interfere. Now that we've discovered another life, it is imperative that we do as little as possible to get in the way. The creature may be primitive or intelligent. It doesn't change a thing. I prefer if we don't have any more contact with the beings. However, should we run into them, I want us to do everything we can before using lethal force? Am I clear?"

"Aye, Commander," Stanton said.

"That goes for everyone," she said. "Do not shoot to kill the alien lifeform unless you have absolutely no other option."

CHAPTER TWENTY-EIGHT

Commander Anara Meyers gathered together the small group inside the colony facility. Amber strobes sent shadows and yellow light spinning everywhere. Thankfully, there was no audible alarm. It must have stopped sometime after initial activation and in the time it took them to arrive on the planet. There was no denying the overall ghost town *feel* was worse inside the empty, grey, metallic hallways than it had been when they were on the outside. She was thankful they'd made it from the shuttle to the colony and were safe, and out of the cold.

"First things first. I'm going to their shuttle hangar. They've got rovers in the bay. I need to get back to our shuttle and pick up Lieutenant Bell. We've been gone longer than expected," she said. "Unless he's managed to repair the systems, he's going to run out of air soon. And then, on our way back, I'm going to retrieve Lieutenant O'Hearn's body. I don't want him left out in the elements. He's already been left alone for far too long. While I am doing this—"

Lieutenant Marshall Weber cleared his throat.

"Weber?" she asked.

"If I may," he said. "I would like to run the rescue. I think it is important you stay here. Find the colonists and figure out what's going on."

"I appreciate the concern," Meyers said.

"As the medic, I just feel—if Bell's been injured, I'm his best chance." Weber nodded, as if he'd just convinced himself of this. He wrung his hands together, but never broke eye contact with the commander.

Meyers chewed on the idea. "I'm not convinced—"

"Commander, I can do this. You're needed here. Captain Stanton doesn't know where the shuttle landed, or where we left O'Hearn. I do. I know where both Bell and O'Hearn are, so I won't have to waste time searching for them." Weber said.

Reluctantly, she nodded. "Okay, Lieutenant. You can run the rescue mission. Our first priority is reaching Bell."

"Understood, Commander," Weber said. "And thank you."

"Remember, we have no idea what's going on. Not out there, and not in here. Don't let your guard down, soldier."

"Aye, Commander."

"But don't shoot to kill. Not if you don't have to," she added. *Neptunites*. She believed her crew, but found it odd nothing had ever been reported about lifeforms prior. The colony had been here for years. Surely, they'd have seen something, and once they saw something, would have informed Euphoric. Right?

Unless reports *had* been filed, and Euphoric was well aware. If the *Neptunites* had been proven harmless, friendly, and not dangerous or hostile . . .

It was a confusing message. Weber's training taught him only to shoot to kill. If someone had a knife, he didn't shoot to injure or disarm. Doing so didn't necessarily eliminate a threat. The only way to ensure one's safety was by shooting to kill. Non-military people didn't always understand. Oftentimes media outlets portrayed the armed forces as the villain or as trigger happy.

The light the media cast on those protecting the freedoms of others was rarely fair or deserved, and almost never just. They fed on stirring the public into a frenzy. Emotions sold editions, boosted subscriptions. Fear. Anger. These two turned the most revenue.

Regardless, basic boot camp tactics remained unchanged.

If you pull your weapon, an instructor would say, you shoot to kill.

Until now.

———

Lieutenant Marshall Weber listened to the sound of his footfalls as he made his way toward the bay where the colonists kept their shuttle and rovers. Running lights lit the way. The overhead lights were dimmer, yellow, or amber, and didn't cast much light at all.

Weber's breathing was quick, shallow. He ignored the beads of sweat forming on his brow. Time was of the essence. Staying calm and focused was essential. He was not thrilled about going back out into the night. He had no idea what Stanton and Ruiz were talking about. Giant snakes with crocodile heads? There was no way something like *that* lived on the planet all of this time undiscovered.

The idea bordered on the edge of ludicrous.

The starfighter pilots had crashed, were running low on oxygen, and their imaginations got the better of them. They saw things. This made the most sense, and who could blame them? With conditions as bad as they were out there, all of them had been thrust into a life and death situation. The mind was apt to go a bit loopy.

That was what it came down to; seeing things.

None of it mattered. Bottom line, he wasn't taking any chances. Whether there was a monster outside or not, Weber had every intention of being prepared. There was no way he'd get caught off-guard. With his sidearm drawn, Webber kept his finger above the trigger where it rested flat on the weapon's barrel.

At the bay hatch door, Weber passed a hand over the detector. The hatch door slid open.

"Lights," Weber said, as he entered the shuttle bay, and the door slowly rolled closed behind him.

The hatch door, once down, sealed.

"Lights," Weber said a second time. For several long seconds, Weber stood statue-still, surrounded by both silence and complete darkness. He heard only the *tha-thud tha-thud* of his heart pounding like a fist knocking on a wooden door. The steady beat throbbed inside his ears.

A loud snap-hiss startled him. He took a step back. The sound came from ballasts above and then a pair of lights came on. Then two more, and two more after that, until the entire bay was lit up bright. There was an overall sterile feel to the bay, despite the smell of synthetic oil and fuel fumes.

The shuttle sat parked on the right. It resembled the vessel they'd come to the planet in. A little larger than *Eclipse's* shuttle, actually. There were clusters of dents and scratches on the hull. Weber traced a finger over areas most heavily marked. He knew the sharp edge, and weight of diamonds were responsible, despite the uncanny resemblance to a shuttle involved in space battles—which was silly, since there had never been a war in space. Yet. Unless you counted pirate ship attacks.

Weber saw several red tool boxes on wheels positioned around the shuttle. He assumed attempts were being made to clean up the cosmetics, as well as ensuring the ship was fully operational.

The floors were clean. No oil or hydraulics leaks he could see under or around the shuttle. This was a most excellent sign. He hoped the colonist mechanics—wherever they were, wherever anyone was—completed any necessary tasks and the shuttle was in good working order. Best he could tell it might be the only other way off the planet at the moment.

Beside the scraped-up shuttle stood two rovers. They were identical. Each had six wheels, three on each side. Lining the frames were double rows of tactical supply cabinets. Weber checked two spacesuits for air supply, put one on, and stored the second on the passenger seat for Bell. He did a quick inventory of the compartments. There was an entire storage area filled with medical supplies. Needles, bandages, a backboard. There were cardiac monitors, oxygen tanks, and IV equipment. He noted a defibrillator in the corner.

After completing the quick checklist, Weber climbed into the driver's seat, started up the rover, and entered the code for lifting the bay door.

As the door rose, red lights came on. A warning alarm sounded. Wind raced into the bay. Blue snow whipped about.

Weber shifted the rover into gear, and once the bay door was fully raised, drove out of the bay. Once outside, he tapped in a different code on the controls. The bay door descended. He waited until it shut behind him before turning his attention to the darkness that stretched on forever in front of him.

He might know where the shuttle had landed, but finding it in the dark would prove more difficult than he had anticipated. Turning on the headlights, which brought some, but only some, consolation, Weber started his journey.

The wind whipped giant blue flakes in every direction. The snow swirled.

The rover bounced, as if threatening to tip on its side.

The ice was Weber's main concern. It was what he feared most at the moment. He needed to stay on land. The weight of the rover might crack the ice. He'd drop into a poisonous ocean. No one would ever find him. There would be no one around to save him. The rover would sink fast, and he'd be swallowed up by the ocean.

An involuntary shiver passed down Weber's spine as he did his best to push the dark thoughts far from the front of his mind, and instead concentrated on the *road* before him.

CHAPTER TWENTY-NINE

Commander Anara Meyers let the others, Angela Ruiz, Adam Stanton, and Danielle Rivers, study the colony layout a moment longer. She wanted them as familiar as possible with the blueprints and comfortable with all of the passageways. They needed to know what lead where. How to get from A to B, and how to get from A to B by using C or D as an alternative.

"You don't think it's strange?" Captain Stanton said. He looked tired as he pressed the web of his hand over the bridge of his nose and rubbed his eyes with his thumb and fingers.

"Don't I think *what* is strange, Captain?" Meyers asked.

Stanton waved an arm. "This. The silence. I mean, we breached doors. I saw the security cameras. The halls are well monitored. Some notification must have signaled our entering the colony through the hatch."

"And your point?" Ruiz asked.

"No one's come looking for us, whether to say hello, or with weapons drawn, or to even ask who we are. Where is everyone?"

Meyers checked her blaster. It was fully charged. "That is why we're here, Captain."

"I don't think I expected no one to be here. I thought there might be some kind of emergency, but—how many people are supposed to be here? Thirty, thirty-five?—where is everyone?" Stanton stood with his back to a wall, eyes locked on the commander.

"There were thirty-five people in the colony, that's correct," Meyers said. "You know, as well as I do, that the distress signal was merely a beacon. Having been unable to hail the colonists on any channel, *Euphoric* sent us to see what's what. Now, obviously, things might be a bit worse than anyone suspected. Or hoped. None of it changes a thing. The job is still the same. Our mission is the same. We're going to explore every inch of this place and try to piece together what happened and where everyone went. We good on that so far, Captain?"

The commander wasn't disciplining Adam Stanton. She tried reeling him back in. It was likely he was in some stage of shock. The trauma of crashing his starfighter, losing half of his squad, and then footing it across the planet surface was more than enough to temporarily impair anyone. She knew her own mind felt off kilter, and more than a little bit rattled.

"Aye, Commander. Good. All good," he said.

She wasn't fully convinced, but his acknowledgment was better than nothing. "Okay. So, we are here. Not far from the bay where Weber is picking up the rover. We have a lot of space to cover. Ruiz, Stanton, I want you two to head this way, east, and make your way all the way around. There is the repair shop, where the colonists keep the machines for harvesting the diamonds, and then the storage facility where the jewels are kept. Rivers and I are going that way. West. We'll search the equipment and supplies area, and the west half of the storage facility. We'll meet up again at the housing sections. There are bunkers, a kitchen with the mess hall, and a recreational room. Those we'll search together, the four of us. The communications room is along the way, as well. Hopefully, we'll be able to contact Windsor on the *Eclipse*." She was near desperate for updated information from her ship. They had been out of contact for too long. She had no idea what might be going through her second's mind. Meyers could barely get her arms around her own wild thoughts.

Danielle Rivers nodded. "Aye, Commander."

Ruiz looked over the blueprints for a moment longer, and then stood up. "Aye," she said.

"Our comlinks should work. We're in close enough quarters. We'll do a check once we start out. Here's the thing. If you encounter any of the colonists, remember they'll more than likely be terrified seeing you. Especially if they have no idea we're here. Keep that in mind. They might mistake us for pirates. It is important we handle the situation with kid gloves."

———

Marshall Weber kept both hands on the steering wheel. It was a nerve-wracking grip. His finger kept opening and closing on the wheel, not too lose, not too tight. The wipers swished back and forth across the front windshield. The rover handled the terrain well. Each large tire operated from an independent axle and suspension. The vehicle rose and fell over mounds of ice and diamonds with surprising simplicity. He made good time.

Before he knew it, the rover headlights shined on something just ahead.

The shuttle.

Weber eased the rover to a stop. The engine idled. The wipers ran smooth back and forth, crossing in arcs over the glass. From where he sat, nose to nose with the shuttle, he couldn't see into the shuttle. The rover headlights bounced back at him. It was almost blinding, despite the darkness between them.

He had the extra spacesuit for Murray Bell.

Weber didn't waste time. He climbed out of the rover, left the motor running, and let his boots grip the ground. With Bell's suit in hand, Weber made his way around the rover, waving toward the shuttle just in case Bell was standing right there and was watching him.

At the shuttle door, Weber paused.

He adjusted the lights on his helmet. There was something in the blue snow. A trail. A red trail. Weber leaned in closer.

It was blood. "Whoa," he said, taking a tentative step backward.

He snatched his blaster out of the holster and turned around. He couldn't see anything behind him. The rover lights lit the night like a small sun. It was a very concentrated area. Everything beyond the reach of the electric rays of light was swallowed in the black.

The blood trail led to the shuttle doors.

Weber tried his comlink communicator. "Bell? Hey, Bell? This is Weber. Do you copy? Over."

Static. Hiss. Silence.

Weber transmitted a second time, hoping to hail his friend. "Bell, are you inside the shuttle? Can you hear me? Over."

There was more static. A second hiss. And, again, silence.

Weber knew he was breathing fast. His breath fogged the faceshield. He could feel his heartbeat inside his ears. With all of that, it was the knot twisting about inside his gut that troubled him most. He didn't feel well at all. Blood. Not a good sign. In fact, it was a bad sign. The worst.

"Weber? Weber, is that you?"

Weber thought his mind was messing with him when the voice filled the inside of his helmet. It came across crisp. Clear. It sounded like music.

"Bell! Bell, are you okay? There's blood out here."

Okay. Not music. Not exactly. Bell didn't sound good. He sounded tired. Weak, maybe.

"Blood? Are you here? Are you at the shuttle?" The man sounded frail. Scared. Weber didn't like the tone of voice. Not one bit.

"Right outside, buddy. I'm right outside. Can I come in? Is it safe to do so?" Weber asked. He had his back to the shuttle door. He remembered Captain Stanton's retelling about his and Ruiz's encounter with some kind of reptile-thing. They'd said there was more than one. They'd seen several.

He had thought them crazy at the time and had done all he could not to eye-roll while Stanton talked. And he'd succeeded. But now, however, he was inclined to believe them. Maybe it wasn't just some tall tale? By the amount of blood out here, he wondered if the creatures on the planet were more than just curious.

"Bell? You still there?"

"Weber? Weber, man. You can come in. Come in."

Weber faced the hatch and entered the pass code. The door opened. He let the barrel of his blaster sweep around inside the shuttle first.

All clear.

He stepped in, closed the door, and re-pressurized the cabin. He kept his helmet on. The display on his faceshield showed very low oxygen. He was just in time. Bell would have suffocated in less than half hour.

"Bell?" Weber called out. Although he held the spacesuit and helmet in one hand, he didn't lower his blaster. The commander expected him to proceed vigilantly, had impressed upon him the importance of not letting his guard down.

The blood outside was a nice reminder.

"Bell?"

"Here, Web. I'm over here."

Weber saw a boot. It was in the area between the cockpit and the cabin. He hurried over.

Bell was on the floor. His eyes were open, but he did not look alert.

There was blood everywhere.

Around Bell's left thigh, just above the knee, a belt stopped circulation to the lower part of the leg.

Except, there was no lower left leg.

It looked as if something had … bitten off the limb.

CHAPTER THIRTY

Adam Stanton and Angela Ruiz walked side by side. The commander sent them off to explore and clear the east side of the colony. They would search the repair shop and half of the storage facility.

Stanton was good with that. He and Ruiz worked well together. They clicked. There was something about sharing a stressful situation that created a special bond. Ruiz was a top pilot and a solid person. His squad had only consisted of people like him, like Ruiz.

He didn't want to think about Lieutenants Reilly and Cornwell.

Not now.

He had to remain focused. There was a job that needed doing. If he let memories flood his mind, he'd lose it. He didn't want to break down in front of Ruiz. It wasn't a macho-masculine thing. If he let his composure slip, it might impact Ruiz's stability. He was the captain. He suspected Ruiz looked up to him. She might not. But it seemed likely. For that reason alone, he stayed stone-faced and appeared unmoved by the loss of half of his squad.

For now.

There would come a time. Then, and only then, would he share his true feelings with Ruiz. In fact, he looked forward to it. They'd share a bottle of something good and swap stories about the team, and maybe have a good cry together.

Later, but not now.

"I mean, what are we looking for?" Ruiz asked.

They walked side by side, bent knees, blasters raised.

"People," he said. "Survivors?"

"That's what it's come to, hasn't it? This isn't so much an investigative mission anymore, or even a rescue mission at this point, is it? It's a recovery, Adam, isn't it? This is a receovery." She didn't mask emotions from her tone of voice. Stanton was glad he'd kept his composure. They couldn't both fall apart. Not at the same time.

"It could be."

"Don't pull my chain. Don't do that to me, Captain."

"Look, I don't know any more than you do. You know that. We were right there when the commander dished out tasks. You and I, we're on the same page. We know the same things."

"You'd tell me, though, Adam? If you knew something more, anything else at all, you'd tell me?"

"You have my word," he said. "I'm not keeping anything from you."

"But it's a recovery mission now, isn't it?"

"Man, I just don't know. It could be," he said. "But I hope not."

He wanted to find the colonists alive. All of them okay and alive. He couldn't trick himself into becoming *that* optimistic. In all likelihood, Ruiz was right.

Chances were better that they would find the colonists dead over finding anyone still alive.

Too much time had passed. The alarm had been activated months ago.

And there were those things outside …

———

"What the hell happened, Bell? Murray? Murray, what happened?"

Marshall Weber leaned his blaster against the wall, set Bell's spacesuit and helmet aside, and knelt alongside his friend. "Hey, man. Bell?"

The lieutenant opened his eyes. Whites. And then he blinked. When he opened them a second time, the dilated pupils. "Weber, I'm not doing so good. I'm, *hey, Web,* I'm not doing so good."

"You're fine. You're gonna be okay, buddy. You are. Tell me what happened. I need to know what happened." Bell had clearly sustained a traumatic injury.

"There was this thing," Bell said.

Weber thought about the story Stanton and Ruiz told. "What thing?"

"It was outside the shuttle. I thought it might be the commander. I went out to look. Make sure everything was alright, you know. And the thing, it just attacked. It came out of nowhere. I wasn't ready for it. The thing is, I went out ready." His skin was pale, pasty, and clammy. He smiled, though. "Okay. Maybe I thought I saw something, and maybe I went to check it out. I know I shouldn't have, but I thought for sure it was one of you guys, you know? The commander coming back for something …"

114

Weber peeled off his gloves and pressed a gloved hand against Bell's forehead. The man had a fever. He wasn't burning up, but it was higher than normal. "Okay, okay, man. I got it. I understand. I just want you to rest, okay? Stay awake. Stay with me, Bell. But rest. No more talking."

"It was an ugly thing." Bell raised an arm, his hand bent at the wrist, his fingers in a fist, with two fingers extended like fangs. "I've never seen anything like it, Web. Never."

"It's okay now. I'm just—I gotta grab the first aid stuff, okay? I got everything I need right outside. You just, look, just don't move. Okay? Don't do anything. I'll be right back."

Bell's hooked hand shot forward. He latched onto Weber's forearm. "Don't leave me, Web. Man, don't—I don't wanna be alone, okay?"

Weber had to break free so he could put his gloves back on. "No, no. I'm not leaving. I just have to get the medical stuff, okay? It's right outside."

Bell's hand, now on Weber's leg, squeezed, tightening his grip on Weber's arm. "You can't go out there. You gotta stay here, you have to stay inside. That thing, it's out there. It's still out there."

Weber imagined a giant anaconda slinking about just outside the *Eclipse* shuttle. "You're still losing blood, Bell. If I don't help you ..."

He stopped himself from stating the obvious. Bell wasn't a fool. They both knew he was in rough shape. The tourniquet was tight but needed readjusting. Bell had done the best he could under the circumstances. The man's quick thinking had kept him alive this long, of that Weber had no doubt.

His friend shook. He was in shock. Weber needed blankets. Bell was in serious trouble. There wasn't time for arguing. He freed himself from Bell, peeling away fingers.

"You can't go out there, Web."

Weber picked up his blaster. "I'm going to be right back, Bell. Stay awake for me, okay? Can you do that?"

"I'm tired, man."

"Gotta keep your eyes open for me," Weber said. "'Kay, Bell? Understand me?"

He couldn't waste more time. Either Bell understood, or he didn't. Weber stepped out of the shuttle. His blaster raised, and his finger on the trigger. Whatever had attacked Bell was not going to get the jump on him.

He was certain Bell hadn't expected an attack and paid the price. Maybe like the Stanton and Ruiz suggested, Bell assumed the thing, the *Neptunite,* was merely curious. He knew his orders from the commander were not to kill alien lifeforms, but everything was different now. Something had attacked and nearly killed Bell. Far as he was concerned the alien lifeform was hostile, a threat, and dangerous. He believed the commander would order him to remove kid-gloves.

Weber, ready and conscientious of his surroundings, made certain nothing hid in the snow, and that nothing was out there waiting for him, before he dashed for the parked rover.

And just as he reached the medical supply compartment, he saw it. Something moved off to his right. He caught sight of it peripherally. When his head swiveled around, but there was nothing there to see.

The rover headlights, and the LED's on his helmet, revealed snow and snow drifts. Little else. Nothing else, actually.

Something gurgled. There was no other way to describe the sound, other than a gurgle; a deep, guttural gurgle. Gravelly and harsh.

Weber spun all the way around this time.

It had certainly sounded as if it had come from behind him.

Now he wasn't so sure. Nothing was there, at least not that he saw.

He fumbled for the compartment latch. His eyes scanned the area, looking up and down and all around. He would never get what he needed if he didn't concentrate. Weber just didn't want to risk looking away. Bell counted on him.

The compartment door opened, lifting. Weber reached in and snatched the medical bag. He unzipped it and then proceeded to stuff it full with as many of the other supplies as he could get his hands on.

He slung the bag over his shoulder and repositioned the blaster using both hands. Finger on the trigger. He was ready to fire bolts at anything that moved.

Shoot first, ask questions later.

An old saying. In a situation like this, it didn't make it any less true. The commander might have preferred a more gentle approach to the native lifeforms, but Weber wasn't having it. Sorry, Commander.

He moved around the rover. The shuttle door was less than ten yards away. Four strides would cover the distance, but at the moment it felt as if empty miles lay between them.

The gurgle. It ended this time with a high-pitched, roaring shriek.

The cry hadn't come from behind him. Not this time.

He knew where the thing was, and so Weber ran forward several steps before he dove into the snow and he rotated around, landing mostly on his back.

He fired two quick bolts into the air.

The thing sat on top of the rover, and just as Weber fired, it had uncoiled and propelled itself through the air, and directly at him. Mouth wide open. Teeth bared.

Weber screamed.

———

Weber fell flat on his back. His left hand held the barrel of the blaster; his right gripped the handle. When he squeezed the trigger, he thought it was too little, too late.

The creature, definitely snake-like, struck like lightning. A good portion of the thing still sat coiled on top of the rover.

Long, bowed fangs grew from the corners of its wide-open mouth. The creature's eyes rolled to the back of its head.

Weber never stopped firing.

Bolts ripped through the rough, layered scales.

Chunks of the thing blew off its body. Weber rolled, but it was not a fast enough getaway.

The bulk of the creature fell onto Weber's left arm.

Weber was surprised by the weight. He used his right arm and pushed the monster off him, rolling it, and then he scrambled back, and away. He was not completely certain the thing was dead.

When he got to his feet, he saw the damage his blaster had done.

A bolt had fired clean through from throat up and out of the top of the alien's skull.

The thing was dead. Had to be. Nothing could survive that kind of a head shot, *Neptunite* or otherwise.

Weber bent forward, breathing hard, and brushed robin-egg-blue snow off his spacesuit. It was almost a casual task, until he remembered something else Stanton had said.

There had been more than one of those things.

As if the monsters hunted in groups, in packs.

Weber snatched up the medical bag and ran into the shuttle.

———

"Hey, Bell. Murray?" Weber knelt alongside Bell, and set the medical bag next to him. Bell's eyes were closed. Weber wasn't sure if his friend had passed out, or worse. He lowered his ear next to Bell's mouth and listened. Bell was breathing. Barely. "Murray?"

Bell's eyes opened. He blinked twice, which looked as if it took tremendous strength to do so, and even harder just keeping them open. "Don't go out there, Web. Please. Stay in here."

Bell didn't realize Weber had gone for the supplies and already returned. "Okay. I won't. I'll stay here. We're going to take care of that leg now, okay?"

There was but half a leg. If Weber couldn't stop the bleeding and clean the wound, Bell would either bleed out or get an infection. Either of those would kill him.

"I thought about being a doctor at one point, did you know that?" Bell said. He patted Weber on the arm.

Weber unzipped the medical bag. Tourniquet only worked on limb injuries, which was what Bell suffered. Weber found a pair of scissors. "I need you to hold still for me, Bell. Understand?"

"I understand."

Weber cut through Bell's tactical pants, from the knee up to the groin, and then with both hands tore the pant leg wide open. "So what got you thinking you wanted to be a doctor, Bell?"

Keep the patient talking; keep his mind off the pain.

Below Bell's knee dangled tasseled strands of flesh, chewed meat, and jagged bone.

Bell actually smiled. "I was a boy, back on Earth, and on my own," he said. "They took my family from me. They were sick. They had the virus, you know? The plague got 'em. The military rounded up anyone infected and shipped them off to internment camps. The quarantine zone, it was explained, you know? But we knew better, didn't we, Web? We knew the truth."

Weber remembered the internment camps when the virus reached a peak. When first opened, the people of Earth were hopeful. A cure must be close. Loved ones would recover and return home. Water shortages, food shortages, and rogue militia groups complicated matters, the way revolutions and famine always do.

"The people in those camps became prisoners, malnourished, and eventually slaughtered in groups," Bell said. "Humane was the buzzword when news leaked about the murders. It was anything but. Do you remember that, Web? They started with mass graves and then just resorted to stacking bodies and burning them. Not all of them were dead when they were thrown in the pile. Did you know that, Web? Some of the poor people, they were still alive, but were discarded like broken pallets and firewood."

"I remember those days." Weber fished out an emergency military tourniquet belt from the bag. It was crafted from sturdy Velcro and a polymer. There was nothing in the supplies he grabbed for pain management. The next few moments were going to prove unbearably painful for Bell, and Weber was filled with sympathy.

It was a distal amputation. *BKA*, below-the-knee.

First, Weber strapped the military belt around the leg, above the knee, and secured it in place by tugging on the belt until tight and the teeth of the buckle caught.

Bell screamed. And cried. His mouth stayed open wide, as he fought for breath.

The best he could do now was work fast. Next, Weber removed the makeshift tourniquet Bell managed to secure around his own upper thigh. The stump spilled some blood as soon as the pressure between the tourniquets released.

"Almost done," Weber soothed, but was lying. "Hang in there, Bell. Stay with me now."

Bell shivered. His hands were balled into fists. He nodded as blood in his drool dripped from the corners of his mouth.

Inside the medical bag, Weber found the two items he looked for. He unsheathed a large bowie knife and turned it over in his hands, inspecting the width of the blade before setting it down. He wished it were bigger. It would have to do.

The second item he'd added to the bag himself was the handheld blowtorch.

"So," Weber said, "you decided you wanted to become a doctor so you could find a cure for the virus?"

Again, and to Weber's surprise, Bell laughed. "No. Nothing that noble. You see, there was this guy, Richard. He'd lost his family. They weren't taken from him the way mine had been. But they suffered a similar fate. The flu killed 'em. He nursed his wife and his daughter until they died. And he took me in, gave me his protection. I was thankful to have it, too."

Weber lit the small torch. A constant blue flame spat from the nozzle. "What happened? Did he get sick, as well?"

"He hid us in an old house. It was in a rural area. The basement wasn't stocked, but there were shelves of canned goods and bottled water in the basement. The two of us could live isolated from the rest of the world for months without worrying about our next meal," Bell said.

Weber passed the flame over the blade of the bowie knife, heating the metal until it began to glow bright orange.

Bell was watching him. Eyes wide.

"And what happened?" Weber asked, trying desperately to keep his friend's mind preoccupied with telling a story.

"Raiders. They came into the house one night."

Weber stopped what he was doing and waited for more.

"Richard had me hide. He'd rigged a false wall and stuffed me inside before confronting the burglars. I begged him to hide with me. He wouldn't. He shook his head, silencing me with his finger and locked me behind the wall.

"I stayed as quiet as I could, but couldn't take my eye away from the small peephole he'd carved in the drywall.

"They beat him. It made no sense. They'd found the food and the other supplies in the basement. There was no reason for hurting the man. He wasn't a threat. They could have just left."

Weber hung on every word.

"They tied him to a kitchen chair. Restraining his arms and legs. Then they pulled off his boots and his socks. One of the guys tipped the chair back, while another used a knife on his feet.

"They cut through the webbing of each of his toes."

Weber's mouth went dry. His tongue felt thick and swollen.

"I've never heard a man scream so loudly in all my life. They didn't even take their time. They just kept cutting and cutting like they were whittling away at a block of wood." Bell closed his eyes and fell silent.

"Murray? Hey. Murray?"

"I'm here. I'm with you," Bell said. "I'm awake. Just—I can't get the images out of my head now. I can't get the sound of his cries out of my head."

"What'd you do, Bell? How'd you help your friend?"

Bell smiled. It was crooked. A half-smile. Weber wondered if the man suffered a stroke.

"I found duct tape, that grey electrical tape? When I was sure the intruders were gone, that they'd left, I came out of my hiding spot and went down to the basement. There was a roll down there.

"They left him for dead, Weber. Or didn't care that he'd die. They took everything. All of the food, and water, and weapons. The cleaned us out," Bell said.

"The tape, Bell. What did you do with the tape?"

"He was unconscious. His feet were bleeding pretty badly. I didn't know if Band-Aids would work. So I just ran the roll around his toes, taped them together. Both feet. Then I remembered he might get an infection. So I had to cut the tape off. I didn't have any water, but I did have a small bottle of hydrogen peroxide."

"Better than water," Weber said, encouraging Bell, as he took the torch to the blade, this time determined not to be distracted. "You pour a good amount on his feet?"

"Was like he took a bath in the stuff," Bell said, laughing.

Once Weber saw the blade was again orange, and bright, he set aside the torch.

"Then I re-taped them up."

"That was when you decided you wanted to be a doctor?"

"Nah. Not then. It was when he died. He still got an infection. Both feet. The toes turned black. Red lines under the skin raced up his legs. I was a kid and I knew that wasn't a good sign. His feet were swollen and hurt. He never recovered. Never got any better."

"You tried, Bell. That's the thing. You tried." Weber wished he could offer more encouragement. He knew it wasn't necessary. Bell was there. He knew the truth. He'd tried, there wasn't more he could have done. It just didn't make accepting the circumstances of the situation any easier.

"Bell, I'm going to help you now. Okay? Listen, Bell? Listen to me. This may hurt some. I want you to bite down on this."

"It's going to hurt a lot, isn't it, Web?" Bell took the strap of leather and wedged it between his teeth. Then removed it, and laughed, shaking his head. "I'm not ready, Web. I'm scared, Web. I'm scared."

It was going to hurt plenty. Bell had every right to be scared. He wasn't going to undermine the man's wits. Instead, Weber placed a hand on Bell's stomach. There was no point in delaying the inevitable. The sooner they got through this, the quicker they could move forward. "On three. Ready?"

Bell put the leather strap in his mouth and bit down, nodding, squeezing his eyes closed.

"One," Weber said. "Two."

Weber skipped three. He placed the hot blade against the bloody stump of Bell's leg. The wound sizzled. Blackened. Smoke rose from the area. The smell of burning flesh filled Weber's nostrils, and he instinctively wrinkled his nose against the assault.

Bell groaned, squirmed, and twisted. He yanked the leather out of his mouth. "What happened to three?"

"I knew I forgot something." Weber tried smiling. He continued pushing down on Bell, holding him as still as possible.

It was going to take cauterizing more than one time to seal the entire area off completely.

Bell blacked out. The pain was too much, overwhelming, but he was still breathing. There was that. Weber removed the blade from the wound, reached for the torch, and set to work heating the knife once again.

CHAPTER THIRTY-ONE

Commander Anara Meyers and Captain Danielle Rivers reached the colony's storage facility. Meyers had overrides for the doors. A single four-digit code that would get them into any of the rooms, halls, or restricted access areas. As a safety measure, she shared the information with Rivers.

When the door opened to the storage facility, the two of them entered the area and then stopped. Even under the emergency amber lights, the mounds of collected diamonds sparkled.

The room was *huge*. That was the best way the commander could think to describe it. It would take weeks transporting the collected diamonds from shuttle to a *Euphoric* barge ship. The diamonds were valuable, though. The drill bits made from jewels were supposedly unbreakable. Depleting natural resources on Earth was unfortunate, indeed. Thankfully, scientists had discovered the same or comparable necessities under the surfaces of neighboring planets.

"Have you ever seen anything like this before?" Rivers did a complete once around while walking deeper into the room.

Meyers said, "Never."

"I was engaged once," Rivers said. They moved, side-by-side, through the area. Weapons raised. Fingers on triggers. "Guy bought me a good-sized diamond for the engagement ring."

Meyers didn't want to interrupt. It was a moment. Someone under her command talking with her. As a person. Opening up. At the beginning of the mission, she worried about developing friendships. She knew missions forged relationships and bonds, but this right now was a first for this trip. She feared if she asked too many questions, or pried, she'd ruin the moment.

"I guess I loved him. Thought I did. Found out he was cheating on me. I called the thing off. Funny thing was, I didn't even care. I mean, I cared. I was humiliated when I had to tell family and friends why I cancelled the wedding, you know? Everyone kept telling me it was better

I learn what kind of a guy he was before getting married. And the ring, you know what I did with the ring?"

"Kept it?" Meyers said. It was a guess. Seemed the most likely. If the guy was cheating, he deserved the financial loss. That was the way she saw it.

"Hell, no," Rivers scoffed. "Flushed it. In front of him."

The commander laughed. "In front of him?"

"Shoulda seen his face!" Rivers said. And then she tried recreating the expression. Eyes wide, nose scrunched up. Lip raised. She laughed.

The commander stood still.

"What?" Rivers said.

"I heard something. Came from over there." Meyers motioned with her weapon. To the right were mounds of diamonds. A small bulldozer sat between them.

The two of them remained silent, listening.

Commander Meyers rotated around. Aimed her blaster in the direction of the noise.

Rivers directed her attention toward where the commander had heard the sound. "Check it out?"

"Right behind you."

Rivers took point. Each step was cautiously taken. Her weapon swiveled left, right, and then left again. Loose diamonds crunched underfoot as they moved toward the mounds and away from the cleared path.

Meyers walked backwards. Kept her back to Rivers' back. She swept her blaster back and forth. Slow. Steady. She took in their surroundings. There wasn't much else to see. Diamonds. Equipment. High, ballooned ceiling.

"What did the noise sound like?" Rivers asked. It didn't sound like she doubted the commander but was just looking for clarification. "Stupid me, I was talking. All caught up in a story about me. I'm sorry, Commander."

Meyers shook her head. "Forget it. You're fine. I heard what I thought sounded like a hollow thud."

Rivers grunted. Furrowed her brow. "Aye, Commander."

They stood still between the piles and beside one of the bulldozers.

"Reminds me of pyramids. The ones that used to stand in Egypt," Meyers said, and wondered if Rivers was too young to know about pyramids. Did they even teach Egyptian History in school anymore? Terrorists decimated the marvels down to nothing but sand centuries ago.

Passing the bulldozer, the angled sides of the piles came into view more and more with each step.

"I'm not seeing anything," Rivers said.

"I've got something." The diamonds were stained a different color. The amber glow made it difficult to identify what color the stain was. "It could be blood."

Rivers looked to her left where Meyers stared. "Looks old. Dried."

They reached the discoloration. Meyers scooped up a handful of diamonds for better inspection. "It's blood," she revealed.

"Commander."

Rivers pointed the end of her blaster at the diamonds.

Meyers saw the cause for alarm. Fingers protruded from the mound.

"Someone under there?" Meyers asked.

Using the nose end of the blaster barrel, Rivers dug at the jewels around the fingers. "I got a hand over here, Commander. But that's it. A hand. Severed at the wrist." Rivers rolled the appendage over. "Chewed off is how it looks, though. Something chewed the hand off the arm."

"Commander Meyers to Captain Stanton?" Meyers clicked her comlink. The hand looked slightly decayed. It wasn't a fresh limb. It had been in the diamond pile a while. There was no chance it belonged to any of her people. While that provided a sliver of relief, it still begged the question: who does the hand belong to?

She waited a moment and then repeated her call.

"This Captain Stanton. Go ahead, Commander."

"Rivers and I are inside the storage area. We've found something. What's your location? Over."

Static. Hiss. "We've just entered the storage area. East end. Where are you? Over."

It could have been the noise she'd heard. Sound traveled funny inside the dome. "We're on the west end. Between two enormous piles of diamonds. There is a bulldozer between the stacks. Over."

"Roger. We see the bulldozer. We're starting your way. Over."

"Roger that."

———

Captain Adam Stanton and Lieutenant Angela Ruiz joined Rivers and the commander. The four of them stood around the severed hand.

"What went down here, Commander?" Ruiz asked.

Meyers shook her head. "I have no idea. We're going to change things up. I don't want us splitting up. I think it's better if we search the rest of the colony together."

"Agreed," Stanton said.

The hand did in fact looked chewed off, as Captain Rivers had pointed out earlier. The questions that came to mind were quite basic. What happened here? And where was the rest of the guy?

"Those things, they got inside, didn't they? Those creatures are inside the colony, aren't they? That's why there is no one around. That's what happened to the colonists. Those things got them." Ruiz looked wild. Her eyes were opened wide, and she kept chewing on her lower lip.

Stanton set a calming hand on Ruiz's shoulder. "We're going to figure this out. The four of us. We've got this. We're trained for this. Okay?"

"I'm most anxious to reach the communications room," Meyers said. She worried what the crew on the *Eclipse* might be up to. The last thing she wanted was them forming a rescue party. They did not need anyone else on the planet. They were safer in space, orbiting around Neptune. "I want to re-establish a connection with my ship. I want to bring Windsor up to speed."

"Aye," Stanton said. "We'll take the lead."

"Commander?" Rivers said. "Do you think there is anyone still alive down here?"

A third, and equally good question. "I don't know, but we're going to find out."

There was a sound. A thud.

"Commander?" Ruiz said.

"I heard that," Meyers said. "It came from back there."

Stanton raised his blaster. "By the door? Sounded to me like it came from the west, from where Ruiz and I came over from."

Meyers said, "The echoes in here, they're throwing things off. It's hard to tell where sound is coming from."

"What was that?" Rivers said.

It sounded as if there was an avalanche of diamonds, but Meyers didn't see any such slide.

They stood in a tactical circle, he four of them had their backs to each other. Weapons raised, always raised.

"We're going to work our way back to the center of the facility," Meyers said and tried not letting the stress get to her. In her mind, the mission was a failure. She'd lost at least three crew members, and until Weber returned with Bell ...

The mission was a bust.

"Move slowly. Watch each other's back," Meyers said.

It didn't matter how *Euphoric* assessed any of this after the fact. The debrief would be a nightmare. It didn't matter that the storm they flew into was beyond her control. She was the commander, the one in charge. Lives were lost. She expected civil hearings, and more than likely termination. There was no one else to blame.

Just her.

They shuffled forward. The crunch of diamonds beneath their boots was almost deafening. There was no quiet way to get through the storage area.

What Meyers needed to do was push the pain, remorse, and guilt aside. If only for the next few hours. The calls were hers to make. The orders were theirs to follow. Until she got them back onto the *Eclipse*, she was the one still responsible for their survival. The responsibility remained heavy on her shoulders.

"I saw something, Commander. There," Ruiz said, using the nose of her barrel to point in the direction where she spotted movement.

Meyers knew there was a shuttle in the colony bay. It would be their ticket back to the *Eclipse*. It was perhaps the one glimmer of hope in what was now one of her darkest moments.

What would the admiral think of her now?

"I'm not seeing anything," Meyers admitted.

The admiral wouldn't be proud. If she managed to save the rest of them, get them back to the *Eclipse* safely, she might—*might*—be able to look him in the eye when she next talked to him.

Eventually.

"I see it. Near the top of that pile. Three o'clock!" Stanton shouted.

Commander Meyers opened fire. Bolts flew through the air. Struck diamonds blew out in all directions from the blasts and rained down around them.

"It's one of those things," Stanton shouted. "They've breached the colony!"

CHAPTER THIRTY-TWO

Captain Adam Stanton took a knee. He knew the others still stood behind him. He lined up his sight. The creature inside the storage facility, inside the colony, moved fast. He squeezed the trigger. The bolt from his blaster slammed into diamonds, missed the target.

"Everyone get out," he shouted, directing them with a waving arm. The only exit available to them was the north exit. It was the direction they wanted to head toward, anyway.

Ruiz clapped him on the shoulder. "Let's go!"

"I'll be right behind you guys. Now go. Move. Move!"

Commander Meyers dropped to a knee beside him. "Let's get this thing."

She opened fire.

"What happened to not killing the locals," Stanton said. Bad joke. Worse timing. He couldn't help himself.

"Hit it, Captain," she ordered.

He kept one eye closed. "It's fast. Freaking fast," he said.

They fired their blasters at the same time. Bolts sizzled through the air.

Commander Meyers yelled, "I hit it."

She may have hit the monster, but the bolt didn't stop it. If anything, the creature got faster, looked pissed off.

"Commander," he stammered.

"Go with the others," she shouted. Her blaster kicked with each shot. Bolts thundered out of the end of the barrel.

The thing was off the mound, on the ground and slithered at them. Its mouth kept opening wide, revealing rows of long, sharp teeth.

Stanton said, "Look at the fangs."

"Kidding me?" she said. "I'm aiming for them."

Stanton chanced a look back.

Ruiz was at the doorway; she waved him on. He wasn't leaving the commander on her own. He focused on the target. Bolts flew from his blaster.

The thing continued at them, somehow moving even faster. Its body snaked this way and that behind a bulbous head. The few legs it had, had feet that were more like three-taloned claws.

"Let's finish it," Stanton said.

"And, there ..." she paused, took aim, and then squeezed the trigger.

A bolt slammed into the creature's mouth. The head exploded. The sound of the chunks of scaled skull clamored against the floor, as if the head were made of metal.

"Man, for a minute there, I was thinking the things were indestructible," Stanton said. "Nice shooting, Commander."

"Why, thank you, Captain." The commander stood up.

Something let loose a gravelly growl, followed it up with a mighty, angry sounding roar.

The two locked eyes.

"More than one of those things is in here," the commander said, it came out in a whisper and sounded filled with disbelief.

Before either of them saw the creature, they turned and ran for the door.

Ruiz still stood where she'd been standing, and ushered them through.

Once past the threshold, Ruiz let the door close.

Rivers said, "Now we know why there's a hand in the diamonds and no body. Damned things ate the guy!"

————

Lieutenant Marshall Weber dressed Murray Bell in the extra spacesuit. He was as gentle as possible pulling the suit over the stump where his left leg had been.

"Air working okay?" he asked.

"Fine," Bell said. He ground his teeth. Even through the faceshield Weber saw the beads of sweat roll down his brow.

"We're going to get out of here, now. Head for the colony. They've got a sick bay there. I can better treat your leg," Weber said.

"We've got to go outside?"

"It's the only way to get to the rover," Weber explained.

He lifted Bell and positioned himself under Bell's left arm. "Lean on me," Weber said. There wasn't another option. They couldn't risk staying at the shuttle any longer. There was no telling how many of those creatures waited for them around the rover. Staying put sounded like a good idea, it just wasn't practical. He didn't like the idea of moving Bell so soon either, but Bell needed more, and better, medical attention.

"That hurts, Web. It really, really hurts."

"I've got you, Murray. No worries, my friend. No worries."

There was plenty to worry about. Holding most of Bell's weight left him incapable of using the blaster. He was forced to use the strap and wear the weapon like a satchel slung across his back. He kept one arm behind Bell's back and his other hand held onto Bell's wrist, which was draped over his shoulder.

The two of them, practically tethered together, hobbled through the back of the shuttle.

"You ever do a three-legged race when you were a kid?" Bell asked.

"Not now, Bell," he said, but smiled. At the hatch, Weber sucked in a deep breath and held it for a count. "Ready?"

"Let's do this," Bell said, no conviction in his tone of voice. At least the sentiment was there.

Weber leaned over, punched in the access code, and when the door opened, he lunged them forward and out of the shuttle. It reminded him of swimming. When he knew the water would be cold. Dipping in a toe prolonged the torture. The only way to get it over with fast was to jump right into the pool.

The ground was icy. The special boots they wore gripped the surface. Bell was far more helpful than Weber would have anticipated. He hobbled the best he could.

At the rover, Weber leaned Bell against the body of the machine and pulled open the passenger door. Bell grabbed onto the handle and set another hand inside on the passenger seat. He, with minimal help from Weber, hoisted himself up and into the cab.

Weber unslung his blaster. So far, so good.

He waved the blaster around as he passed in front of the rover. Bell was inside pounding on the front windshield, garnishing Weber's attention. Bell pointed behind Weber, who then spun around.

It was almost too late.

He had not seen the thing, despite the contrast of its black scales against blue, diamond-crusted snow. The rover headlights highlighted the creature's outline, though. Weber pressed his back against the front hood of the rover and fired his blaster.

Bolts tore through the air, zipped toward the creature.

As if the thing possessed some kind of sixth sense, the creature zigged and zagged. The bolts punched through the ice.

Ocean water sprayed into the air, a geyser burst through the thinning surface, and took out one of the creatures.

The second did not miss a beat.

Weber didn't think he had time to reach the driver's side door, open it, and hop in, before the thing was on him. He dug in his boots, grit his teeth, and fingered the trigger in rapid succession.

The head of the creature was roughly the size of Weber's body. It opened its mouth, as if ready to eat him whole.

Weber screamed into his faceshield as he continued firing his blaster.

Several bolts slammed into the opened mouth. One of the bolts exited the back of the thing's skull.

The creature dropped, eyes open, mouth shut. It slid on the ice, and stopped just shy of Weber's feet.

Weber sighed, and then laughed. "Holy crap, Bell. You see that?"

Behind him, the second creature fell from the sky. It crashed onto the surface. Its legs twitched. Its head moved. It resembled a sleeping animal just moments before waking up. And then the mouth opened. Saliva dripped from elongated fangs. A rattle sound emitted from its throat. The scales along its back quivered, and reverberated.

The fall from the sky must have stunned it.

Inside the rover, Bell waved Weber on, urgently.

Weber, taking advantage of the moment, and not in need of encouragement, raced around the front of the rover. The creature gave chase as Weber pulled open the cab door.

The creature rose on a middle set of legs and rocked its head from side to side, as if shaking off a daze.

Weber pulled himself into the rover, just as the creature uncoiled, and attempted a strike with fangs bared. Weber pulled his legs up and into the vehicle. The head of the creature bit down on air.

Weber reached out for the door and yanked it close. "You okay?"

Bell just nodded. "How about you? You okay?"

"Yeah. Wonderful. Peachy, even."

CHAPTER THIRTY-THREE

"Okay," Commander Meyers said. Her heart still beat fast inside her chest. The run-in with the creatures in the storage facility had unnerved her. It wasn't that she doubted Captain Stanton and Lieutenant Ruiz's report. They claimed they'd seen the creatures on their trek from the starfighters to the colony. A part of her just wasn't positive the retelling wasn't exaggerated some, the way a fisherman's tale of catching fish became more legendary with each rendition. Lesson learned. She would believe her crew until given a reason not to believe them. "Here's what we need to do first. I want to locate the communications room. We need to contact the *Eclipse*."

Rivers raised a hand.

"You don't have to do that," Meyers said.

Lowering her arm, Rivers said, "Don't you think we should head to the colony's shuttle? It's our best chance of getting off the planet. We can fly back to the *Eclipse*. Regroup. Figure out what to do from there."

From somewhere not on Neptune with giant, man-eating creatures, Meyers thought. "We will use their shuttle for safe passage off the planet, yes. But not now. Not before making contact with the *Eclipse*, and not before we finish the exploration of the colony."

"Ma'am?" Ruiz said. "Why are we going to explore the colony?"

"There still could be survivors," Meyers stated.

Stanton said, "It's been months, Commander. Months since the trouble alarm was triggered. I think we know what kind of trouble they ran into." Stanton pointed toward the closed storage room doorway. "They probably went out on a mining expedition. When they were vacuuming up the diamonds, my guess? They brought in some of those creatures. Gave them a ride right into the compound."

"The things may also have attached themselves onto the vacuum vehicles." Meyers thought about it. Could have happened that way. It seemed as if the compound was properly sealed. That could work in their favor. It might mean only a few creatures made it inside. Unless, there was a breach. "Either way, the things went from living out there, to wreaking havoc inside here."

"Which is why we should try and get safely from here back to the bay. I can get that shuttle ready for take-off in less than thirty minutes. We'll punch a path off the planet and rendezvous with the *Eclipse* far, far away from this place," Stanton offered.

"What if when we take-off there's another storm, and we crash again. Then we could be grounded down here for God knows how long. We need an up-to-date weather forecast. They have a Doppler here. And from space, Windsor can report on cloud activity, as well." Meyers wasn't in the mood for arguing. She knew, as Commander, she could shut down the discussion. She was in charge. What she said was what should go.

Except, not listening to her crew was more of a dictator role than a commander one. She wanted rapport with the members of her ship. Trust. Loyalty. The least she could do, the very least, was hear them out.

It was all of their lives on the line now.

Not just her career; her reputation.

"With all due respect, the *Eclipse* didn't catch the storm we flew directly into when we got here, Commander." Stanton held eye contact for a two-count and then lowered his chin. "Forgive me. That was uncalled for."

"Nothing to forgive," Meyers said. "You're right. We didn't see the storm. The planet is far too unstable for us to guess weather patterns. However, I'd still like a best guess before taking any unnecessary risks. The way I see it, we have two shots off this planet. The colony's shuttle, and the second shuttle on the *Eclipse*. If we mess up and crash with the colony's shuttle, whether it is because of some out-of-nowhere storm, or a mechanical issue, or whatever, then we are down to just one last hope. Windsor would have to pilot the second ship, come down here, and pick us up. Based on everything we now know, that would be even more dangerous. Him coming here, picking us up, flying us out. Twice the risk. I appreciate your concern, I do. But right now, I believe our best option, our best chance, is first getting in touch with the *Eclipse*. Let's find out what is going on. Let's give them the information we know so far. *Euphoric* needs to be alerted to what's happend. And we're forgetting one major reason for why we can't just high-tail it out of here right now."

Ruiz said, "And what's that reason?"

"Even if there is just one person left on this planet, we are their last hope for survival. What if they know we're here, but can't reach out to us, and then we just leave? What if that were you? You'd want us to come find you, wouldn't you?" Commander Meyers stood a little taller, jaw set. "I know you are all scared. I'm scared. I've never seen anything like those things. But they can be killed. We can stop them. We *will* get off of this planet."

"Do you think *Euphoric* knew about those things?" Rivers asked. "Do you think they had any idea there were monsters mixed in with the precious diamonds?"

Meyers didn't have an answer to the question, and she did not miss the tone of voice change when the lieutenant said the word *precious*. She pursed her lips, eyebrows arched, and shook her head. "At this point, I really don't know, Danielle."

———

Lieutenant Marshall Weber kept both hands on the wheel. The rover handled nicely. Despite the diamond-paved road, hills, dips, and mounds, it was an overall smooth ride. Bell sat beside him, and although his eyes were open, the man looked slightly lethargic.

"Hanging in there, Mur?" They had known each other a long time. Their friendship stemmed back to when they served together in the North American Alliance Armada. They became friends when they enlisted at about the same time and as privates were sent to the boot camp training facility on Mars. Prisons and boot camps. That was all Mars was good for.

"Want to hear something funny?"

Just the question made Weber smile. "I could go for a joke."

"It's no joke," Bell said. "But my foot itches. My left foot. I don't have a left foot. Not anymore. I swear to you, Web, I swear—the damn thing itches. And you know what I want to do? I want to scratch. Almost reached down, more than once, but stopped myself."

"It's called a phantom itch." Weber knew it was a common thing with amputees. "The nerve that ran through your leg, it's still alive above the knee, and what it does is it sends mixed up messages to your brain."

"So what does that mean? I might keep feeling like I have my whole leg, when I don't?"

"It's possible, Mur. There are meds you can take. Should numb some of that sensation for you," Weber explained. "We'll get you back home, okay? We'll get this sorted out."

"Gotta admit," Bell said. "Some of those prosthetics they have out now, kinda sweet."

Weber nodded. "Yeah. Think of the women you can woo with your tale of battling a monster. You're going to be fighting them off."

"Fight them off? Me? Never. Plenty enough of me to go around, way I see it."

When Bell laughed, Weber joined in. It felt absolutely amazing to be kidding around and moving forward.

The rover jerked to a stop. A pit in the road. Weber thought he'd avoided it. The back tire must have gotten stuck.

Bell placed both hands up on the dash. "What was that?"

"Pothole." Weber gave the rover gas and thought he felt the tire spin. They didn't climb out of the divot.

"You don't want to do that," Bell said. "Rock it backward, and then when it rolls forward, give it a little gas."

Weber dropped the rover into reverse, and then shifted into drive and gave it another push of gas.

The back of the rover sank.

Through the front windshield, Weber saw the ice crack. It spider-webbed out from underneath the rover and extended beyond.

"What do we do now?" Bell asked.

Weber knew what he was thinking. The rover was going to drop into the ocean. There was no way around that. The back tire wasn't going to lift free now. If anything, if Weber applied the gas, the traction would more than likely chew away at what little ice remained. No. The rover was as good as sunk.

"We're going to each open our doors and get out of the rover," Weber said. "Slow like. No fast movements."

"And then what?" Bell had one hand on the door, the other still planted on the dashboard.

"Climb out. Easy does it. And move slowly toward more solid ground," Weber said.

"The ice splits, we're on opposite sides of the ocean, Web."

"We'll be fine."

"And those things are out there," Bell added, needlessly.

"One problem at a time," Weber said.

"How about this one, I climb out of this rover, and I'm going to fall. The ice is already cracked. I can't go hopping on one leg. I'll pogo-stick myself right through the ice."

Weber knew Bell was right. "Lower yourself out of the cab, Mur. Nice and easy. I'll climb out and come around to your side. We'll do this together."

Inside the rover, they heard what sounded like something breaking open. They knew exactly what the sound was.

It was the sound of more ice cracking.

CHAPTER THIRTY-FOUR

The four of them moved together in smooth, tight fashion, as if they'd been part of the same platoon for years. Anara Meyers insisted on taking point. If they came face to face with anything dangerous, she would be the one to square off. Behind her was Danielle Rivers, Adam Stanton, and in the rear, Angela Ruiz.

Green sight laser from the four blasters cut through the dim amber glow along metallic hallways. The beams flashed over nooks and crannies. Should they encounter another one of the *Neptunite* monsters, the laser would help lock onto the fast, slippery targets. Meyers explained the scaly shell might not be bolt-proof, but hitting the back of the head through the inside of an opened mouth worked wonderfully.

"Aside from that guy's hand in the storage area, has anyone seen any sign of anyone else?" Stanton asked.

Meyers shot a look over her shoulder.

"I'm just asking. There was supposed to be like thirty-five people down here. We've come across, like, one hand."

Rivers said, "The hand's all I've seen."

Ruiz added, "Same."

"Best chance of finding survivors, if there are any, is going to be the north end of the compound," Meyers said.

They weren't moving fast, but they maintained an almost shared singularity among the four of them.

"Why the north end?" Ruiz asked.

"Two reasons I can think of," Meyers said. "That's where the food is, and that's where the communications room is."

"That's all well and good, in theory," Stanton said. "But, if the communicators are this way, then why hasn't anyone reached out for help? The trouble alarm was activated months ago. We all know *Euphoric* tried unsuccessfully to reach a live person for details, and when they couldn't, we were deployed. I'm hoping you're right, Commander, and when we get to the north end of the colony we find them, all thirty-five alive and well."

But he would be surprised if that was the case, Stanton thought, but left it unsaid.

"Thirty-four," Rivers said.

"We found a hand," Meyers added, without missing a beat. "We don't know that the man who lost it is dead. We just know what we know at this point. But I'll tell all of you this. Me? I'm remaining optimistic."

Stanton didn't think the commander sounded it. He, internally, applauded her every effort at staying positive. She had the right approach, regardless of the surrounding crummy circumstances. He knew a good leader when he saw one. "I'm with you, Commander. Let's get where we are going, help those who need rescuing, and get off of this planet."

Meyers caught his eye. Stanton clearly caught the moment that passed between them, and when she gave a slight nod, he knew he'd earned her approval. He just hoped she knew she'd in turn had also earned his.

A few more yards down the hall and Meyers stopped. "This is the communications center," she said. The top half of the door was thick glass. Communications stenciled in black. Meyers tried the handle; it was locked. She cupped her hands and peered into the room.

"What do you see?" Rivers asked, her back to the door.

Stanton noticed Rivers stood in a ready-position. Her knees were bent and her eyes continued scanning up and down the hallway. She silently asserted nothing would sneak up on them if she could help it.

"Dark inside. I don't see computer lights or anything," Meyers said, as she entered the door code to access the room. "Everyone, stand back. Blasters ready."

The door opened. Commander Meyers stepped into the room. Her green laser passed across the empty area. "Lights," she said.

The light fixtures stuttered, and then came on.

Meyers pointed left and then right. Stanton went left, Ruiz and Rivers went right.

"Clear," Stanton said.

"Clear," Ruiz said.

Meyers closed the door, lowered her weapon so that it dangled from the strap around her shoulder. "Ruiz, stand guard. Nothing gets in here. Got it?"

"Aye, Commander," Ruiz said.

"Okay." Meyers made her way around the room. She pulled out the chair by the communications equipment. She looked over the system in front of her as she sat down. "Let's see if we can get this communicator up and running."

CHAPTER THIRTY-FIVE

"We are going to do this real slow, but not take all day about it," Marshall Weber said. The rover was stuck in a hole on the ice, and the ice was cracking. In moments he knew the rover would plunge down through the ice and into the toxic ocean. He and Murray Bell were moments away from an almost certain death. They needed to act fast, but slowly. "Okay? Slow, but fast. Am I clear?"

For several long moments, they sat motionless in the rover while Weber talked through the plan.

Bell said, "As mud, lieutenant."

Weber smiled, despite the situation. "Okay. Good. Just sit there, okay. I'm going to get out of the rover."

It didn't even matter how lethal the water was. Once underneath the surface, the current would grab them. They'd be pulled under the ice still intact and trapped until they drowned. The ammonia, well, that just made a bad day worse.

Reaching for the door with his left hand, Weber sat as still as possible. He didn't even turn his head. Eyes forward. His fingers found the handle. He lifted the lever. The lock disengaged. The door popped open a fraction. Easing the door outward, Weber let his left leg slide down from the driver's seat. The toe of his boot touched the running board. He shifted his weight onto his left leg.

The ice moaned in protest.

"Web."

"I know. I know. Stay still."

"I'm not moving, Web. Barely breathing over here."

Weber continued to climb out of the rover. Time was running out. The ice wouldn't support the weight of a rover much longer.

Once both feet were out of the rover, and he was firmly on unstable ice, he allowed a short sigh. Relief washed over him. "Halfway there," he whispered.

"Says you," Bell said.

Leaning back, Weber maneuvered himself out of the way of the door as he brought it around to close it. Standing on the ice, he felt exposed. Vulnerable.

He wished he had eyes in the back of his head. His mind convinced him those things were slithering up to him, coiled, about to strike.

He resisted the urge to spin around. If he didn't get Bell out of the rover before they fell through the ice, it was over for the both of them, regardless of the creatures. If one of the creatures attacked, it was over. The creature had become just one of far too many variables. Weber kept his palms on the rover and sidestepped around the front of the vehicle.

The likelihood of them surviving this was closer to zero than Weber was ready to admit.

Breathing slow and shallow breaths, Weber found himself where he needed to be, on the passenger side of the rover. A second, equally satisfying wave of relief came along and Weber inhaled it with relish.

Bell pushed open his door.

Weber was on the wrong side. "Whoa, whoa, Bell!"

Bell pulled the door closed. The door slammed shut.

Weber saw Bell cringe inside the rover.

"It's okay, man. It's alright," Weber said, speaking softly. He knew Bell could hear him just fine inside his helmet. "Relax. Breathe easy. In. Out."

"I am relaxed. My breathing's fine," Bell responded.

"I'm talking to myself, Bell. Not everything's about you," Weber said, grinning. Did he have any regrets? Or many?

Weber's mind spiraled. The past raced directly at him. It wasn't the time. His body demanded his attention. His memories were winning out. *Regrets.* That's what came to the forefront.

K.C. and he had been together close to a year, had met after he'd completed his service with the NAAA and just started working for *Euphoric Enterprises* on the Nebula Way Station.

One morning, he saw in the wastepaper basket in the bathroom a home pregnancy test. It was positive. She was going to have his baby. Like a coward, he'd left for work—a menial security detail for *Euphoric* consisting of hours locked in a room watching rows of monitors from closed-circuit cameras stationed around the home office—and spent the next several days avoiding her calls.

When she demanded they talk, he ended things with her over the phone. Explained how things just weren't working out. That the problem was him and not her. A cliché he tried his best to make sound sincere and authentic. The key was he never gave her a chance to share her news with him. This way, it looked like he'd broken things off before ever knowing she was pregnant.

After a week apart, he realized his mistake. He did, in fact, love K.C. Leaving her had been a bad move. The idea of being a father at such a young age terrified him. He was barely making enough money to take care of himself. How was he going to support three people? Regardless, he knew he'd been wrong and wanted to make things right.

K.C. agreed to meet for drinks.

She agreed they could get back together, give things a second shot.

And he waited for her to tell him she was pregnant.

And waited.

After two months passed and she didn't show any sign of a baby growing inside of her, had never mentioned the pregnancy test she'd taken, he was compelled to bring up what he'd found, what he'd done, and how he was thankful she'd taken him back.

K.C. listened without saying a word. Her eyes welled up with tears, though.

"Baby, what's wrong?"

Then she told him what happened in between the days they'd been apart. "I was scared," she said, her lower lip trembling. "I made an appointment with my doctor. I had the baby removed."

Weber felt his heart crushed inside his chest.

She kept apologizing.

It wasn't her fault. It had been his. All of it.

Making matters worse, he joined with *Euphoric's* patrol, assigned to work under Commander Meyers and deployed on the *Eclipse* two weeks later.

Again, he left K.C. with no real goodbye and no explanation.

He knew she blamed herself for everything that went wrong. It was because he could no longer look her in the eyes; because he no longer felt good about himself that he had to leave this time.

Shame.

He despised himself.

"Web? Web, man? You in there?"

Weber shook his head, doing his best to clear the pain from his heart and the horrific memory from his mind. "We're going to do this," he said.

There was no reason K.C. should give him a third chance. He didn't deserve her love nor her forgiveness. If survived this predicament, though, he was at least going to apologize. Again.

He wouldn't tell her that he still loved her; wouldn't tell her that he missed her; wouldn't tell her that he thought about her all of the time.

She didn't need to hear any of that. It would only confuse things. He'd already done plenty to mess with her life. But an apology, she deserved at least that much.

Weber opened Bell's door, reached into the cab …

Below them the cracks in the ice spread, and resembled a bizarre frozen lightning storm underfoot.

The back end of the rover fell through the ice. The front end lifted into the air.

Weber gripped Bell with both hands and yanked him out of the passenger seat just as the cab door swung closed.

The rover's front grill pointed toward the sky. The vehicle bobbed on the space of ocean occupied. Some ice still surrounded the back end of the rover, wedging it somewhat in place. The hold wouldn't last.

Weber knew they were still on an unstable surface. He got to his feet, spun around, reached down, and picked up Bell's right leg near the ankle.

And then, as best he could, he ran.

The cracks in the ice grew longer, deeper, and raced after them.

There was an area of diamond shaped mountains. If they could just reach them, reach that area, Weber suspected they'd be safe.

Dragging Bell on the ice was much easier than the two of them trying to hobble toward safety.

Chancing a look back, Weber caught sight of a block of ice rolling. Reminded him of film he'd seen on icebergs in the Antarctica, long before the massive bodies of water began drying up on Earth.

The rolling berg toppled down on the rover and pushed it underwater.

They'd reached what could quite possibly be land, and even if it wasn't, Weber could not do anymore. He was winded and the muscles in his legs burned.

The cracks in the ice stopped ten, fifteen yards behind them.

The rover was gone. Submerged. And now either sinking to the bottom of what must seem a bottomless ocean, or was being swept around the planet on some unnatural, and foreign current.

Weber laughed. Slow, at first, and he ignored the way Bell stared at him. As his giggling escalated, Bell finally joined in.

"We made it," Weber said, over and over again.

"I can't believe we didn't drown inside that thing!"

"I know, right? But we didn't. We made it. We got out of there!" Weber could hardly wait to get back to the *Eclipse*. He resolved to record an apology video. He'd send it on ahead of their return to Nebula.

It wouldn't be perfect. It would not repair a single thing. K.C. deserved that much, and maybe, just maybe it could be a start.

"I'm just amazed! We're still alive!"

"Nothing can stop us now, Bell. You hear me? Nothing."

Something snarled. A low groan grew into a terrible growl.

Weber patted a hand against his thigh. Slapped a palm on the ice.

He panicked, thinking he didn't have his blaster, that he had left it inside the rover.

The growl came again. Only this time it was closer.

And the sound came from behind them.

CHAPTER THIRTY-SIX

Commander Anara Meyers fit a bud into her ear, tapped the end. It glowed a soft blue. Then she blew into the microphone in front of her. She looked around for a way to transmit, and touched the microphone base. Nothing.

Danielle Rivers pointed underneath the table. "You use the foot pedals. Press down on it when you want to talk. Lift off when you are done."

"Seems a bit archaic. Have you done this?" Meyers asked.

"First degree I earned was in communications and broadcasting," Rivers explained.

Meyers stood up. "Please. Have a seat. See if you can reach the *Eclipse*."

"Aye, Commander." Rivers sat down. She typed on the keyboard. Lights flashed on the system in front of her. "This is the transmitter over here. It turns electrical signals into radio waves with an antenna. The radio waves can travel indefinitely."

"Do we have an antenna?"

"Saw one outside. Noticed it when we were getting close to the colony. It was actually one of the first things I saw. That's good news," Rivers said and tapped more keys. She twisted knobs, repositioned herself in the chair, and adjusted the bud she placed inside her ear. "It was there. Standing tall. One less thing we have to worry about. Okay. Let's see what we can do."

Meyers nodded. "Ready when you are."

Rivers depressed the pedal underneath the table. "This is Lieutenant Danielle Rivers, trying to reach the *Eclipse*. *Eclipse*, come in. Over."

———

Officer Nathaniel Gaines stood up. "We're being hailed."

Mark Windsor, who'd been pouring over every detail of Officer Mandy Kadera's report, looked up from his pad. "Say again?"

Gaines pointed to his ear and was smiling. "Solid signal. Coming from the colony. It's Captain Rivers. She's trying to reach you."

"Have you replied?" Windsor set aside his pad. "Never mind. Put them through."

Gaines nodded. "And go."

"This is First Officer Mark Windsor. Captain Rivers, do you copy? Over."

Those on the bridge watched the officer, hope on their expressions. Eyes wide.

"Officer Windsor. This is Captain Rivers. How are you reading me? Over."

"Loud and clear," he said. "Over."

"You're loud and clear, as well. I am here with Commander Meyers, Captain Stanton, and Lieutenant Angela Ruiz," she said. "We're inside the colony, in their communications room."

Windsor felt a knot twist in is gut. "And the others?"

"We have a confirmed fatality. Lieutenant Gordon O'Hearn. Lieutenant Murray Bell is with our shuttle. We broke through the atmosphere and were side-swept by a storm. It took our shuttle and the starfighters down. Our medic, Lieutenant Weber, is en-route to pick up Bell at the shuttle and retrieve O'Hearn's corpse," Rivers explained. "We've not heard from pilots Reilly or Jane Cornwell. Over."

Windsor cupped his forehead between the web of his thumb and finger. Three casualties. That was far too many. He didn't imagine any of this sat well with the commander. "How did you make it to the colony, Lieutenant?"

"We walked," she said.

"And what about the colonists?"

"So far, we've not encountered anyone else," she said.

"No one?"

There was a pause. "No one, sir. However, we have engaged with an aggressive alien lifeform. This being, almost reptilian, could quite possibly be responsible for the colonists sounding the alarms."

Windsor wasn't sure what Rivers was saying. He tried imagining a lizard wreaking havoc on the planet. It concerned him because Rivers indicated the reptiles might be the cause of the alarms, but people oftentimes overreacted. It was human nature. What weighed heaviest on his mind was locating the colonists. They must be holed up somewhere on the compound. "How much of the compound have you explored?"

"Nearly half. The commander is confident they are here. Over."

That was good news. It confirmed his suspicions that the colonists were hiding somewhere. He knew *Euphoric* gave up hope anyone was still alive on the planet, thinking too much time had passed. He wasn't as quick at dismissing the colonists or their will to survive.

Once the *Eclipse* team found them, they could set things straight and head home. The loss of life to members of the crew was tragic, and he wanted his commander and the others back on the ship as soon as possible. "Is the commander close?"

"Standing right beside me. Over."

"Commander Meyers, this is First Officer Windsor. I have an updated priority memo from *Euphoric*. Is there a pad close by where I can transmit the information to you?"

"We have access to the computers here. We're accessing the database now, seeing if we can get it online," Rivers said. "And . . . we are ready for the transmission."

"Okay. Standby," he said. Windsor was not thrilled about passing along the new, altered directive. It was cold and heartless. If the *Eclipse* crew could sort things out, get the colonists back on their feet, and the mining operation up and running again, then everything would be set straight. He found the memorandum and sent it to the colony's database. "Sent."

"The commander wants to know how everything is on the *Eclipse*. Over," Rivers asked.

"We're fine. Planning for your return home. We can send the shuttle to retrieve you, and any of the colonists you may still encounter." He wanted to convey optimism. Was it possible something horrible had happened to every single one of the colonists? That would be catastrophic. People back home would riot. *Euphoric* would wind up a defendant in a liability class-action lawsuit. It wouldn't matter if release forms had been signed. The right to sue still existed. Bad press might more than cripple the corporation, it could bankrupt them.

"What's the meaning of this?" It was Commander Meyers.

"The directive came from the home office."

"I can see that. Are they out of their minds? We're here to check on the colonists, not collect up the diamonds and bring them back to Nebula," she shouted.

Windsor winced. "Understood, Commander. Loud and clear."

"Here's what we're going to do, Windsor. We're going to complete our search of the facility. A thorough search. If we find any of the colonists, we will bring them back to the *Eclipse* with us. If we don't find anyone, then my team and I are returning to the ship. Without any diamonds. If *Euphoric* has a problem with that, they can take it up with me when I return. There are serious threats down here, and I will not put my crew in danger any longer than is necessary to complete our initial objective!"

Windsor said, "I can ready the second shuttle. Say the word and I'll fly down to retrieve all of you."

"You can ready the shuttle, Windsor. That would be great. We have the colonist's shuttle here. It might be easier, safer, if we just exit the surface in that," Meyers said. "But, as a contingency, should something go wrong, we'd definitely appreciate your assistance."

"Aye, Commander. I'll be ready."

"We'll be in touch, Windsor. Over and out."

Windsor signed off. He sat back in his chair, dropped the pad into his lap, and sighed. He suddenly felt wonderful. He'd gotten to a point where if contact hadn't been made soon, he would have choices to consider and decisions to make.

Thankfully, that was no longer the case. Windsor stood up and pulled on the ends of his uniform shirt, straightening out wrinkles.

"Gaines," he said. "Let Officer Kadera know I'm heading down to see her. We've got to ready the second shuttle for a possible rescue mission."

Gains did not try hiding his grin. "Aye. I'll alert her immediately."

CHAPTER THIRTY-SEVEN

Aroldis D'Rukker tried blocking memories from his mind, oftentimes with little success. He felt like remembering some things did little good. They didn't move him forward, and therefore, couldn't be useful. If anything, memories were a deterrent, forcing him to lose focus. Unable to stay focused was a dangerous way to live your life in space. Too much depended on concentration. It wasn't just his own life he was responsible for, either. He had his crew to think about. They were his family and depended on him.

And yet, at times, it just happened, and he remembered.

D'Rukker knew he promised the crew much more than he delivered, but they got by. The idea of adventure and action was, in fact, mostly time spent searching for replacement parts for ship repairs, and pulling off larcenies so they didn't starve or run out of fuel. It was seemingly endless and fruitless expeditions that rarely lacked any significant payment. But it was what he'd made of his life and hoped if his father ever found out, he wouldn't be too disappointed.

He missed his father. For as long as he could remember, it had always been just the two of them.

His mother jumped ship shortly after he'd been born. Although his father never talked bad about his mother, he one time found a letter his father had hidden inside a desk drawer. His mother claimed she was too young to be a mother, and a child wasn't really what she wanted in life. There was too much left to do, so much out there still to explore. Aldoris' mother said she wasn't ready to give up on living her own life first. Having a family wasn't at, or even near, the top of her priorities. That was what she had written.

And then, apparently, she'd left.

Aldoris wasn't sure how a woman walked out on a family, just gave up, and quit. It's what his mother had done, though. He knew it wasn't the norm, and that when you got down to it, his mother had been a heartless, emotionless, and selfish woman. The exact polar opposite of his father.

He wasn't some textbook guy with mommy issues. Aldoris would fire a blaster bolt into the forehead of anyone who suggested such a preposterous, unsubstantiated psychological babble. If anything, and he'd admit, willingly, he was a son who always admired his father. It was more than just placing him on a pedestal he didn't deserve. He didn't worship the man, but definitely loved, admired, and missed him.

Brandt D'Rukker had been a galactic marshal. He worked a sector on Nova, operated by a chunk of the more mid-sized corporations in charge of the Way Station. It was during a string of assaults and a subsequent murder when Galactic assigned more marshals as investigative resources.

The only commonality linking the spurt of criminal activity together was one specific company that employed each of them. Aroldis remembered the long hours his father worked. Even when not at work, the case was all he talked about. He loved every minute. His father involved him. They would sit around the table, his notes between them, and they would talk through the points of the case. He always wanted Aroldis' take, asked his opinion often. As a teenager, he felt like he was an *un*badged marshal.

Best part, at one point, they'd gotten close. The two of them didn't have the thing solved, but Aroldis' father had definitely drawn some lines and connected some dots. There wasn't a painted picture, but some broad strokes had been brushed, and Brandt was confident they were now closer to solving the crimes than they had been before. He'd been so excited, in fact, that he contacted his supervisor with the new connections he'd identified.

It was then—maybe two days later—when a new cop, a kid fresh from the academy, came across an oddity in records when checking over the company's books. The kid had been green, and this had been a major investigation. The kid had been, Brandt thought, assigned to basement work based on the rookie status. Pouring over documents and more or less mindless legwork that rarely had him leaving his seat seemed like an appropriate assignment for a newbie. The kid never complained. Aroldis remembered his father recalling the excitement the new marshal expressed over just becoming part of the investigative team. It was not something he'd forget, because he understood how that new marshal must have felt. It was probably exactly the same way he felt each time he worked into the middle of the night at the kitchen table with his father.

This kid, it turned out, had uncovered a recent series of rather large monetary transfers into a private account. Closer inspection revealed the account had been set up a few weeks prior to the start of the corruption.

Although there had been no name attached, the I.P. address and software tracking led the marshals directly to Brandt's door.

The following year became a blur, a nightmare. He'd never forget the day the Galactic sent an entire armed team to bust through their door. His father had been in the shower. He had been cooking dinner for the two of them. The marshals never attempted knocking.

Aroldis sold their place and used the money to hire an expensive criminal defense attorney. There was no way some court-appointed hack was going to represent his father during the trial. He never told his father he'd sold the place, though. Brandt didn't need to know that. He had enough on his mind. When first arrested, the judge denied the request for bail. (Which, at that hearing, Brandt had been represented by a court-appointed attorney). Hence, the sale.

The charges Brandt faced spanned from theft and assault to murder.

Someone was pinning the spree of crime on his father. It was clearly a set-up. Somehow, Brandt had become the fall-guy, the patsy. The trial was a joke. The prosecution produced less than even circumstantial evidence. And while the defense attorney did her best, nothing helped. Aroldis figured the conspiracy went too deep, went too high. There was no telling who was involved, but Aroldis suspected the galactic marshals as part of the cover-up.

Brandt was sentenced to twenty-five years to life on Mars.

There was no getting off Mars. Everyone knew that. It was as good as a death sentence.

At first, Aroldis promised his father he'd find out the truth and clear his name, get him out, get him off that desolate planet ... He meant it when he said it, but soon after his father was gone and on Mars, the realization of *everything* set in.

Aroldis did not have the authority or ability to investigate the corporate crimes on his own. Just sixteen, he tried looking for work. It wasn't as simple as walking into a place and asking for a job. People knew who he was, who his father was. Sympathy wasn't in abundance for the D'Rukkers on Nova.

Aroldis stayed with friends when he could and on the "streets" when he had nowhere else to go. The Nova Way Station didn't tolerate or accommodate the homeless. If picked up for vagrancy, or loitering even, he'd find himself on an earthbound shuttle in no time. It often happened to those who couldn't prove residency.

Broke and hungry, Aroldis did what needed doing to survive.

He stole his first ship.

———

D'Rukker stretched, yawned, and gave the *Cutlass* controls a cursory glance. Erinne was the best co-pilot he could ever remember having. The kid had a way with the *Cutlass* that made her flying seem effortless. It wasn't easy, or often, that D'Rukker felt comfortable with giving over control. That required trust. Trusting was not one of his strong points.

Everything looked fine, and yet, something had interrupted his sleep. Not Erinne's though. Because she hadn't been sleeping. "What have we got?" he asked.

She shushed him and spun a dial.

"Officer Windsor. This Captain Rivers. How are you reading me?"

"Hot damn," Erinne said, slapped the dash, and fine-tuned the same dial next to her communicator. "Yeah, looks like someone from the mining colony is trying to reach out to the *Eclipse.*"

D'Rukker sat forward. *"Euphoric,* eh? Looks like communications have been restored. They hailing from the planet surface?"

"Seems that way." Erinne sat back in her seat, hands on the arm rests. "How long are we going to just sit here?"

"I've been thinking about that."

"You've been sleeping."

D'Rukker shot Erinne a grim look. She might be the only person who could get away with talking to him that way. No. She was the only person he knew who could get away with talking to him that way. "I do some of my best thinking that way."

"And snoring."

"I don't snore."

"Then your nose is broken," she said and laughed.

D'Rukker crossed his arms.

"Sorry. As you were saying?"

"My best guess, that colony down there got overwhelmed by storms. Too much to handle all at once. Must have been more than they were expecting."

Erinne said, "Nice place to visit, but I wouldn't want to live there."

"Exactly," D'Rukker said. "So they had set up this fancy compound with minimal research beforehand, because when you think about it, they don't care about the people."

"It's the diamonds they want."

D'Rukker nodded. "Exactly. Planet that size, filled with jewels, Nebula's only got money on the mind. Not safety."

"Okay. But we *kinda* figured all of that."

"We did. But see, we know it's true now. So, this distress signal gets sent out from the planet, right? And Nebula sends the *Eclipse* to investigate the situation."

"Which they are doing," she added.

D'Rukker said, "Which they are doing, but minimally. They sent down one shuttle, with four starfighters. Radio contact has been down for …"

"Over seventeen hours."

"Over seventeen hours and the *Eclipse* hasn't done anything but follow around in orbit," D'Rukker said.

"I don't get it."

"Tells me they have a bare bones staff left, a skeleton crew. They don't have enough resources to send down another party to check on the status of the first party. We know they got walloped when they broke the atmosphere. And what? And nothing. No one came for them, not even after hours of communicator salience," D'Rukker explained. "Do you see where I'm going with this?"

Erinne kept nodding her head, but said, "Ah, no. I have absolutely no idea where you're going with this."

D'Rukker pursed his lips and puffed out his cheeks. "Way I see it, we've got two choices."

"I'm listening." Erinne propped her left elbow on the arm of her chair, made a metallic fist, and dropped her chin onto robotic knuckles.

"We swoop in now, no way of telling what we're up against. *Euphoric's* people will be armed. I'm sure everyone on the *Eclipse* has a brand new blaster and whatever newest weaponry is out there nowadays. It's not that I'm afraid of a fight," he said, actually without much enthusiasm. Had been a long time since he'd last been in a fight. In a way, he kind of craved some confrontation. Floating around in space was the epitome of boredom. "But I just can't qualify putting my crew in danger when I don't have to."

"Qualify?"

She enjoyed giving him a hard time. He kept reminding himself he loved her like a daughter. If he didn't, he might end up killing her. "We should wait."

"Wait?"

"Let the *Eclipse* complete their assessment. We keep monitoring the communicators, figure out what they know, see what's going on—what *went* on, and when they're gone, then we'll head in."

"We know what went on. Bad weather. Plant's one big storm globe."

"We think we know what happened. We don't know anything. Not yet."

"So we wait?"

"We wait, and when the *Eclipse* is long gone, all we will have to deal with is some miners and scientists." D'Rukker grinned. "Can't get any easier than that."

"*... we have engaged with an aggressive alien lifeform. This being, almost reptilian, could quite possibly be responsible for the colonists sounding the alarms.*"

"Wait. Did you hear that?" D'Rukker said. The look on Erinne's face made it clear she'd heard the transmission also, and yet he struggled with comprehension. "What did they just say?"

"Now what?" she asked.

He sat silent for a moment. A game changer. It shouldn't be, and yet it was. The thoughts of his father are what filled his head. Everything his dad had ever taught him was in direct conflict with the way D'Rukker lived his life. Aroldis drew lines, though. He made things as black and white as he could. Eliminated as much of the grey as was possible. He stole things. Generally, he robbed those who could afford to lose some. While he didn't give loot to the poor, he still felt he identified with the classic literature character. He couldn't remember the name. Some guy living in a forest. Had a band of merry men. That guy stole from the rich, gave to the poor. Thing was, he was poor. So, in a way ... But this. People were in danger. They were close enough to help. They had the means to help. The question was simple. Did they have an obligation to help?

If he played the game, what would my father do in this situation, there really wouldn't be much of a game. He knew the answer.

"Aroldis?"

He sucked in a deep breath and then exhaled. "Now, I've got to rethink this."

"I guess that means I should say goodnight?" she said.

CHAPTER THIRTY-EIGHT

The sense of victory Commander Anara Meyers felt was short lived.

The four of them, Adam Stanton, Danielle Rivers, and Angela Ruiz, were still inside the communications room. They managed to get the radios up and working, made contact with the *Eclipse*, and at least had some kind of a plan in place for moving forward.

Meyers didn't care about *Euphoric's* altered agenda. Retrieving diamonds was furthest from her mind. If management had an issue with her disobeying the order, they could write her up when she got back home. They weren't here. They didn't see what was going on. Of course, the new order came before she'd made contact with *Eclipse*. Once Windsor relayed the situation back to *Euphoric*, she was certain her employer would see things differently.

They would have to see things differently. People were missing and dead. There were giant reptile-like creatures on the planet that, as best she could tell, no one had known a thing about. (And if she found out *Euphoric* did know about the monsters . . .) And the creatures were tough to kill. Something about the snake-like scaly plating deflected or absorbed bolts fired from blasters. Only way to knock them down and out was by hitting them in exposed, soft spots.

An open mouth has proved effective.

She had shared that tidbit with her team. Right now, it was the best she could do.

"Okay," Ruiz said, "so are we going to explore the rest of the colony together?"

"We are," Meyers said. "The dorms, the kitchen, the rec room. Those are our next stops. Looks like, based on the layout, in that order. We stay close. We watch each other's backs."

"You think there are more of those things in here, inside the compound?" Stanton looked over his blaster. The weapon still held a near-full charge. He touched his fingertips to the bowie knife in the sheath strapped against his thigh.

"I have no reason to think there aren't any more," the commander said. Her mind raced through scenarios that might have played out on the colony months ago. If one or two of those things were loose inside the compound, the miners and scientists never stood a chance. They might have a few weapons down here, but it wasn't like everyone had been on high alert the way a para-military crew would have been. In actuality, the colonists were defenseless against an alien attack.

Only on Neptune, Meyers knew all too well, *they* were the aliens.

"In here? Inside the compound?" Rivers asked.

Meyers said, "It's not much of a stretch. Something caused the colonists to set off the alarm. We get here, and what do we find? Place is like a ghost town." She thought about the hand they'd found in the mound of mined diamonds. "We haven't run into one person. It's possible we're the only four people here."

"Alive, you mean?" Ruiz said. "The only four people here still alive."

Meyers nodded. "So we're going to search this place. We're going to search the place good, too. And then we're out of here. We're getting off this planet. Right now, I am mostly concerned with our safety. Us. My crew. Is that understood?"

"Aye," they said, in unison.

"I'm going to want one person to stay back. This room is a lifeline. It needs protection." Meyers made brief eye contact with the three of them. She didn't want one of those things getting into the communications room. She imagined a creature like that could do untold amounts of damage. This room was their link to the *Eclipse*. If things didn't go as easily as she had planned, they may need to get a hold of Windsor. She didn't trust the portables, not with the unstable weather. The signal might not reach her ship, and the crew on board would have no idea they were in any kind of trouble.

Rivers raised a hand. "I've got this, Commander," she said, straightening her back and standing tall.

Meyers gave the lieutenant a slight nod. "You stay inside this room, Lieutenant. Once we step out, you lock that door. No one gets inside. Not alien, not even a colonist. We have no idea what the entire situation is. Someone shows up you get a hold of us on the comlink. Nothing comes inside this room."

"Aye, Commander."

"Okay. Good. The rest of you, let's get this search over and done. I've got point. Everyone else fall in behind me. I don't think I need to say this, but eyes open. Stay alert. Let's move!"

There was a quick moment where the only sound was off the *Eclipse* crew lock and loading blasters. Meyers stepped out of the communications room. "Last one out, make sure the door is closed."

The commander's comlink crackled. "Commander Meyers? Commander Meyers?" The tone of voice sounded panicked. "Hello? Anyone?"

It was their medic. Marshall Weber. Meyers responded, speaking slow, calm, and clear. Meyers knew the importance of defusing the situation as best she could. While she wasn't with Weber, the way she spoke with him on the radio might help reassure him that everything would be okay. If she matched his level of intensity, he'd feel less secure. It wasn't easy, but the commander stayed relaxed. "I read you, Lieutenant Weber. Go ahead."

The four of them stood silently waiting for the next transmission. They anxiously looked from one to the other. It was almost as if no one wanted to say a word, except, Weber wasn't talking either.

Meyers knew the mission had come unraveled from the moment they pierced the planet's atmosphere. Space exploration was dangerous from the get-go. Everyone knew that, accepted it. Danger came with the job. It was also why a lot of people signed up. It wasn't just the healthy *Euphoric* paychecks and benefits that were the draw. There was something to be said for living on the edge.

Problem with that way of thinking was most people considered themselves somewhat immortal. Meyers always thought the admiral was going to live forever. Until recently, until the last time she saw him. He had become quite thin. His skin was loose on his bones. There was a tremor in his hand. She noticed it when he poured himself a cup of coffee the last morning she spent visiting with him just prior to the Neptune mission.

He was going to die. The admiral, the strongest man she'd ever known, would not live forever. And now, she knew with equal conviction that *she* would not live forever. It was okay, but she didn't want to die out here. Not on Neptune. And not with at least getting the chance to say goodbye to her father.

"Weber?" Commander Meyers said.

"We're surrounded, Commander. Surrounded." Marshall Weber whispered. He sounded cold, scared. There was an audible tremor in his tone of voice.

Stanton and Meyers locked eyes. No words.

Meyers said, "Weber, where are you? Do you have Bell? Is Bell with you, Weber?"

"They're everywhere, Commander. We—we're not going to get out of this."

CHAPTER THIRTY-NINE

Lieutenant Marshall Weber positioned himself behind Murray Bell. They were on the icy ground. Bell lay between Weber's legs, his head on Weber's thigh. Weber kept letting go of the barrel of his blaster, patting Bell on the shoulder. It was for reassurance, although there was nothing at all reassuring about the situation.

They'd made it out of the shuttle and into the rover. The escaped a sinking rover, only to wind up stranded on the ice. And now they were surrounded by serpent-like creatures. They were hideously frightening, and moving closer, and closer.

Weber knew they must look as alien to the creatures as the creatures did to him. For some reason, the things didn't immediately attack. It might suggest a level of intelligence. Perhaps the things were just curious and investigating.

On Earth, people would have done the same thing.

Eventually, they would kill the unknown *whatever*, and autopsy it, or cage it.

Yeah. On Earth, they'd mess with anything alien, anything new and never before seen. Why? Because people thought they were superior over everything else. Entitled.

Why should a natural inhabitant of Neptune feel any differently?

The creature things were all around them.

One, coiled less than fifty yards away, raised its croc-like head. The eyes never blinked. The mouth opened wide as cords in the back of its throat vibrated. A prehistoric scream erupted. If Weber was forced to explain what the sound meant, to translate, he'd have sworn he just heard the first alien battle cry.

"Web, man. Shoot it. I don't know what you're waiting for. Shoot the thing!"

Shoot it. Made the most sense, if there had been just one of the creatures in front of them. He counted five, no, six. Sticking with the idea the creatures housed some sort of intellect, Weber didn't want to appear like the aggressor in the situation. If these things were just slithering in for a closer look, satisfying a curious itch, the last thing he wanted to do is inflame a possible peaceful circumstance.

"They haven't done anything, Bell. We've invaded their planet. We're the ones who shouldn't be here. I start sending bolts at them, then who's the one at fault?" Weber said. Inside his own mind, it made sense. It wasn't him being passive, as much as responsible.

"Have you seen my leg?" Bell waved a hand over what was left of his leg. "They've attacked, partner. They have already drawn first blood on us, on our race. And if you ask me, Web, if you ask me? They like the way we taste! They're probably damned tired of a diet consisting of eating whatever else lives under this ice. Bored senseless with the local cuisine. And then what? Low and behold, here we come like a meat buffet on legs. A meat buffet, Web."

Marshall Weber knew Bell was crying. He heard the sniffles echo inside his own helmet between their transmissions. Weber wouldn't call him on it. He knew the man was afraid, terrified. Hell, he was terrified.

"Shoot them, Web. Shoot them."

He lifted the strap of his blaster up and over his head. He held the rifle in his arms, finger on the trigger. "Bell, I can't just open fire—"

"Give me your blaster, then. If you can't do it, I will." Murray Bell reached for the weapon.

Weber tugged free, fell backward. Bell rolled out from between Weber's legs. He stayed on his stomach, perched up on his elbows. "Shoot the damned things, Weber!"

Marshall Weber saw the look on Bell's face through the faceplate; there was no denying the torment and pain in his friend's eyes.

Bell was right.

They were in danger. They would never get anywhere safe, and would never make it back to the colony with so many creatures around them. This might be it. This could be the end.

He did not want to infuriate the creatures. This was their last stand, no doubt. If there was another choice, he'd take it. He didn't see any other options. Resigned, Weber raised the blaster.

The coiled creature looked to be the most aggressive. Maybe that one was the leader. Take out the biggest guy in a fight, and the others might back off. That had always been something his father had taught him. Go up to the biggest. baddest guy and break his nose. It sends a message. It lets everyone else know you are not playing around.

Weber still wasn't convinced making the first move was the best idea.

The options remainedweren't just limited, they were nil.

Shoot the things where they sat coiled or get eaten.

That was about it.

And while Weber wasn't in a hurry to become the main dish on an alien smorgasbord, his finger still hesitated on squeezing the trigger.

The creatures must have sensed the mood swing, the increased hostility in his action when he raised his weapon and pointed it directly at the main monster, because they all raised their heads. Jaws spread wide. They let out screeches and growls.

The best Weber could compare the action to would be a pack of wolves howling.

Weber's heart raged behind his ribcage. It was now the moment of truth. Although he was para-military, had extensive weapon training, he considered himself a paramedic, a healer. A helper.

He closed his eyes for just a second, a moment to regroup.

When he opened them, he placed the head of the largest creature in blaster crosshairs. He squeezed the trigger.

The segmented red laser bolts flew through the air and struck the target below the head.

The thing cried out. It could have been in pain, or it might just have been angry.

His actions didn't deter the other creatures. They all shrieked their own kind of howling, with heads back and jaws opened wide. Worse than the sound, they all uncoiled and started moving. The motions were unnerving. An attack was now imminent, and Weber couldn't help realizing it might be a battle he actually started.

Like a pit of snakes, vipers, the creatures slithered about making their way closer and closer. None came directly at Weber and Bell, though. It was as if the aliens insisted on utilizing as much caution as possible. Slow, and calculating. In a roundabout way, however, the things were shortening the distance between them; tightening the noose.

"Don't stop! You can't stop," Bell yelled. He kept leaning his weight on one forearm, and then the other. He craned his neck this way and that. The man was doing his best to see all around him at once. His jerky movements were making Weber dizzy. "They're coming!"

Weber shouted, "I know they're coming. I can see them!"

Trying his best at lining up the next shot, aiming just for the head of the closest creature, Weber let bolts fly. The air sizzled as the red laser zipped out of the end of his blaster.

As if realizing, learning, and understanding that the bolts were dangerous, deadly, the creatures dropped their heads low. It made them harder targets.

And they moved fast.

The creatures serpentined this way and that.

"We're not going to make it," Bell screamed.

"We're going to make," Weber responded, but inside his head, his own brain agreed one hundred percent with Bell. There was not a chance in hell they'd make it.

They were going to die.

For a fleeting moment, Weber considered putting a bolt through Bell's head and then firing one up through his own chin and into his skull.

Death would be swift that way. Hopefully, painless.

Weber figured, even if it hurt *some*, a murder/suicide would deliver far better results than getting devoured by one of the creatures.

It would have to be better.

Weber, in a crouch, spun around and sent an almost endless stream of bolts at the enemy, because that was what they were now. The enemy.

Most of his shots missed. The hot bolts passed through the ice, kicking up sprays of diamonds and poisonous ocean water.

The blaster stuttered, kicking out a handful of bolts, and then nothing.

The charge was depleted.

The weapon was rendered useless.

It was as if the creatures, when they saw Weber lower his weapon for closure inspection, were confused by the gesture. They paused. Hissed.

And then, as if they understood the significance—their enemy was now defenseless, the voice of the creatures, as one, resounded with an ear-piercing cry. More like snakes than even when they sat coiled, the creatures slithered and raised their heads poised to strike ...

CHAPTER FORTY

Captain Adam Stanton stayed behind Commander Meyers and Lieutenant Ruiz. It wasn't that he didn't trust Ruiz watching his back, because he did, it was just that he thought he could watch all of their backs better. It was the same when it came down to anything. He just naturally trusted his own skills and talents more than he trusted anyone else's.

Commander Anara Meyers moved slowly through the halls. They had an entire half of the compound left to explore. The expectation was coming across survivors and getting the heck off the planet. Quick. Simple. Stanton knew better. Planning and execution rarely worked out the way one thought. Regardless, Stanton remained as optimistically hopeful as possible. Success was more than fifty percent mental. The other fifty percent rested in his hands and the hands of his teams. They had gelled as a team, too; had grown together over the long months on this first mission as a crew with the *Eclipse*.

They moved as one, silent, except for their shallow breaths and the sound of their boots on the metallic floor. The amber lights kept them in an almost constant dismal setting. Stanton ignored all of it as best he could, although the sounds of them letting out ragged breaths and the somber lighting took a mental toll.

He walked backwards, more or less, sidestepped and pivoted. His blaster swiveled left and right with him. He swept the area, and aimed the barrel with his finger on the trigger ready to pull at all times. If he saw one of those things coming after them, he would annihilate the thing before it even got close. The creature would be hating life once Stanton opened fire and the bolts blasted holes through its crusty scales.

Anytime they approached an intersection of passageways, the commander stopped. They'd group close together. She would inspect the passages carefully before moving forward.

They knew nothing about the creatures. Could they scale walls? Squeeze into tight places? Camouflage scaly skin with plaid backgrounds? Nothing. They knew not a thing. While Stanton applauded the commander's tenacious efforts, he was also a bit unnerved, maybe even agitated. The slow moving was certainly cautious—especially with how much they didn't know about their newly discovered advisory—but it was eating up the clock.

Time kept ticking away. He wouldn't say he was homesick, but right about now all he wanted was off the planet and to be back on the *Eclipse*. He didn't consider that an unreasonable wish. However, Stanton stayed focus, concentrating more on his responsibilities of back watching and less on dreams. Inside his mind, he couldn't help but replay the recent transmission exchange between Weber and the commander.

His friends were stuck outside the compound, surrounded by the evil snake-things.

No one asked to go and help. Had they have asked, the commander would have denied the request. And rightly so.

The four of them were deep inside the colony. They would have to backtrack through the compound, go back out into the elements, and then search for Weber and Bell. Although, the faceshield would display a location, potentially...

Something moved. "Hold it," Stanton said. He'd seen a shadow, or thought he had.

Ruiz spun around, dropped to one knee, and raised her blaster. She had one eye squeezed shut, the other wide open and staring through her scope. The green site laser from her weapon played on the floor, wall, ceiling. "I'm not seeing anything."

"It was something. Just around the bend," Stanton said. A part of him felt foolish. Maybe he had spoken too soon? Perhaps he should have waited until he was certain something was behind them.

No. No, it was better safe than sorry. Not the other way around. A distant early warning was better than an ambush. "Stay here," Stanton said and took a step forward.

The commander reached out. Her hand locked on his arm. "You stay here. I'll have a look."

"With all due respect, Commander, no."

"No?" Meyers said.

Stanton didn't wait and hash out the issue. He continued on, backtracking the way they'd just walked. His respect for the commander continually grew. She didn't send her people out to do things while she hung back as a spectator. She walked the line. Front line. She put herself, or tried, in the dangerous situations. She might not be as fearless as she pretended to be, but Meyers was brave. There was no denying that much.

Adam Stanton kept his knees bent. Arms high. The butt of the blaster crammed against into the crock of right shoulder. Left hand on the barrel. He didn't have a scope on the weapon but used the sight on the nose of the barrel for lining up targets.

As he came upon the corner, Stanton slowed his steps even more. He listened intently for any sound out of the ordinary. Although, being new inside the compound, he had no clue what normal sounded like.

He pressed his back against the wall. The amber lights spun, made small shadows grow and dance. His hiding spot was cast onto the wall across from him. If one of the creatures was on the turn, and was smart enough to understand shadows, his element of surprise was shot.

Stanton almost laughed at the thought. He knew he was personifying some alien being, giving the thing far more credit than it deserved. The creatures were anything but intelligent. They were primitive, basic. He figured the things slept, hunted, and ate. Life didn't get any more elementary.

Sucking in a deep breath and holding it, Stanton dropped to a knee as he pivoted his body around the corner. Weapon trained on whatever might be waiting directly in front of him.

As his knee hit the floor, he took a fraction of a moment and inventoried the situation.

He counted at least six of the creatures. They were slithering toward him. Some were on the walls. They definitely had small legs and webbed feet with taloned toes. The talons gripped the wall, digging into the metal. He also heard the clicking of those sharp toenails on the square floor tiles.

His mind reeled. The potential scenarios played out in his mind's eye. He couldn't differentiate a winning plan from the options. His was one blaster against a half dozen dangerous, violent aliens.

"What have you got?" Commander Meyers' voice whispered in his ear. It was such a crisp transmission, for a moment he thought she might be standing directly behind him. He almost turned around to check but knew better. Might be better all-around if she were directly behind him. The two of them could deliver an unforgettable punishment on the creatures. On his own ...

"Six *unfriendlies* making their way toward us," Stanton whispered. He believed his sudden appearance went undetected. The creatures seemed preoccupied with each other. Their jaws opened and snapped closed, making back-throat gargles and tongue clicks. "Commander, if I didn't know better, I'd say they were communicating with each other."

So much for unintelligent alien lifeforms, Stanton thought. This changed things. Drastically.

"Can you get out of there?" Meyers asked.

Stanton knew he'd been lucky to drop in without alerting them to his position. He feared anymore movement might draw unwanted attention. He suspected their eyes worked in a fashion similar to other reptiles, picking up prey based on motion. "Not positive, Commander. I feel like if I stay still, they aren't seeing me," he said.

He saw two options, limited options at that. The creatures crept closer and closer. If Stanton waited too long to do anything, they would be on him in less than a minute. It would be far too late to kill all of them by then, maybe too late to kill even one. If he backed away, made it around the corner, they would most likely see him, and then they'd come at him fast. He would be leading them directly toward his commander.

"Permission to engage," Stanton said.

"Permission granted," Commander Meyers said.

Stanton looked to his right. Commander Meyers stood there. She held her blaster in her right hand, barrel aiming up. She gave him a nod, raised her left hand so he could see as she counted down, lowering a finger at a time. She mouthed the words, "Three. Two. One."

Commander Meyers launched herself off the wall, slid to a knee beside Stanton, and the two of them immediately opened fire.

CHAPTER FORTY-ONE

The creatures were all around Lieutenants Marshall Weber and Murray Bell. The rover was gone, sunk into Neptune's ocean. The vehicle had been the only safety net available. The snake-like creatures were everywhere. They were surrounded.

Bell, with a missing leg and no weapon, was defenseless and panicking. "Web, man, shoot!"

"Web, man, what are you waiting for?"

The creatures came at them fast.

Weber sighed. "The charge is gone. I'm out. The blaster's useless."

The two of them locked eyes. They were going to die. The resolve washed over their expressions, the somber emotion of one matched the other as if looking into a mirror.

The biggest of the creatures came in close and coiled its body as the head rose in the air above them. The jaws opened wide. The rattling roar from the back of the creature's throat nearly shook the ground. The sound hurt Weber's ears. He couldn't plug them with his hands, not with a helmet on, so instead was forced to just close his eyes and wait for the horrible cry to end.

Bell rolled onto his back. It was as if he didn't want to die if he couldn't see it coming.

Something whistled.

It came from above them. Weber looked up.

He saw a light spray from a cluster of clouds. His first thought was another freak storm. He hated this stupid planet; hated everything about it!

On the tail of the beam of light was a ship that cut a path through the sky.

It wasn't the *Eclipse* or a shuttle. It was like nothing he had seen before. It flew like an inverted V with layered wings. The ship opened fire. Lasers blasted the snow and ice around them.

"Take cover!" Weber shouted. He dove forward, draping his body over Bell.

Weber heard more shots fired. The creatures chortled out throaty, gravelly cries. Weber watched as the ship made a second pass. Most of the creatures were down. Injured pools of blood around the long, round bodies. They weren't dead. Dying, though. "Whoa-who!"

Bell pushed Weber off, tried sitting up.

As the large ship swooped in, weapons blazing, Weber knocked Bell back down. He covered Bell with his own body.

"What in the hell are you doing?" Bell screamed. "I can't see what's going on!"

"What if they miss?"

"Your body isn't going to protect either of us from a blast out of a ship that size. Look at the size of their cannons." Bell, once again, shoved Weber off and sat up.

Bell had a point.

Weber held his useless blaster in his hands, wished his charger wasn't dead. He wanted in on the action. He suddenly felt the flicker of hope stir inside his chest.

The ship spun around above them, hovered in place.

The underside cannon swiveled, bolts fired. A creature's body exploded. Blood and innards sprayed. The cannon swiveled. Bolts fired. The blast hit a creature's neck just below the croc-like head. The head fell away, severed from the rest of the body in a clean, sizzling, slice.

Weber had been certain they would never get out of this. Those creatures had them, dead to nuts, as his friends in military training had been known to say. Dead to nuts.

He had no idea who piloted the ship rescuing them, and at the moment, he didn't care. They could be pirates for all he cared.

"Web!"

Marshall Weber looked at Bell and noticed Bell was looking behind Weber. His eyes were wide. Weber's stomach dropped. He knew one of the creatures was closing in.

Without hesitating, Weber snatched his bowie knife from the sheath strapped to his thigh. He dropped onto his arm and rolled away. The ground crunched under his weight. His rapid breathing fogged the inside faceshield.

When Weber stopped rolling, he got up onto his knees, knife in a right-hand grip so that the blade ran along his forearm and he'd be ready to block and slash at the same time; in one fluid motion.

Except, the thing—the creature—wasn't poised to strike … him.

Bell lay on his back on the ground with both arms crossed in a block above his chest. The creature had one of its feet on Bell's legs. Pinning the man in place.

Weber jumped up onto his feet and sprinted forward. He rotated the Bowie handle. The blade arched forward as he leapt into the air. Before he realized what he was doing, Weber found himself straddling the back of the creature and driving the Bowie blade deep into the thing's flesh, piercing between the scaly plates.

The creature bucked and shook, attempting to get him off of its back. It slithered away from Bell, which was a good sign. However, it was headed for a break in the ice, not far from where the rover had sunk.

Weber fought to free his blade from the creature's neck.

They were close to the edge of the ice and Weber saw clearly the steady ripple of the ocean current.

Without overthinking it, Weber rolled off. He crashed hard on the ice. Had something in his shoulder popped? It was dislocated. Thankfully, it was his left arm. It didn't matter. His blaster was empty and his Bowie was lodged in the creature's neck.

At the last second, Weber jumped.

The back tail of the creature whipped back and forth, as the snake-thing serpentined toward freedom, headed for the ocean. He didn't clear the jump. The toes of his boots kicked the monster. It sent Weber flailing. Again, he came down fast and hard on the ice. With his left arm dangling, Weber got to his feet and ran back toward where he'd left Bell.

"Weber!" Bell was pointing.

Weber chanced a look back. The creature realized he was no longer riding on its back, and perhaps understood that he was now injured. It had spun around. The ocean no longer seemed like its target.

The thing growled and roared as it tucked its head down and then using the ice to its advantage slid fast and furious toward him.

The V-shaped ship dropped out of the sky, rotated so the point of the V was aimed directly at Weber.

Weber looked back a second time. The serpent was nearly on him, its jaws were wide open. He could not believe the size of the curved teeth jutting from its mouth. The thought of those teeth biting through his flesh made him run faster, his legs pumping as hard as they could.

It seemed useless; he couldn't run faster than it could slither.

He wondered what the ship was waiting for. Why weren't they blasting the thing off the planet? And then he realized what the hold-up was: they didn't have a clear shot. He was blocking the way.

Weber dove onto the ice.

It was a calculated risk, because if the ship didn't fire immediately, then he'd just sacrificed himself for nothing.

How he managed to land on his left arm was beyond him. He screamed at the sharp pain coursing through his arm, back, and neck. It almost felt as if his skin were on fire.

The ship opened fire.

Weber didn't stay put. Instead, he got onto all fours, well ... all three working limbs, and kept his left arm cradled as close to his chest as he could, and then dog-crawled his way toward Bell.

The ship passed overhead, just as he reached Bell.

Bell was clapping him on the back. Pulled him in. "You're okay!"

"Thought I was going to die," Weber said.

"I thought you were, too." Bell didn't sugarcoat a thing. He said what he thought. Blunt was better than most, Weber thought.

Bell pointed. "Check that out."

The ship was close to the surface. From the back of the V, a hatch opened, a mechanical ramp lowered, and standing on the edge of the ramp was a woman in a tight spacesuit, waving them over.

"What do we do?" Bell asked.

"We'll never make the colony, not with so many of those creatures out. Not with you missing a leg," Weber said.

"Ouch."

"It's the truth, Mur. It's the truth, so I say we take our chance with these folks. They saved our lives just now."

"They did at that. Help me up," Bell said.

Weber lifted Bell onto his leg and got under the man's arm. They ran with three legs for the back of the ship.

The woman waiting waved them on in a most frantic fashion.

Weber didn't need to look behind them to understand her sudden panic.

"Faster, Bell!" Weber encouraged.

"Going as fast as a one-legged man can run," he said.

Weber almost laughed. If he hadn't been scared out of his mind, he might have. The situation needed some humor. There had to be a break in the terror that had gripped them the last several hours.

On the horizon, the sun was rising. The sun was just a small white orb. Even some three billion miles away, the sun managed to light the sky and chase away the night.

The woman raised a blaster, firing over their heads, let bolts fly.

Instinctively, Weber lowered his head, and tucked his chin closer to his chest.

Bell stumbled, as if the sudden blaster bolts flying overhead close enough to singe hair had they not been wearing helmets, and tripped him up.

Weber readjusted his hold. He grit his teeth since he had his left arm and shoulder pressed tight against Bell's body. With his eyes cast down, he watched their feet. There was nothing graceful about their run. It was clumsy at best, pathetic otherwise. They didn't stop, though. "Faster, Mur. We've got to reach the ship!"

"Ya think?" Bell did laugh, sort of. "I'm trying."

The woman fired three quick blasts overhead.

"I know you are."

Weber kept waiting for the sound of the creature chasing them to start screaming. He knew the things were hard to hit and even harder to kill. He figured, once again, he was in the line of fire, preventing the woman from striking and killing the creature with a bolt or two. There was no diving out of the way this time, not with his arm, and not with Bell in his condition.

The woman held her blaster with both hands now. She stood with feet shoulder-length apart and knees bent. She looked like she meant business. Weber was thankful she appeared to be on their side. He didn't know a thing about the lady in front of them, other than she did not seem like someone to mess with.

Weber and Bell reached the lip of the ramp.

The woman's right arm shot out. Her palm slapped a red button.

The ramp began rising.

Weber lost his balance. He pitched Bell forward. His friend tried staying up, hopping on one leg, but as the ship tipped lifting into the air, he stumbled, arms out, and fell.

Weber slid down the closing hatch. His legs dangled outside.

The woman punched the red button, halting the closing process. She dropped onto her belly and extended an arm.

Weber latched onto her hand. It felt like metal under her suit. Her grip was like a vice. He worried she might crush bones.

She tugged, pulling him into the ship.

Weber used his legs, his knee getting a hold on the lip of the ramp, and hoisted himself into the ship the rest of the way.

Rolling onto his back, an arm draped over his rising and falling chest, Weber finally allowed himself a moment to laugh.

The woman, also lying down and breathing heavy, said, "Did I miss something? What's so funny?"

"Nothing," he said. "Not a damn thing. I'm Weber. Lieutenant Marshall Weber. And that guy back there, he's Lieutenant Murray Bell."

"My names Cohn. Erinne Cohn."

"It's a pleasure to meet you, Cohn," Webber said.

"A real pleasure, ma'am," Bell added.

CHAPTER FORTY-THREE

Commander Meyers' blaster fired bolt after bolt. The red laser bolts cut through the air and slammed into a creature. Only a few missed, scarring the walls and floor with black burn marks. Smoke rose from the scorched areas and from the armored scales protecting the creatures from the blasts. Stanton had been brave enough to back step from the way they'd come to search a corner corridor. They had all heard strange noises, and even if given only one guess, they each knew it had to be one of those creatures following them after they'd left the communications room.

When Stanton indicated there was more than one, Meyers ordered Ruiz through a hatch while she ran to help her captain.

Now the two knelt side-by-side, shoulder to shoulder, and fired on a hallway filled with those snake-*ish* creatures.

Stanton's aim was equally on point. His bolts hit the targets he tried hitting. It looked as if only ricochets burned scars into the floor, walls, and ceiling. Otherwise, his aim was spot-on. The creatures just refused to die. They did, however, retreat some. That alone had to be considered some kind of small victory. Except, they would have to save any celebration for later.

The things were no longer in attack mode. They didn't flee, but neither did they advance. Again, another good sign.

Meyers was worried about the blaster charges. The weapons held a charge for some time, but not indefinitely. "We're going to run," Meyers announced between shots. "There's a chamber door not far from where we were. It's where I sent Ruiz. It separates the living quarters from the rest of the colony." The compound was set up in segments. Although each segment was attached to the next, people could easily divorce themselves from a specific area. This way, if there were any kind of hull breach, the residents would be safe until a team could repair damages.

"I'm ready when you are," Stanton said.

She slapped him on the shoulder before she took off running.

Stanton didn't hesitate. He let two more bolts fly, and then turned and fled.

The two of them raced toward the door. Spacesuit boots, made special to keep them from floating away, but light enough to wear comfortably, pounded the metal floor. The fast-tempo of each footfall created a peculiar sounding drum roll. They were neck and neck. Ruiz was just inside, and offered up hand waves of encouragement.

Meyers' nostrils were filled with the smell of burnt creature. The odor from the fired bolts filled the passages. What made her stomach churn most was the fact that it didn't smell horrible.

When had she last eaten? When had any of them eaten, or had something to drink? She knew, then, that she was tired. Losing focus. If she didn't concentrate, she was going to get tripped up and tumble, and those things would feast on *her*. No. They would not catch her. She was not going to become their next meal!

Meyers didn't have to look back. She knew they were being chased. The things were fast. If she had to guess, she and Stanton were moments shy of being gobbled up alive. "Move it, Captain!"

She ran all out, giving it everything she had. There was no conserving energy at this point. As far as she was concerned, right now was the end of the race. Kicking it into gear, her strides grew, arms pumped, and within a half of a heartbeat, Meyers pulled ahead. It wasn't about beating Stanton, it was meant to inspire.

The technique worked.

Adam Stanton fought for the lead.

It became a game. She thought she could see him smile, maybe heard him giggle in an inadvertent transmission. "Never going to beat me, Captain," she egged him on, and again edged out in front of him.

Something behind them growled, and despite the spacesuit, Meyers thought she felt a spray of hot breath on her back.

Stanton—if he had been smiling—no longer smiled. His brow furrowed and jaw set.

The hatch doorway was five yards ahead of them.

Meyers wasn't prepared when Stanton pushed her from behind. She flew forward, losing her balance, but crossed the threshold. She went down hard, but immediately rolled onto her back and propped herself up onto an elbow.

Stanton, right behind Meyers, spun around and helped pull closed the hatch door with Ruiz. They cranked the wheel lock on the center of the door and effectively sealed themselves off from the south half of the compound. This was confirmed when a red light above the doorway turned green.

Panting, bent forward, with hands on his knees, Stanton said, "You are fast, Commander. Like a cheetah. You have some cheetah blood running through you?"

"A quarter. On my mother's side," she said, grinning.

Something big and heavy slammed into the opposite side of the hatch door.

Stanton jumped. Ruiz laughed at him.

"Don't worry," Meyers said. "We're going to get out of this."

The commander was certain other ways back through the compound existed. She remembered seeing them on the colony blueprints. There weren't multiple routes leading everywhere like some kind of crazy maze. There were two. There were only two, and now this one was blocked.

The best she could tell, they weren't isolated or trapped at the north end. They were just inconvenienced. Restricted. Limited, even.

The thing on the other side of the sealed hatch door slammed into it a second time.

And then a third.

The three of them stood motionless, staring at the door. Meyers knew the same question ran through their minds. It certainly ran through hers. Can those things break down that steel door? "Those hatches are built to withstand a direct hit from a meteor, people," the commander said. "Some hybrid snake-thing is not going to ram its crocodile head through steel that thick. Just not going to happen."

The next thud looked as if the hinges rattled. Had a screw come loose?

"Let's get going, The faster we complete our search, the sooner we can get off this ..." her mind searched for some word to describe the hell they were now in, but settled for simple, and said, "planet."

Stanton gave her a wink. A curious thing, and then he took off at a jog toward what she believed was the mess hall. Ruiz followed him.

Meyers, staring at the hatch door a moment longer, thought she saw the wheel lock move. There was no way, with those small legs and taloned claws, those things could be smart enough to unlock the hatch.

It just couldn't be possible. These were reptile-like animals. Nothing more.

Unless—no, no, it couldn't be—unless they were synonymous with the humans of Earth, an intelligent alien race?

CHAPTER FORTY-FOUR

Captain Danielle Rivers, guarding the communications room, stood by the door. She stared out the thick glass but could see only the amber-lit hallway. She heard the sound of a great gunfight and hoped beyond hope that the rest of her team was okay.

She knew protecting the communications room was an important assignment, but it didn't feel right. She wanted to be with the commander and the others, fighting.

She stood on tiptoes and strained seeing down the hallway, and then, when she could, she wished she hadn't.

A horde of the serpent creatures slithered her way. One scaled the walls in a serpentine fashion, slithering faster than the others. Its head snaked up and down, and then it stopped. It was perched on the wall opposite the door to the communications room. Its eyes locked on hers.

Recognition.

She moved away from the door, turned her head away from the scene. She pressed her back to the wall and tried controlling her breathing.

Her brow, covered in beads of sweat, was ignored. The sweat rolled down the bridge of her nose. The salt stung the inner corners of her eyes. "This isn't good. This isn't good. This isn't good."

Rivers contemplated calling for help. The radios were right there in front of her.

She had no idea how the others fared in the gunfight. Were they okay?

Would it be selfish calling them back to help her?

Did she need help? Wasn't she safe inside the locked room? So the thing saw her. That didn't mean it could get inside the room with her. She stayed still and regulated her breathing. Out of sight, out of mind.

However, she was tempted to turn and look out the glass window. Had the things moved on, or were they waiting for her?

She was freaking out. Her chest rose and fell fast. The quick and shallow breaths were going to make her hyperventilate.

This was just a nightmare. It was how she tried to convince herself everything would be okay. They would all survive and get off this crazy planet and be back in the safety of the *Eclipse* in no time at all.

That is, if the creatures didn't kill the commander and the others moments ago.

No. They were okay. They'd made it to the next section of the colony, she was certain.

Her comlink squawked. "Captain Rivers?"

It was the commander. A flood of relief overcame Rivers. Her body shook, and she almost laughed. "Commander? Commander, come in?"

"We are isolated in the north half of the compound, Rivers. Over."

"But you're okay? Over."

"We're all okay," the commander said. "How are you? Over."

Rivers sucked in a deep breath and chanced a look. It was fast. A turn of her head. She saw at least four creatures; three were coiled and hissing just outside of the communication room door. The fourth was crawling over the others, and then she lost sight of it.

Until its head popped up on the other side of the glass.

Rivers screamed.

"Lieutenant?" the commander's voice came over the comlink.

Rivers moved back, and away from the door. She couldn't look away from the thing trying to get in.

The creature's head smashed into the glass. The glass didn't crack or shatter this time. "I'm a—" she said. "It's good. I'm okay."

"We engaged the alien, but they may be headed in your direction." Rivers heard the concern in the commander's transmission.

"They're here, Commander. At least four. They're outside the communications room," Rivers said. She had backed herself up to the table with the radios.

The snake-thing slammed its head against the glass again. Rivers shuddered.

"Are you okay?"

"They're trying to get in; one of them is trying to smash the glass."

The commander did not respond.

"Commander? Are you still there?"

"You have your blaster?"

"Aye, Commander. I do."

There was another long pause in communications. Rivers knew the other three were discussing what to do next. She hoped they agreed to come to her rescue. She didn't want to be alone anymore. Fear ran through her body like blood in her veins. "Commander?"

"We can't come back," Meyers said. "You are going to have to defend the room until we can get to you. We've just a few places left to search, and then ..."

"I understand, Commander. I won't let them in," she said. There was no way she could stop the things if they smashed through the glass. She raised her blaster, as if at any moment the communications room would be breached.

Rivers' finger twitched over the trigger.

The beads of sweat now irritated her eyes. She used a forearm and ran it across her face, swiping away the perspiration as best she could. "Nothing's getting in here, Commander."

She conveyed way more confidence and determination than she felt.

"We'll be back for you, Lieutenant. Soon. Very soon," the commander said.

"Aye, Commander. Over and out."

CHAPTER FORTY-FIVE

On board the Cutlass

"It is kind of claustrophobic in here." Lieutenant Marshall Weber stood with his back to the wall on the bridge of the *Cutlass* but considered it more of a cockpit. Murray Bell sat on the floor beside him. He didn't look too good. His stump, where his leg had been, was bleeding again. The blood wasn't gushing, but the man needed medical help and soon.

The ship's captain, Aroldis D'Rukker, stood like a statue. Large arms folded across his chest. "If you don't like it, we can drop you back on the planet surface. Anywhere you'd like."

Weber arched an eyebrow at Erinne Cohn. "What I mean is, it's cozy in here. Very welcoming."

D'Rukker didn't seem to buy it.

"Look," Weber said. "Bell and I appreciate your help. And we thank you."

D'Rukker bought that. "We're not in the business of saving people."

"No? What business are you in?"

They were on a pirate ship. Weber knew that much.

The captain went back to giving him a stoic expression.

"Is there any chance you can drop us off? There's a colony not far from here—"

D'Rukker said, "We know where it is."

"Wonderful. That's, well, that's just wonderful. So, I'm thinking it won't be much of a problem giving us a lift there?"

Looking at Erinne Cohn, D'Rukker said, "We look like a taxi service to you?"

Erinne shook her head, "No, boss."

"Didn't think so."

Weber held up both hands, a surrendering gesture. "I'm just saying, I—we—we appreciate what you guys did for us. Don't get me wrong, but we've got to get back to our crew. They may be in similar danger."

"Not our problem," D'Rukker said.

"But, the way I see it, it kind of is," Weber said.

D'Rukker shifted his weight. He was indeed a beefy guy. "And how is it you see things, Lieutenant?"

"I mean, unless you plan on keeping Bell and I as prisoners—"

"You're not prisoners. At any point since you have been on my ship have I, or anyone else on the *Cutlass* made you feel like a prisoner?" D'Rukker made his point.

"Well, no. But—"

"You and your friend are free to leave at any time," he said. "There is just one small issue we need to settle. A matter of payment."

"Payment? Like, you think I'm carrying a ton of currency on me? We're on Neptune, sir. I don't have anything valuable to offer."

"You have diamonds, Lieutenant." D'Rukker offered up a half-sided smile. It was clearly him making his intentions known and insisting Weber understood what was now on the table.

"Diamonds." Weber shook his head. "That's what you want? Diamonds?"

"We were going to patiently wait for your party to leave the planet before visiting the colony to see what the distress signal was all about." He shrugged, as if heroism turned him modest.

"You planned to help them, the way you helped my friend and I?"

"You could say that," D'Rukker said.

"That's mighty generous and selfless of you," Weber said.

D'Rukker grunted. "You think this is funny?"

"I don't care one way or the other about diamonds. Take some, take them all. That's not my game. I'm more concerned about getting back to the compound. You want to negotiate some form of settlement for our safe return, I'll even advocate for a large sum on your behalf. How's that?" Weber asked.

"Now I think we are closer to reaching an understanding."

"How wonderful," Weber said. "In the meantime, my friend here is bleeding, and I'd really like to have a look at his leg." Weber pointed down at Bell. Bell was not alert. His eyelids fluttered. "Hey, Bell? Bell?"

Weber dropped to his knees. He placed his hands on Bell's chest and then touched two fingers to the side of Bell's throat. "I've got a pulse. But it's weak. Do you have a sick bay on this ship?"

D'Rukker eyed Cohn.

Weber snapped. "Hey, this man is going to die if I can't give him some help. Please, is there a sick bay on the ship?"

D'Rukker said, "Let's get him down to Higgs."

Weber draped one of Bell's arms over his shoulder. Erinne Cohn knelt on the other side of Bell and took Bell's arm over her shoulder. The metallic hand touched Weber.

He looked over at her. Their eyes met.

"Sorry," she offered up.

He returned a half smile. "Lift on three," he said.

"Follow me," she said, shifting Bell's weight as best she could, sharing the burden between the two of them.

"We're not done discussing things," D'Rukker said, as the two ambled off the bridge.

Weber knew there was more to discuss. D'Rukker might think he's intimidating, and, well, maybe he was a bit imposing, but Weber didn't scare easily. He knew the man had some kind of heart, or the *Cutlass* never would have swooped in to rescue them in the first place. D'Rukker and his crew could have let them perish, and then there would be that much left to deal with when stealing the diamonds.

No. D'Rukker wasn't half as bad a person as he wanted others to believe.

And so, Weber did not reply.

———

Warren "Higgs" Higashioka was the *Cutlass* medic. Asian descent, he had straight black hair and pale skin. He wore thick glasses with black frames. His shirt was half tucked into his pants and one sleeve was rolled up his forearm.

Bell lay on a table in the ship's sick bay. His clothes had been stripped off him.

"He might have an infection," Higgs said.

Weber stood on the opposite side of the table, across from Higgs. Cohn stood at the foot of the table, watching everything with intent.

"I was worried about that," Weber said.

Higgs wore latex gloves. He removed a rectangle bag from a drawer. Working effortlessly, Higgs held the bag upside down, so that a thin, but coiled tube hung from the end. After suspending the bag on a hook over the table, Higgs uncoiled the tubing. On the open end was a silver needle that, after tapping Bell's forearm, Higgs pierced into Bell's skin, inserting the needle into a vein. He used medical tape to secure the needle flat against Bell's skin, and then twisted a knob to start fluids flowing from the bag into Bell's arm. "This antibiotic should work fast and help fight the infection. Won't be long before we see if it is helping," Higgs said. "In the meantime, why don't we clean the leg and re-cauterize the wound? I'm assuming you can help me with the procedure, Lieutenant?"

"Sure, Doc," Weber said. "Thank you."

"Will he be alright?" Erinne asked.

Higgs traced a finger over the infected area, leaning in close for a better look. "I can't say for certain. Could be touch and go, Erinne. Touch and go."

Erinne grabbed a black, thermal blanket and covered Bell, her eyes never looked away from Weber.

CHAPTER FORTY-SIX

Captain Danielle Rivers screamed.

The pit of creatures swarmed the area outside of the communications room. Rivers knew she was on her own. The things kept smashing into the door, into the glass. The glass began cracking, spider-webbing.

They were going to get in. It was just a matter of time. It seemed as if the more they tried to crash through the door, the more enraptured the creatures became. Her scream didn't help. The outburst served only to rile the things all the more.

Rivers cupped a trembling hand over her mouth.

She felt the warm wet tears stop on the edges of her fingers, where those fingers lay across her cheeks. Her eyes darted left and right. There were no other escape exits. Just the one door, she knew as much, but right now she'd settle for an air shaft, or anything she could crawl into and hide.

There were two grates near the ceiling. They were small and rectangular, and far too narrow to fit through.

No. She was trapped.

She was trapped, and soon the glass would shatter, and the creatures would slither into the communications room and devour her.

She remembered the hand they'd found in the mountain of ice in the storage area.

Rivers did not want to die.

Holding her blaster in the ready, she did the one thing she could do and waited.

The wait was short.

One of the creatures slammed its head against the glass and the glass gave. Beads of glass rained onto the floor. Outside the door, the creature hissed as if exclaiming victory. Its head tipped back and its mouth opened wide. The growl was long and loud. The sound sent shivers running up and down Rivers' spine and along her arms.

There was no holding back now. Rivers knew the time to defend the room had arrived. Without delay, she squeezed the trigger. The blaster barked in response. Red laser bolts flew from the mouth of the barrel. She hit the door below and above the missing window.

Her hands shook, and the quivers impacted her aim.

She knew she was crying, sobbing, but needed somehow to remain calm. It was difficult, far more easily said than done when the first of the creatures snaked its head and then its body through the opening.

Without a moment to spare, Rivers opened fire again. She fired round after round.

She wasn't just crying, but screaming, now.

Anger filled her body.

It was what she needed most. The anger caused a flood of adrenaline to course through her body. Her training kicked in, her conditioning. Fear ebbed away and was replaced by the calm she'd been searching for.

Resolved, Rivers closed an eye, let her green laser touch the head of the creature as it fit the last of its body through the opening, and fired three quick bolts. The blasts struck the creature in the snout. It roared.

The second bolt melted the creature's left eye.

And the third took the creature in the throat. A gooey, opal fluid sprayed from the gaping wound. It was down, dead, or dying, but didn't appear to be a viable threat any longer.

Her mild triumph was short-lived. A second creature filled the gap in the door and was squeezing its way into the communications room. Rivers, determined to defend the area, now hopeful and more confident, worked at repeating her strategy—a simple, and basic plan—to kill these creepy things before they killed her!

She fired bolt after bolt.

The second creature, much shorter than the first, crawled through the window and dropped into the room much quicker than the first. The thing found cover behind the corpse of the first creature, as a third began to crawl through the spot where the glass once served as an ideal barrier between Rivers and the creatures.

Charged with two targets, Rivers knew the one in the room with her was more of a danger. After all, it was the one inside the communications room.

The bolts didn't do much damage. She couldn't get a clear shot at its head or neck. The thing kept its mouth closed, as if it understood the inside of the mouth was vulnerable to bolts while the plated scales encasing its body was not.

It was also as if the thing had learned from watching the demise of the other snake-crocs and now knew the importance of protecting the chinks in the armor. Guard the weaknesses. So it kept its head down, kept its mouth closed and protecting the throat.

It slithered toward her, as the third thing fit the rest of its body into the room.

She was locked in the communications room with two of those things, while yet another fit its head into the space on the door.

Rivers backed toward a corner.

The shorter creature of the two was the faster. It moved past the corpse and the larger thing and scurried under the communications table. Then it rose up, lifting and overturning the table.

Communications equipment crashed onto the floor. Sparks flew and sizzled as a small fire started. The flames rose in a whoosh, activating the overhead sprinkler system. White foam sprayed down from the heads.

The creatures cried out, perhaps confused by what was happening, but not impaired by the foam.

The smallest of the three now inside the room lifted its head, tiny arms with sharp talons scraped at air menacingly. The threat was well conveyed. It meant to shred her first.

In doing so, it left open a soft spot. Rivers set the green laser against the thing's throat and fired a bolt. The creature twisted to the left, lowered its head, unscathed, but enraged. The scales along its length quivered, rattled together. The sound was like nothing Rivers had ever heard before.

She wanted to plug her hands over her ears. She was losing it, she knew, her mind unraveling. With her own death right in front of her, she wasn't sure how much longer she could hold on. Surrendering almost seemed easier.

The other two serpent-things must have smelled her fear, her submission. They advanced on her. Slow and cautious, but advanced nonetheless.

There were only a few feet between them. She was on her backside, propped up on elbows. She had dropped her blaster when the table overturned. She unsheathed her bowie knife and held it in both hands while her eyes searched for the blaster.

Over an accumulated inch of foam from the sprinklers covered the ground. The blaster was as good as gone. Buried.

The smallest of the three creatures struck. Unblinking, the thing seemed to watch her as, at the last moment, its jaws stretched wide. Rivers saw the black eyes of the thing roll back, revealing only the whites, before the fangs sank into her thigh.

The creature shook its head, a violent tussle. Flesh ripped from the bone. Rivers, the knife forgotten, threw her head back and howled in pain. Her screams sent the vipers into a frenzy.

The other two attacked, taking bites out of her legs.

Rivers saw a fourth, or fifth, or sixth creature crawling into the room through the spot where a window once protected her from any attack.

She was losing blood.

The pain stopped. The lower half of her body went numb.

Or was gone.

She stopped crying out for help; for them to stop ripping her apart, and while she died, she silently watched the creatures feast on her body.

The smaller of the creatures slithered up alongside her shoulder.

Was it smiling down at her?

Before her mind could formulate an answer, the creature snapped its jaws over her face. Rivers felt the teeth puncture the top of her skull and through her jaw before complete darkness surrounded her, before death, a welcomed next step, took her.

PART III

THE RESCUE

CHAPTER FORTY-SEVEN

"Commander! Over here," Ruiz shouted. She was just down the hallway. Standing with her blaster aimed toward the ground, Ruiz pointed at something in front of her.

Stanton and Meyers rushed over.

"The mess hall," Meyers said.

There was a section of wall that was eight by four of thick, reinforced glass. In what looked like blood someone had written a message from the inside.

Help! We're In Here.

"Is that blood?" Stanton asked.

"Catsup," Meyers said.

"Think there are survivors inside?" Ruiz asked.

"Be the best place to hole up and wait for a rescue. Got restrooms. Food. Some space to move around to prevent cabin fever," Meyers said, pointing at the inside of the cafeteria. "This is definitely an ideal place to hide!"

"Let's check it out," Stanton said, lifting his blaster.

Meyers approached the door. She punched in the code. The door slid open. Stanton entered first. He swept his blaster right and left. His finger over the trigger.

There were several long tables with chairs. The floors and walls were white. The amber lights were off. Someone had disassembled them. The casings and bulbs were stacked on one table. It took a moment for Stanton's eyes to adjust to normal lighting.

The commander closed and secured the door behind them.

The swinging doors leading, presumably, into the kitchen swung open, and a woman wielding a chef's knife came running out.

Ruiz and Stanton trained a green laser on the woman. Center mass.

Meyers held up her hands. "It's okay! We're here to help you!"

The woman gave pause. She never lowered the knife. "Who are you?"

"We're from *Euphoric*. They sent us to investigate the distress signal," Meyers explained.

"That was almost a year ago," the woman said, shaking her head. Her hair was in knots. She was thin, pale. Her arm came down, slowly, little by little until the knife was at her side, the blade running the length of her thigh. "You're here to rescue me, to get me off this planet?"

"That's right," Meyers said. She spoke softly, gentle. Her calm tone of voice diffused the tension. "We are going to get you out of here. Where are the others?"

The woman dropped the knife. It clanked and clattered on the floor. "I don't know. I don—there's me. I think there's just me."

Stanton hid his shock. There were thirty-five people stationed on the colony. Had been. Now there was one. "Those things, those snakes, is that what happened?"

The woman's knees wobbled.

Ruiz ran forward, her blaster dangled from the shoulder strap, and caught the woman before she fainted. "Commander?"

"She's in shock. Put her on the floor. Gently," Meyers said.

"Can there really only be one person left?" Stanton asked.

Meyers looked around the room, studied the long window behind them. "We've seen those things fight. They're fast, strong, and relentless. Over the course of six months, doesn't it seem more likely that no one would have survived?"

"Who is she?" Ruiz asked.

"Could be one of the miners or a scientist. I don't know. It doesn't really matter." Meyers shook her head. "Commander Meyers to Captain Rivers, come in?"

Rivers had been on Stanton's mind, as well. He did not like the idea of leaving her behind. The need to protect the communications room made sense. He did not argue the commander's call. But then her last transmission … She should remain safe as long as she stayed locked inside with the radios. "She's not answering."

"Give her a minute," Ruiz said.

Meyers tried again. "This is Commander Meyers. Come in, Captain Rivers?" When there was still no response, Meyers said, "Stanton, check in back, see if there is anything we can use to cover her. Anything."

"Aye, Commander," he said and took off. He wasn't worried about finding a creature on the other side of the swinging doors. That was where the woman had come from. However, he was not about to let his guard down. He entered through the doors using extreme caution. He checked every corner carefully, looking on the sides of the stoves and around the large refrigerators. There was a pantry, as well. He pulled open the doors and jumped back.

Inside, wrapped in a blood-soaked tablecloth, was a body. Male or female, he didn't know. Nor was he about to check. The person was dead, beyond help. He closed the doors and backed away.

He slung his blaster over his back and checked the drawers. Utensils. Seasonings. More utensils. Table cloths.

Stanton grabbed two and ran back into the dining area. "There's a body back there," he said.

The woman was sitting up. She looked dazed, lethargic, but at least her eyes were open. She had a hand pressed against her forehead, as if it might help regain balance. "That's Friedrichs. Calvin Friedrichs. He was my assistant."

Ruiz asked, "What happened to him?"

"When everything started, it was Hewer. Ralph Johnson. We called him Hewer," the woman said.

"That's the name of a person who breaks up rocks. A mining term?" Stanton said.

The woman smiled. It was brief. Her lips barely moved, but Stanton saw it. "You're right," she said.

"I'm sorry. I didn't mean to interrupt."

"It's okay," she said. Now, as she started talking again, she only looked Stanton in the eyes, as if he were the only person in the room with her. "The audible alarm was activated. Calvin and I were in the lab at the time. The siren was loud, it was so loud. We knew a vacuuming operation just went out. They went out once, sometimes twice a day. They didn't stay out long. The days are so short here. We didn't want the men out when it got dark. The weather is more unpredictable than we initially anticipated. The limited land on the surface was even more unstable. There were geysers that erupted without warning. The chemical makeup of the ocean and the sharp edges of the diamonds, it was dangerous. Every vacuuming operation, I worried about the safety of the colonists," the woman said. "I went down to the storage facility; if something was wrong, I thought I might be able to help."

"What happened?" Stanton said. "How did they get inside the compound?"

The woman took his hand in both of hers. She was shaking, cold. "There were these ... things. These monsters, they were inside the storage area. The men ... I saw the monsters chasing them down. The things moved so fast. They had swarmed the vacuum machine, attacked it while it was out mining minerals. And when the driver made a hasty retreat back to the colony, they got inside. They rushed through the opened bay doors before Hewer could close them again. There were so many of them. It was like they must have been watching the operation and determined the best time to strike. They came through the opened doors and ..."

"Hewer, he'd locked himself in the control room. He sealed off the storage area as best he could. I couldn't get inside. I wanted to help them, and I couldn't get inside. But, I didn't really want to go in there, I didn't want those things getting me. I wanted to help them, but what could I have done? What could I have done to help them?"

"It's okay, you tried," Stanton said. "If Hewer opened the doors, if he'd have let you, then you would be dead right now."

"I ran back to my lab," she said. Eye contact broken. She released his hand. Now she frantically brushed fingers through her knotted hair. "Calvin was panicking. He wanted to know what was going on. I tried to tell him. I was crying and hysterical. I think I was even hyperventilating. He had me sit down. I remember that. He had me sit down and poured me a glass of water. And I told him we needed to find somewhere safe to hide. We were yelling, trying to talk and be heard over the screaming alarm. Somehow, I don't know how, but somehow I managed to tell him what I'd found, what I'd seen. I don't think he believed me, or maybe because of how overwrought I was, he believed me, but couldn't believe something he hadn't seen with his own eyes. I convinced him the mess hall would be the best place to hide, the safest. I explained we'd have everything we'd need to last a few days until help came."

The woman rolled her eyes. She chuckled. Her hands fisted her hair. She tugged at the ends as if trying to pull the roots out from her head. "After a week, we started rationing food. I realized, we realized, no one was coming. No one was going to come."

"We're here now," Stanton said. "We came."

She began sobbing. "What took you so long?"

Commander Meyers said, "But what happened to Calvin?"

"He tried going to the communications room. He wanted to attempt contacting *Euphoric*. He said that was our best chance. Maybe our only chance. I didn't want him to go. I begged him to stay with me. He said he wouldn't be long. He'd be right back." Her eyes glossed over. She had a vacant stare about her. Her tongue licked dry lips. "And he wasn't. He wasn't gone long at all. Before I knew it, he was at the door, pounding on it. I let him in. He was crazed, yelling for me to seal it. To shut the door and seal it closed. He was covered in blood. He was missing an arm, and I—I tried to help him, but he'd lost so much blood. I tried to save him."

"What is your name?" Stanton asked.

"Carter. Sandra Carter. I am the astrophysicist *Euphoric* hired for this mission."

Commander Meyers asked, "So you are the only one still in the compound?"

"There's no one here. There is no one left," she said, her eyes moved from one person to the next. "There is no one left. I'm the only one still alive."

CHAPTER FORTY-EIGHT

Erinne Cohn wasn't comfortable with the *Euphoric* lieutenant standing behind her while she sat at the *Cutlass* controls. "Either sit co-pilot with me, or get lost," she said.

"Sorry," Weber said and sat down in the co-pilot chair beside Erinne. "I just—this is a nice ship."

She snorted. "It's alright. Aroldis works on it night and day. Always making modifications. He's installed some cool stuff. She flies sweet. I think that's more because of the pilot, not the mechanics. I'm biased though, since I'm the pilot."

Weber laughed.

Erinne smiled. "I'm sure she's nothing like your ship."

"The *Eclipse*? That's pretty state-of-the-art. That's for sure. But my dad, when I was younger, like a little kid? He used to tell me about how he and his father re-built a ship together. They lived on Earth. It was a shell of a fighter they picked up together from some metal scrap yard, a cemetery for fighters and shuttles and stuff. They loaded the thing on a rented flatbed and brought it out to my grandfather's barn. He lived on like fifty acres, and even though he had the money to buy a new ship without breaking the bank, he bought a piece of junk," Weber said.

"So he and his son could work on it together?"

"Exactly," Weber said. "They spent three years finding parts and putting her together, and then one day, when it was all done, the two of them took it for a ride. They cruised around between the troposphere and stratosphere, you know space license requirements and all of that, but my father would tell me it was the best ship he'd ever been on. None flew better, ever."

"Did you and your dad ever build a ship together?"

Weber pursed his lips. "We talked about it, but he died. The virus got him. He was one of the few people on Nova who became infected with the Earth disease. They had him quarantined on a medical wing. They wouldn't even let me visit him. He spent his last months alive alone. We video chatted every day, but that wasn't the same. Not to a ten-year-old kid, you know?"

Erinne had no idea why this stranger was opening up. She thought it odd someone would be so forthcoming with someone they'd just met. Always keeping her own emotions guarded, even around D'Rukker, she wasn't sure how she felt about the lieutenant's unsolicited sharing. "That's too bad," she said.

"It wasn't easy. I always told myself, though, if I ever had a kid I'd do the same —find the shell of a machine and rebuild it with my child in my grandfather's barn."

"Your grandfather's still alive?"

Weber shook his head. "No, no he's not, but the farm is mine. He left it to my father, and my father left it to me."

"You have land on Earth?"

"I do. I sometimes think about leaving *Euphoric*, leaving the Nebula Way Station, and going home. There are times where a simpler life just seems more appealing, you know?" he said.

She knew. "But I like to fly."

"I'd like to re-build a fighter in my grandfather's barn," Weber said. "Maybe someday, if I meet the right one. Get married. Settle down. You know, have little guys running around. I think then I would want to build up a ship in that barn, but ..."

"But?"

Weber waved a hand around. "I'm here. Middle of space. I chose a different life."

"You didn't choose to stay on the farm?"

"I enlisted. Military. Soon as I turned eighteen. I needed something ... different."

"And what? Now those other dreams can't happen?"

"*Euphoric* has kind of a set policy on who can fly long-term space missions. Anyone with an immediate family is discouraged from even applying. Maybe I like flying too much, too. I don't know." And then after a moment of nothing, he added: "What happened there ...?" He tapped a finger on his left arm and nodded his head toward hers.

Erinne ignored him. She wasn't playing this game, his game. You talk, I talk. It wasn't going to work on her. Who did he think he was? This guy couldn't just plop down next to her and ask all kinds of personal questions just because he'd told her some sentimental garbage about his father and grandfather working on an engine.

"Another time, perhaps," he said. "There!"

Erinne almost jumped out of her seat.

Weber was up and pointing out the front porthole. "The colony."

"I knew where the colony was," she said, flying over the compound. On the second pass, she came in low, and slow. "Place looks deserted."

"We have to get in there."

"And the diamonds?"

Weber spun around.

Erinne didn't need to turn. She'd heard Aroldis come on the bridge. "Should we land by the bay?"

"Close as you can get," D'Rukker said. "I want minimal exposure. I have no idea how many of those creatures are close by. Last thing is an attack as we break for the bay hatch."

"Understood. I could put us down so close our ramp will be like a red carpet to their front door," she said.

"And that is why you fly my ship!"

"Bringing her around," Erinne said, her hands doing different things on separate control panels. Toggles flipped, buttons depressed, levers pulled. "Lowering flaps. Reducing speeds."

"Watch out!" Weber gripped the dash.

D'Rukker called out Erinne's name.

Erinne Cohn saw it. A geyser erupted in front of them. A thick spray shot into the air, clipping the right wing on the *Cutlass*. "Hold on," Erinne shouted.

It was too late. They were flying too slowly, too close to the surface.

The *Cutlass* toppled, spiraling out of control.

D'Rukker stumbled and fell, crashing onto the floor. The *Cutlass* hit the ground, and the power inside the ship flickered and shut off.

"Erinne?" Weber said, spitting blood from his mouth, and then wiping his lips with the back of his sleeve. "Erinne?"

CHAPTER FORTY-NINE

"Okay, we're going to get out of here." Commander Anara Meyers knelt beside the scientist. She held the woman's hand. Sandra Carter kept nodding her head. Meyers couldn't tell if Sandra understood, or if the woman was still in shock. It didn't matter now. All that mattered was getting off the planet. All of them.

"We can't leave him though," Sandra said.

"Can't leave who?" Meyers asked. "You said there was no one else on the compound."

"Calvin," Sandra said, looking over her shoulder, eyes on the doors leading into the kitchen. "I can't leave him."

"He's gone, Sandra," Meyers said. "There's nothing we can do for him."

"Commander?" Ruiz said.

"Yeah?"

"I've been trying to hail Lieutenant Weber. He's not responding," she said.

First Captain Rivers wasn't responding, now Lieutenant Weber. Her mind attempted to force away obvious thoughts. She couldn't afford to dwell on what might have happened to them both. The mission had become worse than any nightmare she'd ever had. When she worried about failing her first time out on the *Eclipse*, this was never what she imagined. Telling herself that none of this was her fault didn't help, not in the slightest. "We're inside the compound. Transmissions are bound to be skewed."

It was a lie. She had no idea what the reception was like. Her job as commander was keeping everyone calm, cool, and level-headed. She couldn't do that if she gave in to her own fears and fantasies.

"Sandra, can you stand up?"

"What about Calvin?"

Meyers got nose to nose with the scientist. "We've gone over this, Sandra. Calvin is gone. We can't do anything for him. Right now, we need to leave this area. We need to get back to the compound bay. There's a shuttle in there. It is our only way off of Neptune. Do you understand me?"

Sandra Carter was violently shaking. "We are going to get off of the planet?"

"That's right. I have a ship waiting for us in orbit. We're leaving."

"We're leaving."

Meyers still couldn't tell if Sandra understood anything being said. The woman was simply repeating everything. It was close enough, she supposed. "Stanton, help her to her feet. Stick close to her, understood?"

"Aye, Commander."

Meyers didn't want to return the way they'd come, but the hatch door they'd sealed off was the quickest way back to the communications room. She only hoped the creatures had grown bored waiting and moved on.

As long as Rivers was holding down the fort, they'd be able to send Mark Windsor word they'd soon be on their way and to keep an eye out for the returning shuttle. Meyers insisted on remaining optimistic. Rivers might not have answered their call for a multitude of reasons. "Ruiz, I want you on point. I am going to follow these two."

"Aye, Commander." Ruiz swung her blaster around. She held the barrel in her left hand, her right around the grip, finger by the trigger. "Ready when you are, Commander."

Stanton had Sandra on her feet. "Captain?"

"We're good, Commander. We're ready."

"Let's do this, then. Let's get back to the bay." The commander readied her own blaster. She noticed the gauge. Her blaster was nearly out of energy. She needed a recharge pack. There wasn't one. Without asking, she knew Ruiz and Stanton's weapons would be in a similar situation. They were almost out of ammunition, and there was a lot of ground to cover.

Optimistic.

"Ruiz, lead the way."

———

They would need space suits. Soon.

Lieutenant Marshall Weber had no idea how long life support on the *Cutlass* would last. It looked as if everything had shut down. They'd crashed hard. There could be a breach in the hull.

Weber didn't even want to think about that.

A breach would mean he had even less time than he thought. And right now, he thought he might only have an hour or less before the breathable air was used up.

He touched Erinne's arm.

She was breathing, but hadn't moved. Her forehead was bleeding, but he couldn't see more than a small gash. The head bled a lot. That was normal and not necessarily dangerous. It would depend how hard she hit and whether she suffered a concussion or not. The fact she still was out cold, however, was not a good sign.

"Erinne? Hey," he said, giving her shoulder a gentle nudge.

She stirred. Eyes opened. Closed. Eyelids fluttered.

"That's good. You're good," he said. "Erinne?"

"We crashed."

"That's right. We crashed. Here, sit up," he said, helping her back into her seat. He squatted down in front of her. "I want you to follow my finger with your eyes only. Okay? Don't move your head."

"Good. I won't. It feels like my head was just smashed with a boulder."

Weber removed a penlight from his belt. He flashed it toward, but not directly into Erinne's eyes. Her pupils weren't dilated and looked about the same size. They responded appropriately to light.

"What are you looking for?" she asked.

"Well. Thirty areas of the brain and most of the cranial nerves deal with your vision," Weber explained, moving his finger past Erinne's field of vision. Her eyes followed the finger. Her head stayed still. "You want the good news or the bad news?"

"I don't know—"

"The good news your head should be okay. The bad news, this ship ain't going anywhere anytime soon," he said. "Sit still. I want to check on your captain."

"D'Rukker's not my captain. We don't operate that way. He's my boss," she said.

"Well, let me check on your boss." Weber's sleeve had a rip in it. He made it larger and then tore a piece off, handing it over to Erinne. "Press this on your forehead. Apply pressure. Don't keep lifting it off to see if you are still bleeding. Got it?"

She nodded and touched the cloth to her wound.

Weber reached up and pressed her hand hard against her own forehead. "Tight. Apply pressure."

"Okay, okay, I got it."

Weber scrambled toward D'Rukker. Same issue. Bump on his head. No blood. He must have knocked himself out. Head hit the wall.

He used a finger and thumb to peel open one of D'Rukker's eyes, shining a light next to the eyeball.

The man's eyes opened wide. His arms shot up. His large hands latched onto Weber's wrist.

"Whoa, man! Good reflexes." Weber winced. "It's okay! You're okay."

There was a fraction of a second where Weber strongly suspected he was about to get punched, but then D'Rukker's brow creased and softened. Confusion overcome by memories? "Erinne?"

When D'Rukker released Weber's wrists, Weber shook them to start circulation flowing again. "She's fine."

"I'm right here, Aroldis."

D'Rukker moved Weber out of the way, sat up, and then stood up.

Weber reached out with the intent of steadying the man, should his legs give, and he started toppling.

No such thing happened.

"Systems shut down," Weber said. "I have no idea if there is a hull breach. We're going to want to get into some spacesuits as soon as possible."

"I have to check on the rest of my crew." D'Rukker touched the top of Erinne's head, moving her hair aside.

Erinne lifted the torn cloth off the wound to show her boss.

"Hey," Weber said. "Constant pressure."

She slapped the cloth back in place. "Owww. Sorry."

D'Rukker said, "You stay here. Run diagnostics. I need you to figure out what we're working with, what's broke, and what we can and cannot fix. Weber and I are going to check on the crew. We'll be back with spacesuits if spacesuits are needed. I don't want you to move. Are we clear?"

"Crystal, Aroldis."

CHAPTER FIFTY

Captain Adam Stanton kept an eye on Ruiz's back. He felt vulnerable helping Sandra Carter since his blaster was out of reach, slung across his back. It was almost as if he was naked or exposed, and he didn't like it one bit.

They had made it down the main passage without incident. At the hatch door they'd sealed, the four of them stopped.

Stanton stared at the door. "They could be waiting on the other side for us," he said, stating the obvious.

Commander Meyers moved front and center. She let her blaster hang off the shoulder strap and grabbed onto the wheel lock. "If we go the other route, we might as well be miles away from Rivers. We'd have to circle around the entire compound before reaching the communications room again. That could take hours. There might be more of those things on the other side. We just don't know."

But we know there were almost half a dozen on the opposite side of this hatch, Stanton thought. *That much we do know.* "I want you to stand over here, Sandra. You understand me? You stand right here."

With Sandra Carter out of the way, Stanton retrieved his blaster. It felt wonderful in his hands, as natural as if it were an extended part of his body. A fifth limb. "Commander, I'm low on a charge. I've got my sidearm, but that blaster doesn't have half the power these rifles do. And these rifles blasters barely break skin on those things."

Ruiz twisted her blaster over in her hands and checked the gauge on her weapon. "Worse. Mine's dead." Ruiz tossed aside the blaster and unholstered her sidearm. "This will have to get 'er done."

The commander just nodded. "Glad you double checked, Ruiz. Look, we're just going to have to be conservative with our shots. Quality and not quantity this go-around," she instructed.

Stanton took three quick breaths as the commander began spinning the wheel lock counterclockwise. He felt as if he were getting ready to go underwater and knew the water was icy cold, that it would shock his system once submerged. He gritted his teeth. "Ready, Commander!"

The latch clicked. The door was unlocked.

The commander looked back at them. Stanton saw the anxiety on her expression. Her eyes were opened a little wider, her brows a bit arched, and her lips pulled thin as muscles in her mouth and neck stretched taut. She gave a silent count, numbered by slight bobs of her head. She pulled open the hatch door and jumped back as her hands re-secured her weapon.

The three of them stood side-by-side, prepared to open fire, and …

"They're gone," Ruiz said.

The commander stepped forward. She checked beyond the threshold, left, and then right. "Clear," she said.

Stanton decided to leave his rifle blaster slung over his shoulder, conserving what energy the weapon had left, and drew his sidearm. It felt comfortable in his hands, but, like they'd said, the bolts were less powerful. He'd have to make do. "Come on." Stanton guided the scientist, his left hand on the small of her back. "We are going to keep close with the others. No falling behind. You got that?"

Sandra nodded.

"Say it. I want to hear you say it."

"No falling behind."

"No falling behind," Stanton said, affirming the statement. "We've got this. Okay? We're getting out of here. We're going home. Okay?"

She nodded.

"Say it."

"We're getting out of here. We're going home," she said, a bit more conviction in her tone of voice. Might even have been a hint of confidence to boot.

Stanton gave her a smile. "That's right."

Ahead, the commander and Ruiz slowed. They were at a bend. If his memory served correctly, just beyond the bend was the communications room. And Danielle Rivers. She would be thrilled to see them.

Meyers held up a fist. Ruiz and Stanton halted.

Meyers checked around the corner. It was fast. Then she lowered herself onto a knee and checked a second time. Slower and more carefully. Standing up and facing the others, she said, "There are two down the hall. Just outside the communications room. I don't know. They weren't moving at all. I couldn't tell if they were alive, dead, or sleeping."

Stanton took the news as good. "That means Rivers is safe behind a locked door. We need to get those things away from there. Or kill them. I'm okay with either. As long as we do something and get rid of them."

"Settle down, Captain," Meyers said. "We're on the same page. We've got an advantage right now. I don't want to lose it. If those things are asleep, maybe we can get off kill shots without a fight."

"How do you propose we do that?" Ruiz wrinkled her nose and shifted her weight from one foot to the other. "Are we going to sneak up on them? Put a bolt in the back of their heads?"

Meyers said, "That's exactly what we're going to do."

Stanton raised a hand. He figured the commander would volunteer. She'd been taking point the entire time. "I'll do it."

"I've got your back," Ruiz said, two hands on the grip of her sidearm.

"You wait here with the commander." Stanton had a hand on her shoulder. Contact made her seem more responsive.

The commander nodded, and Stanton moved forward. He took it slow. Small steps, edging his way down the hallway. He kept an eye on the immobile targets. If one of them so much as yawned, he was prepared to open fire.

He felt cold beads of sweat roll down his back and pool behind his knees. He had his right arm extended. The sidearm in his grip, his left hand under his right hand for balance and sustained support.

The green laser was locked on the back of the head of the closest creature. The closer he was to it, the more deadly the shot. He wanted to press the shirt barrel into its flesh and then pull the trigger. Even armored plates, like the ones that seemed to scale the creature's body, would be hard-pressed resisting such an up and close bolt.

The second creature was smaller than the first. Although both lay coiled, it was easy enough to see there was a considerably shorter difference in girth and length. Taking out the bigger of the two made the most sense.

Stanton re-gripped the butt of his sidearm. He felt the sweat on his palms. Although he'd spent eight years serving, he never saw war. There were some tense confrontations, but the situations were all diffused before firefights broke out. Mostly he'd been deployed to hostile areas as a prop; a presence. The military oftentimes used its people as a show of force, which more than not worked as a powerful deterrent.

The smaller creature stirred.

It lifted its head and looked around.

Stanton stopped, standing statue-still. His lifted his finger off the button that activated the laser, and he held his breath. Inside his mind, he counted off the seconds. One. Two. Three. The thing lowered its head. Stanton stayed put, continued holding his breath.

After a full minute, and his lungs feeling as if they'd caught on fire, Stanton sucked in air. Shallow, slow breaths. The reality before him was clear. There was a good chance, a very good chance, this was it for him.

Even if he were to kill the first, large creature, the thing's thrashing death would alert the smaller, equally dangerous creature. With just a sidearm, he knew he didn't stand much of a chance. The people behind him, his commander, the lieutenant, and the doctor stood a better chance of surviving this ordeal if he at least killed one, and, if luck decided in his favor, he at least wounded the second before his death.

That was the plan. Kill one. Injure the other.

Die.

Okay, it wasn't the best plan. Stanton did not have a death wish. If there was a way out of this, if he saw one, he would take it. Naturally. He was just being practical. Preparing his mind for what might come of this mess.

And then there was Captain Rivers.

He didn't want to let her down. She was trapped inside the communications room. Getting her out safely was just as important. More so.

He wasn't sure when he'd started walking forward again, but he was.

He now stood over the snake-thing's body.

Its head, at the center of the coil, was just feet away.

Stanton leveled his sidearm, sucked in a deep breath, and opened fire.

Both creatures responded immediately. They uncoiled, rising; towered over him. He continued firing his weapon. The bolts sizzled, cutting through the air, the short distance working in his favor. The bolts left black scars on plated scales.

The larger creature shrieked.

Stanton fired a bolt into its gaping mouth. The head imploded.

The neck and cylindrical body gyrated. It spit blood everywhere. Stanton, thrilled at the results, turned his weapon on the smaller of the two creatures. The thing moved fast. It slithered around, claws with sharp nails gripping the other creature as it scurried over the dying beast.

Firing bolt after bolt, the creature dodged the spray.

Stanton's eyes darted toward the door to the communications room. He saw the smashed glass and his heart sank. Was Rivers okay?

"Rivers?" Stanton shouted her name over and over as he backed away from the lunging creature.

Ruiz sprinted down the hallway, slid on her knees, her sidearm raised, firing bolts at the creature.

The thing, perhaps injured, possibly realizing it was outnumbered, let out a shrill cry, and then retreated. With its head low to the floor, it sped away. It was headed toward the storage facility. That was not good. That would be where they'd need to head next.

One problem at a time.

Panting, Stanton bent forward and put trembling hands on unsteady knees.

"Are you okay?" Ruiz asked.

"Rivers," was his only reply.

CHAPTER FIFTY-ONE

Commander Anara Meyers guided Sandra Carter into the communications room.

"Stand there," Ruiz warned. She and Adam Stanton knelt beside what was left of Captain Danielle Rivers.

Carter cried out. Shaking, her hands went to her face.

"Sandra. Sandy, you need to get a hold of yourself," Meyers said. She tried turning the scientist away from the carnage. Carter struggled, as if she couldn't look the other way.

Rivers had been shredded. The creatures had torn her apart. Stanton had the captain's head in his lap.

"She fought to protect this room," he said. "She stayed behind and died defending this stupid room!"

Ruiz touched his shoulder, and he shook the hand off.

"We need to keep moving," Meyers said. "We know there are more of those things. That one that got away could just be rounding up reinforcements."

Stanton stared at her, and it was unnerving. She saw blame in his eyes. Stanton thought Rivers' death was her fault. Maybe it was. "Captain," Meyers said.

"Aye, Commander," he said.

She watched as Stanton gently laid Rivers' head on the floor. He bowed his head, was maybe saying a short prayer for the woman, before he stood up.

Ruiz tried a second time, touching the captain. This time, he allowed it. He looked defeated, deflated.

It was how she felt.

Ruiz scooped up Rivers' blaster, checked the charge, and then threw the weapon back onto the floor. "We're not getting out of here, are we, Commander?"

"Yes, we are," Meyers said. She heard the lack of conviction in her own tone of voice. "You're all going to follow me. We're going to stay close, and we're going to move fast. We need to get through the storage area and back to where we came in for our helmets. In the bay is a shuttle. We'll touch base with Lieutenant Weber, and then we're gone.

We'll launch and head for the *Eclipse*. We're going to do this. We're getting off of Neptune."

She knew she'd made the plan sound short and simple. The thing was the plan was short and simple. They needed to get through the storage area and to the bay. Point A. Point B. Shortest distance. The problem was execution. They had driven those creatures back, which seemed like a victory. Except now, the creatures might all be holed up in one section just waiting for their return. One or two of those things could kill the four of them easily. A nest of those vipers would ...

———

Erinne Cohn did not mind everyone cramming into the *Cutlass* bridge. Aroldis D'Rukker and Weber returned with Higgs, and a weak, but awake and alert Murray Bell. Brett Serverino looked a bit battered, beaten up, but otherwise okay. Serverino was the ship's engineer and mechanic. Between him and D'Rukker, they could repair, modify, or create anything that needed doing.

"Erinne," Serverino said.

"You okay, Brett?"

"Glorious. You?"

Erinne smiled. "Sure. Glorious," she said.

"What did you find?" D'Rukker asked.

"That geyser slammed right into the undercarriage. Clipped the wing. That mineral-rich water sprayed the engines. Doused 'em good, I'm thinking," Erinne said. "The excessive heat from the engines hardened the frozen water almost instantly. I could have flown, recovering from getting hit by the blast, but that's what brought us down. The diamonds blocked gears, ruining anything and everything it came in contact with."

Serverino nodded. "She's right. I put out fires in the engine room. The damage is, around here, *unpreparable*."

Erinne watched D'Rukker for a reaction. There wasn't one.

"We need to get inside the colony," D'Rukker said. "They'll have what we need to fix the ship."

"What we need is a new engine," Serverino said.

"They'll have everything we need," D'Rukker said.

And there was the reaction Erinne expected. Denial. He wasn't going to leave his ship stranded on this desolate planet. He would die out here trying to fix it, instead. Stubborn. The man was inconsolably stubborn. There was no point arguing with him. She doubt she'd be able to change his mind. Erinne would never allow it, though. Either they'd all get off of Neptune, or they'd all stay.

She'd stay.

No one could ever convince her to leave D'Rukker alone. The man wasn't just her savior, and it came down to more than loyalty. Aroldis was like a father. D'Rukker would never leave her alone anywhere. She knew he would stand by her side always. He would never have to ask, but should know, that she would always stand by his.

"We're going to suit up," D'Rukker said.

Erinne beamed. "I managed to bring us down close to the colony, still. Maybe not red-carpet distance. But we're not that far."

"That's why I let you fly, my baby," D'Rukker said.

"Guys, I don't want to speak out of turn," Weber said.

"And yet you are." D'Rukker shook his head. "What is it?"

"Remember, not that long ago? It was like, oh, I don't know, an hour back? When my friend and I were surrounded by giant snakes with crocodile heads and these creepy claws?"

D'Rukker laughed.

Weber cocked his head to the side and planted fists on his waist. "Am I missing the joke?"

"You had a *Euphoric* blaster and a knife," D'Rukker said. "That, my friend, that's what is so funny."

CHAPTER FIFTY-TWO

Sandra Carter, the astrophysicist, stayed sandwiched between the crew of the *Eclipse* as the team made their way through the compound. Although the spinning amber lights showed shadows racing across walls, they moved slow but steady. Each step brought them closer to salvation: the colony's one shuttle.

Ruiz and Stanton had sidearms drawn and ready, while Commander Anara Meyers still had enough charge left in her blaster rifle to inflict some serious damage should a creature cross their path.

They reached the doors to the storage area without incident. The fact the door leading into the storage area stood open was immediate cause for concern.

"We didn't leave it that way, did we?" Stanton said.

"We did not," Ruiz said.

"What? Those things, they opened doors? They got the door open?" Carter looked like she might start crying. Her hands shook and she held them up near her face, as if at any minute she'd start chewing away at fingernails.

"We don't know what they can do," Meyers admitted. She eyed Captain Stanton, a knowing look passing between them.

Just because the creatures were alien didn't mean they weren't intelligent. They might look prehistoric, but that didn't prove anything. In fact, the way the creatures behaved was anything but primitive. The commander suspected they communicated and worked together planning attacks.

The shrieking came from behind them. All four turned and stared down the shaft of the hallway. The first things visible were the racing shadows cast onto the walls from the spinning amber lights. Meyers counted at least three raised heads.

"They're coming," Ruiz shouted.

Meyers waved them through the door and into the storage area. Her mind flashed back to an image of the hand they'd found stashed in one of the gigantic mounds of diamonds. She pictured Captain Danielle Rivers ripped apart in the communications room. Every instinct inside her gut screamed that this was a trap. She had the feeling they were now being herded, purposely forced into the storage area. What other choice did they have?

Stanton said, "Stay close to the wall. We'll circle around the facility. It will be far less vulnerable than passing directly through the center. If we do that, we have to defend every side. This way, we only have to watch three. In front of, behind, and across from. Got it? Backs to the wall!"

Ruiz took point and Carter stayed close behind. Fear gave the scientist motivation. For once, she moved with purpose. The commander had no doubt the woman's entire body was racked with fear. Thankfully, Carter found the strength to push past it for the moment. They all had dug deep and were operating on fumes, she had to believe. She knew she was. She was hungry—starving—and thirsty, and she wouldn't pass up an opportunity to use a bathroom.

Meyers shook her head in an attempt to knock free distracting thoughts. She closed the storage area door and fired a bolt into the lock box. It sprayed sparks, crackled, and burst into flames. The fire died out quickly. With the sensors fried, the creatures wouldn't be able to get into the storage area through the door. That didn't mean they were locked out. She had noticed air ducts above. They encircled the room, one about every twenty or thirty feet. Of course, the assumption was the creatures were aware of the blueprint for the compound. She'd much rather error on the side of caution and expect them to know the ins and outs of the place. The alternative was getting caught off guard.

"There! Up top!" Stanton pointed with the barrel of his sidearm. His laser reflected off the diamonds. He stopped using the guide and closed an eye. He lined the head of a creature in his site and fired off a bolt. Then another.

The creature growled, jaws open, fangs exposed. The roar echoed inside the chamber. That was the last thing they wanted.

Meyers fired off a bolt. It struck the creature in the side, knocking it over. The creature rolled down the diamonds, starting a small avalanche of gems in its wake. As it fell, it coiled, uncoiled. The claws along its body struggled for a foothold. When it reached bottom, it would pounce. "Run!"

Ruiz grabbed Carter's arm and took off.

Stanton let loose several more shots. They struck diamonds, sending a spray of gems into the air.

Meyers pushed him along. He was wasting the charge on his weapon shooting at a flailing creature. They needed to conserve ammunition as best as they could. Who knew how many were still inside the compound? How many were lying in wait? If they ran out of power charges, they'd be as good as dead.

If they weren't dead men walking already.

Between two mountainous piles, Ruiz stopped and screamed. She dropped to a knee and fired ahead of her.

Stanton yelled, "Commander, behind you!"

She threw herself back against the wall.

Stanton barely waited for her to be out of the way before he opened fire.

Meyers saw one of the creatures cresting the top of the hill she stood closest to and raised her blaster.

This was it. The last stand?

Commander Meyers thought of her father. If the admiral were here, he'd give out a war cry and charge into the thick of the battle.

Ruiz moved between the piles, toward the center of the storage area, and the scientist followed her. She covered her head with her hands and was screaming.

Stanton had Ruiz's back, following behind, but walking backwards.

Meyers had no option but to stay close. They shouldn't separate.

Going into the center of the area was the worst possible move, though. It was as if the creatures knew it and were flushing them out.

Ruiz shook her weapon. Batted a palm against the barrel, and shouted, "I'm out!"

They were now surrounded.

There were creatures all around them.

Stanton pushed the scientist and Ruiz down onto their knees, and then stood over them. He pivoted around, firing bolts at anything that moved and anything that didn't move.

Meyers joined him, and they stood back to back.

She felt the recoil of his shots through his back muscles. She trained her laser on targets and unleashed a flood of bolts, her finger squeezing the trigger as fast as she could.

Their shots hit home more than not. And a creature or two even died.

The monstrosities advanced on them, diving into the piles of diamonds and swimming through the gems like sharks sneaking up on prey. Meyers kept expecting she'd see a dorsal fin coming at them.

"I'm out," Stanton shouted.

Instinctively, Meyers checked her gauge.

She ignored what she saw, raised her weapon, and fired on the creatures closest to them. They were everywhere.

More were coming into the storage area through the ducts.

The four of them were dead center in the room. There was nowhere they could run. There wasn't any place to hide.

She squeezed the trigger on her blaster and nothing happened. She gave the weapon a shake and tried again.

Nothing.

The things were so close she could see the oblong pupils of their eyeballs.

Jaws opened. Fanged teeth bared. Taloned claws clicked and clacked on the ground. Tails whipped back and forth in a dangerous frenzy.

CHAPTER FIFTY-THREE

Aroldis D'Rukker ran through the doorway once it swooshed open. His blaster had double barrels. When he fired the weapon, lasers shot from the mouth, making the air around crackle.

Lieutenant Weber joined in immediately. His blaster was similar to D'Rukker's. Heavy and solid. It definitely took both hands and all of his strength to hold. The kick was severe. He knew his shoulder and forearm would be bruised when this battle was over. His bolts went wild as he struggled for control of the weapon. Diamonds sprayed up and all over the place as he hit the mounds of gems instead of the heads of the creatures.

Beside him stood Brett Serverino. He held the large blaster in on hand and fired laser bolts with accuracy, splattering creature heads with nearly every shot.

"Come on!" Weber shouted.

Commander Meyers ushered everyone forward. Lieutenant Angela Ruiz guided some woman Weber had never seen. Behind them was Captain Stanton, and lastly, the commander followed.

The four of them ran, bent forward, heads down.

Creatures scurried toward them, screeching, angry, in attack mode. One was directly behind the commander. Weber planted both feet and aimed his weapon. If he missed, he'd hit Anara Meyers. The bolt would obliterate his commander.

If he didn't do something, the creature would be on her and then she would be dead, regardless.

Weber squeezed the trigger, a smooth action, his finger taking the trigger all the way back without jerking it. A single laser bolt flew out of the mouth of the barrel. The bolt burned a hole through the creature's head as it rose off the ground and prepared to devour the commander.

Meyers was showered in a spray of its blood. She ran faster, though. She never stopped.

Getting behind D'Rukker and Webber, the commander didn't pause. "We're going to the shuttle!"

"Erinne is getting her ready. Go! We'll meet you there!" Weber responded. "Go, go!"

Serverino made his way into the storage area, never letting up on his shooting. D'Rukker moved out, stood beside him, and fired on the creatures relentlessly.

Weber saw the creatures retreating, scrambling to get away from the gunfight. Some scaled the piles of diamonds and were escaping into the air ducts. He let out a "Whoa-who!"

D'Rukker turned his head slightly, eyebrow cocked.

Weber said, "Sorry. Got a little caught up in the moment."

"Go and join your friends. We'll hold them here until the shuttle takes off."

"Wait, you're not coming with us?"

D'Rukker laughed. "And leave my ship? I don't think so."

"But what are you going to—?"

"Everything we need to fix her will be somewhere in this compound," D'Rukker explained.

"Yeah, with a million hungry monsters that want to eat you," Weber said.

"Do we look worried?"

They did not look worried at all. "I just—"

"Well *just* someplace else. Get out of here. Now!"

———

Weber returned to the bay. Through the front porthole, he saw Erinne Cohn at the controls.

"Someone is inside the shuttle," Captain Stanton said.

"She's okay," Weber said. "She's with me. These guys saved Bell and I out on the ice."

"They're pirates," Meyers said.

"Does it matter?" Weber asked.

Erinne was at the shuttle door. She stood with her arms out, holding on to either side. "What are you guys waiting for? Engine's prepped. Tank's full. She's good to go."

Erinne stepped off the shuttle.

Weber went up to her as the others climbed into the shuttle. "You've got to come with us," he said.

"I told you. Aroldis is never going to leave his ship, and I'll never leave him. We're family. He is all the family I have left." The pirate smiled at him. "Come with you where? Back to your ship? Back to Nebula? Web, that's not who I am."

"But it could be," he said.

"What's the alternative? A small farm on Earth? Be your wife? Raise a family for you so you and your kid can build a starfighter in a barn?"

"It's not that small of a farm," Weber said, speaking in an almost whisper.

"Weber, let's go!" Ruiz stood where Erinne had stood inside the shuttle and called out to him.

"I want to fly ships still. Not just build them." Her eyes bore into him. Weber knew she was looking deep into his heart through his own eyes. She touched the side of his face. "Are you going back to Earth when you get out of here?"

Weber looked over at the shuttle. "No. I'm not."

Erinne smiled. "Good."

"Why is that good?"

"It means there's a good chance I'll run into you again somewhere out in the middle of nowhere."

There was little chance they'd cross paths again. Space was infinite. She kissed him.

"Yo, Romeo, let's move."

Erinne said, "Murray's all strapped in. Ran an IV from the medical bag on the shuttle. Try to keep him still until you get back to your ship."

"I will," he said.

"Until next time." Erinne swiveled her blaster up from the strap where it hung over her shoulder and without another word ran toward the sound of the fight still raging on.

Weber started toward the shuttle.

Captain Stanton appeared at the door.

"I'm coming," Weber said.

"Get down!" Stanton shouted.

Weber dropped to the floor and rolled. Dropping from the ceiling was a small creature—small compared to the ones they'd just fought in the storage area. It didn't look any less dangerous or deadly, though.

Crab crawling, Weber scurried away from the thing as fast as he could, dragging D'Rukker's blaster with him. His hands and feet were moving too fast for him to pick up the weapon. If he took even a moment to grab for it, the creature would be on him.

A laser bolt passed over his exposed torso.

Weber dropped flat onto his back.

Another bolt flew past him and struck the creature in an eye socket. Blood oozed from the wound for just a moment. It was as if the heat from the laser had extolled damage, but also cauterized the wound at the same time. It rose into the air, shrieking, clearly in pain.

A third bolt stuck home, hitting the creature in the mouth and exiting out of the back of the throat. The creature stood where it was for a long second and then toppled over.

Weber felt a hand slip under his arm, and he was hoisted up onto his feet.

Ruiz raced with him back onto the shuttle.

"Where are the others?" Stanton asked. He held a standard *Euphoric* issue blaster in his arms. It must have been on the shuttle.

"They're not coming," Weber said.

"They're not, what?"

"They're not coming. They're staying. Get us out of here!"

"We didn't get to thank them? How are we just going to leave them here? Those things are everywhere."

"They can take care of themselves," Weber said but wasn't sure he believed it.

The woman Weber did not recognize was tending to Murray. She had strapped herself in beside the lieutenant and was holding his hand.

Ruiz went to the front of the shuttle and shouted to the commander, and then turned around. "She said buckle in."

In front of them, the shuttle the bay doors slowly opened. The shuttle engines roared.

Weber did not want to see the planet surface. His mind imagined more creatures out there waiting to get into the compound. He couldn't handle that thought. It would make Erinne's chances of survival less likely, and right now, he needed something good to hold onto.

The shuttle eased out of the bay, and then behind them, the bay door descended.

Stanton sat next to Weber, securing the belts around his waist and chest. "We're going home."

They were going to another spaceship in the planet's orbit. And then they would return to Nebula. Neither was home.

CHAPTER FIFTY-FOUR

On Board the Eclipse

First Officer Mark Windsor stood on the bridge. He could not take his eyes off the porthole. The sight of the *Euphoric* shuttle approaching the *Eclipse* was one of the best things he'd ever seen. Communications were up and running between them, and although the commander had only given him a brief debrief, he was anxious for the rest of the details. It could wait.

A celebratory meal was being prepared because Commander Meyers had stressed repeatedly that the crew was starving.

Chief Engineer Mandy Kadera, standing beside Windsor, bounced on the balls on her feet. "I knew they were going to make it. I just knew it. Didn't I tell you? I know I told you. That new commander, she's going to work out just fine."

Windsor hadn't been too sure, on either account. He kept the negative thoughts to himself. In fact, he'd already replaced them with loyalty and confidence in his new team. Their first mission might not be considered a success in the eyes of the suits back at *Euphoric*, but as far as Windsor was concerned, it was.

"With permission, Commander, I'm going down to supervise the shuttle landing," Kadera said.

"I believe I will join you."

"Aye," Kadera said, still smiling.

EPILOGUE

The *Eclipse* sped toward home. From where they were in the galaxy, they had a wonderful view of Earth and both Way Stations. The Way Stations were mirror-copies of each other. The further of the two was Nova. The closest, Nebula. The center of Nebula was cylindrical. Three arms jutted out and on the ends of each arm were three rings. Each ring spun independently, as did the center. Everything Earth once had was contained on Nebula. Hydroponic gardens, stores, businesses, virtual vacation spots, and residential neighborhoods.

Once the *Eclipse* docked, a man stood in the bay and fidgeted. He adjusted his shirt collar and tried looking both calm and official. "Commander Meyers! I am so happy you've made it home safely! I am Crispin Gunther. Your liaison for the Neptune mission. And this is my assistant, E.G.O.R."

He held out a hand.

Meyers ignored it.

"A pleasure to meet you, Commander," E.G.O.R. said.

Meyers eyed the robot, before turning her attention back on Gunther.

Reining his arm back, he said, "We have some things to go over. The corporate higher-ups are in a conference room and look forward to your debriefing."

"The crew and I are tired, Mr. Gunther—"

"Crispin. Please."

"They need to spend time with friends and family, *Mr. Gunther*. We lost four crew members on that mission. Four friends. I have been coordinating time to meet those families so I can deliver to them the devastating news," she said.

Gunther held up both hands. "We have people that will do that unpleasant business on your behalf. You needn't worry about that. Instead, the corporate higher—"

"As commander of the *Eclipse*, it is my responsibility to tell those waiting family members about what happened on that planet, about how their loved ones died heroes, and convince them it wasn't all for nothing. It is my responsibility, and it is my privilege, Mr. Gunther. Now if you'll excuse me, I know many of the families are already here, waiting to speak with me," she said.

"Of course, Commander. It's just that first you should debrief with the corporate higher—"

"Mr. Gunther, if you don't get out of my way," she said, and left the threat unsaid, as she shouldered past the corporate liaison.

"It's just that the diamonds, Commander," Gunther said.

She stopped, shook her head. She couldn't believe the brass ones on this guy. Slowly, she turned back around and faced him. There was no hiding the vile displeasure on her facial expression. "The what?"

"The diamonds. You did get the updated objective sent, did you not?"

"I did," she said, taking steps back toward the little man.

Behind her was the crew from the *Eclipse*. She hadn't realized they'd assembled and were watching the exchange. This wasn't meant for them to hear. She was embarrassed by her outbursts, but it couldn't be helped. Professional or not.

"You see, it's just that, you didn't bring any back." Gunther had taken steps backwards, away from the commander.

He stopped when he backed into Captain Stanton. He looked up at the captain over his shoulder. He offered up a weak smile that quickly vanished as if he'd seen something dangerous in the captain's eyes.

The commander puckered her lips and let her tongue brush along the back of her teeth as she contemplated her next words.

When she could find none, she did the next best thing.

Curling fingers into a first, Commander Anara Meyers unleashed a punch that clocked Crispin Gunther square in the nose.

It wasn't Gunther's fault, she was certain. He was just doing as he was told.

Her job came with risks, and apparently, so did Gunther's.

Bleeding, Gunther fell onto the floor.

"Well, that was rude," E.G.O.R. said.

"Shut it, tin can!" Commander Meyers helped the man onto his feet.

"And that was more rude," the robot said.

Ignoring the assistant, Meyers said, "Will you explain to the corporation I will be along to debrief them as soon as I can? And please, ask them to have ready all the information they previously obtained about the mission to Neptune. I want to hear firsthand whether or not they knew the planet was infested with creatures that had emerged from the toxic oceans, because they knew. Didn't they? They knew. They sent us over there without as much as an inclination into the dangers that awaited us. Have them have that information ready for me, Crispin. Will you do that for me?"

"Of course, Commander. Shouldn't be a problem," Gunther said. Most of his words were garbled. He must have some blood in the back of his throat. Broken noses tended to do that.

"Wonderful. That's wonderful," she said. She clapped Gunther on the back as she kind of shoved him forward. "Appreciate your *liaisoning* for us, Mr. Gunther. I really do. Top notch. Unparalleled by any other, I am certain. Nice work."

"Thank you, Commander," Gunther said, hurrying away. She wondered if he missed the tone of sarcasm in her voice. She didn't see how he could. Her words had dripped with mockery.

"Commander Meyers!"

The voice boomed around her. Meyers snapped to attention. Back rigid. Arms at her side, as did the rest of the crew in front of her.

The sound of the voice came from behind her.

She didn't need to turn around to see who approached. Had the admiral seen her punch Mr. Gunther? It could cost her job. She could be arrested for assault. Her actions could bring utter disgrace to the Meyers name. Why had she done that? Why had she let her emotions get the better of her?

She had to face him. She turned around. "Admiral," she said. While he looked thinner than even the last time she saw him, gaunt, almost, his voice had lost none of its power, and command. The authority was as strong and as apparent as ever.

"Was that a corporation man you just punched in the nose, Commander?"

"But, Daddy, I can explain," she said. Daddy. Why had she called him that? Why, as an adult, as a commander, did she let him always make her feel like a child?

"From what I just observed, sounds to me like he had it coming."

What? Meyers felt shocked. She wasn't sure she'd heard her father correctly.

"And what I can remember from when I returned from a long mission like yours, was the desire to eat some real food."

The crew behind Anara agreed. She didn't have to see them to know they'd be rubbing their stomachs and nodding vigorously.

"I've booked us a banquet room at the Mandrake. Spared no expense. My daughter has returned home from her first major solo mission. That calls for a celebration in my book!" He looked at the ancient pocket watch he carried on a chain. "They should be ready for us right about now."

Captain Stanton said, "All of us, Admiral?"

"The entire crew, and Dr. Sandra Carter, if she is inclined to join?"

"Food on the ship was good, but ..." The scientist raised her eyebrows. "I could eat."

Everyone laughed.

Anara Meyers wasn't sure what was even funny about what Sandra said. Maybe nothing was funny. It was possible the laughter came from relief. They were home, back on Nebula. Safe, and alive, but home.

"Admiral, I will meet you there as soon as possible," Anara Meyers said. Over his shoulder, she saw Captain Danielle Rivers' husband and son. The man stood behind the boy, hands on the pre-teens shoulders. A celebration did not seem appropriate. They had endured, and survived a traumatic event, but a celebration? "I just have some people I need to talk with first."

The admiral nodded. "I know you do. I've rented the room for the evening. Please, join us when you are finished."

First Officer Mark Windsor stepped forward. "Commander, would you like me to accompany you?"

She did. She really did want Windsor with her. Anara had no idea how she was going to tell so many people that their loved one was dead. She didn't want to do it alone. "No, but thank you. You join the others. I will be there just as soon as I can."

Without looking the captain in the eye, never looking away from Rivers' husband and son, Anara began walking toward them.

They became something of a blur the closer she got to them, but it was only because she was crying and refused to wipe away the tears.

―――――

Lieutenant Murray Bell sat up in the hospital bed. His legs dangled over the side. He kept kicking out his metallic prosthetic. "I mean, the good thing is, I won't have to shave it when I wear shorts."

Weber and Ruiz laughed.

Bell edged himself off of the bed. He winced when he stood.

"That hurt?" Weber asked.

"The nub is sore. Going to take some time getting used to it. They wired nerves and screwed in bones. Docs tell me this leg is going to be so much better than the original I'm going to contemplate lopping off the other for a matching pair." Bell took a few steps, and then a few more. He stood in front of a full-length mirror that hung on the back of his door. "I'm like a freaking robot. How's your arm?"

Weber rolled his shoulder around. "Wearing the sling on the way home helped. I should be fine, no bionic arms for me." Weber couldn't help but think of Erinne and her arm. She never got around to telling him what happened, how she'd wound up with a prosthetic. He wanted the attention diverted. Bell was the man of the hour in his book. "We're going to have to come up with some kind of new nickname for you, like … like … I got nothing."

Ruiz laughed again. "Shorty. Eileen. iHop."

Bell pointed at the lieutenant. "Oh, she's full of them!"

———

Weber tried calling K.C. Her voice mail picked up. Before leaving a message, he disconnected the call. A message felt inappropriate. To do this right, he needed to talk with her in person.

There was one person on his mind, one he also wished he could reach out to.

Erinne. She preoccupied his attention in a way he'd not felt in a long, long time.

He wondered if by playing around with radio frequencies he'd be able to track down the *Cutlass*.

Would she want to hear from him, though?

———

"Just so we're clear. You returned from Neptune without a single diamond?"

Commander Anara Meyers stood in the center of a room. The corporate heads were holograms, and they stood around her, judgmental.

"That's correct," she said. No explanation given. Everyone was well aware by now what the crew of the *Eclipse* faced once on Neptune.

"You did receive the updated information, requesting you salvage as much of mined gems making trips and filling the hull of the *Eclipse*."

"Or are we mistaken?"

"I did receive the amended information. That is correct," she said.

"And yet, you disobeyed the order?"

"I disobeyed the order, and would again, sir," she said. Meyers wasn't sure which person was talking to her. The questions came from all around her. In fact, the experience was quite dizzying.

"Do you have anything to say for yourself?"

"My crew and I went blind into a dangerous situation. We followed the initial objective to the letter. We put the lives of those on the compound first. Although we only managed to rescue Sandra Carter, it was because she was the only person out of thirty-three still alive. My crew worked together as a team, and despite the loss of four crewmen, we made it off the planet, and back to Nebula. Despite the odds stacked against us with no thanks from *Euphoric's* intel, I consider the rescue mission a success."

"Oh, you do, do you?"

"Yes, sir. I do."

They didn't counter, or argue. Neither did they have any of the information Crispin Gunther promised they would. "Thank you. That is all. You may leave. Our ruling will be handed down shortly."

For a moment, Anara Meyers stood where she was, before realizing they had actually dismissed her. She turned and left the room, but walked out with her back straight and head high.

Outside the conference room her father, the admiral, waited for her. "How did it go?"

"They're deciding my fate as we speak," she said.

"Are you okay?"

"I am, Daddy. I don't care what decision they come to, I know we all did what was right," she said.

The admiral wrapped an arm around her shoulder. "I'm proud of you. How about I take you for a drink."

"I think I'm supposed to wait here for their ruling," she said.

The admiral looked back at the closed door. "If they fire you, then you are fired, and going for a drink with your father won't make much difference, will it? And if they just hand down some disciplinary action, then so be it. Either way, going for a cocktail with me isn't going to change the outcome one way or another. Is it?"

Anara looked back the closed door, as well. Then she smiled. "No. No, it won't. Let's go have that drink."

THE END

ABOUT THE AUTHOR

Phillip Tomasso is an award-winning, Amazon Best Selling author of more than twenty novels. He works full-time as a Fire / EMS Dispatcher for 911. Aside from writing, and time spent with family, Tomasso enjoys playing guitar, and singing. However, to hear him sing you might disagree. As always, Tomasso is at work on his next novel. Please be

sure to visit his website, follow him on Twitter, and Like his Author Page on Facebook. You can also email Tomasso with any reviews, comments, or requests for Guest Speaking at: phillip@philliptomasso.com
www.philliptomasso.com
www.twitter.com/P_Tomasso
 www.facebook.com/authorphilliptomasso

Special Thanks

I want to give special thanks to Brian Bennington and Adrian DeJesus. They, on numerous occasions, helped me flesh out the ideas for this novel, read countless drafts, provided feedback, aided in direction, and were patient with my constant babble while writing the story. Additionally, I would like to thank my editor K.P., and Gary Lucas with Severed Press. They continue to see value in my tales, and for that—for them—I am grateful.

Other Titles by Phillip Tomasso

Assassin's Promise
Queens of Osiris
Wizard's War
Wizard's Rise
Young Blood: The Nightbreed
Extinction (A Novella)
Blood River
Damn the Dead
Preservation
Evacuation
Vaccination
Pigeon Drop
Convicted

Jay Walker: Case of the
Impractical Prankster
Jay Walker: Case of the Missing
Action Figure
Treasure Island: A Zombie
Novella
Sounds of Silence
Pulse of Evil
The Molech Prophecy
(written as Thomas Philips)
Adverse Impact
Johnny Blade
Third Ring
Tenth House
Mind Play

CHECK OUT OTHER GREAT SCIENCE FICTION BOOKS

DERELICT: MARINES
by **Paul E. Cooley**

Fifty years ago, Mira, humanity's last hope to find new resources, exited the solar system bound for Proxima Centauri b. Seven years into her mission, all transmissions ceased without warning. Mira and her crew were presumed lost. Humanity, unified during her construction, splintered into insurgency and rebellion.

Now, an outpost orbiting Pluto has detected a distress call from an unpowered object entering Sol space: Mira has returned. When all attempts at communications fail, S&R Black, a Sol Federation Marine Corps search and rescue vessel, is dispatched from Trident Station to intercept, investigate, and tow the beleaguered Mira to Neptune.

As the marines prepare for the journey, uncertainty and conspiracy fomented by Trident Station's governing AIs, begin to take their toll. Upon reaching Mira, they discover they've been sent on a mission that will almost certainly end in catastrophe.

ALLIANCE MARINES
by John Mierau

One by one, all of Earth's colonies have gone dark and silent. Reach, the last colony, teeters on the verge of civil war against its Earth-loyal overlords...and Reach-born rebel Lee Zhang has sworn to push the planet over the edge.

As the colony descends into total war, a convoy from Earth races across the galaxy, carrying news of a threat unlike anything mankind has faced before. The colonies have all been destroyed by a vast alien horde, and now Earth has fallen, too. Time is running out for sworn enemies to learn to trust and unite, or the human race is extinct. The Takers are coming to destroy mankind. If we don't do the job for them first.

CHECK OUT OTHER GREAT SCIENCE FICTION BOOKS

MAUSOLEUM 2069
by Rick Jones

Political dignitaries including the President of the Federation gather for a ceremony onboard Mausoleum 2069. But when a cloud of interstellar dust passes through the galaxy and eclipses Earth, the tenants within the walls of Mausoleum 2069 are reborn and the undead begin to rise. As the struggle between life and death onboard the mausoleum develops, Eriq Wyman, a one-time member of a Special ops team called the Force Elite, is given the task to lead the President to the safety of Earth. But is Earth like Mausoleum 2069? A landscape of the living dead? Has the war of the Apocalypse finally begun? With so many questions there is only one certainty: in space there is nowhere to run and nowhere to hide.

RED CARBON
by D.J. Goodman

Diamonds have been discovered on Mars.

After years of neglect to space programs around the world, a ruthless corporation has made it to the Red Planet first, establishing their own mining operation with its own rules and laws, its own class system, and little oversight from Earth. Conditions are harsh, but its people have learned how to make the Martian colony home.

But something has gone catastrophically wrong on Earth. As the colony leaders try to cover it up, hacker Leah Hartnup is getting suspicious. Her boundless curiosity will lead her to a horrifying truth: they are cut off, possibly forever. There are no more supplies coming. There will be no more support. There is no more mission to accomplish. All that's left is one goal: survival.

CHECK OUT OTHER GREAT SCIENCE FICTION BOOKS

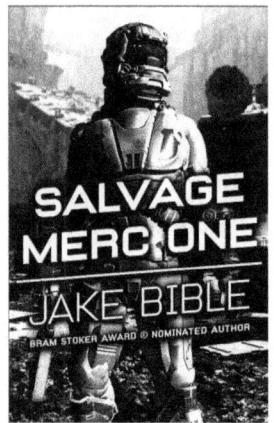

SALVAGE MERC ONE
by Jake Bible

Joseph Laribeau was born to be a Marine in the Galactic Fleet. He was born to fight the alien enemies known as the Skrang Alliance and travel the galaxy doing his duty as a Marine Sergeant. But when the War ended and Joe found himself medically discharged, the best job ever was over and he never thought he'd find his way again.

Then a beautiful alien walked into his life and offered him a chance at something even greater than the Fleet, a chance to serve with the Salvage Merc Corp.

Now known as Salvage Merc One Eighty-Four, Joe Laribeau is given the ultimate assignment by the SMC bosses. To his surprise it is neither a military nor a corporate salvage. Rather, Joe has to risk his life for one of his own. He has to find and bring back the legend that started the Corp.

SERENGETI
by J.B. Rockwell

It was supposed to be an easy job: find the Dark Star Revolution Starships, destroy them, and go home. But a booby-trapped vessel decimates the Meridian Alliance fleet, leaving Serengeti—a Valkyrie class warship with a sentient AI brain—on her own; wrecked and abandoned in an empty expanse of space. On the edge of total failure, Serengeti thinks only of her crew. She herds the survivors into a lifeboat, intending to sling them into space. But the escape pod sticks in her belly, locking the cryogenically frozen crew inside.

Then a scavenger ship arrives to pick Serengeti's bones clean. Her engines dead, her guns long silenced, Serengeti and her last two robots must find a way to fight the scavengers off and save the crew trapped inside her.

www.ingramcontent.com/pod-product-compliance
Lightning Source LLC
Chambersburg PA
CBHW071305210626
46818CB00015B/3004